Melting

Rogues & Gentlemen, Book 17

By Emma V. Leech

****

Published By: Emma V. Leech.

Copyright (c) Emma V. Leech 2019

Cover Art: Victoria Cooper

ASIN No.: B07V5WCLBF

ISBN No.: 9781696970020

Table of Contents

Chapter 1

"Wherein we meet our heroine and family, sinners of quality"

1ˢᵗ September 1820.

Marie de Wynn was a spectacular whore.

There was no getting away from it, though Gwenn knew the words were her mother's own, and said with pride.

Even on the wrong side of forty, Marie de Wynn was still a breathtakingly beautiful woman, the kind for whom men fought duels. Helen of Troy must have been cast in a similar mould to have caused such a great deal of aggravation.

Where Marie went, excitement and drama inevitably followed.

Gwenn considered her mother now, her dark tresses artfully coiled in a complicated style that looked just a little dishevelled, as if she'd been recently ravished.

It was a look Marie had spent a lifetime perfecting, and one she'd taught her daughter. For, at the age of nineteen, Gwenn was to inherit Marie's legacy and become the greatest courtesan England had ever seen. Whether she liked it or not.

As it happened, she did not.

There was very little point in remonstrating. It had taken all of Gwenn's considerable powers of persuasion to delay her fate this long, as her mother had wanted to launch her into society last year. Though Gwenn had no objection to entering society, it was the outcome that they disagreed on. She had tried on numerous occasions to suggest that perhaps she might simply catch a wealthy husband and settle down, rather than follow Marie's path. Her mother would turn to her, an expression of outrage in her eyes, as if Gwenn had suggested the possibility of turning into a unicorn.

That exact expression was facing Gwenn at this moment. She'd known it was futile, but some perverse part of her nature seemed to enjoy banging her head against the brick wall that was her mother.

"You are the strangest and most ungrateful child," Marie lamented, shaking her head and making the heavy ruby earrings she wore sway against her neck. "Why on earth would you want to shackle yourself to a man who will own you like a pair of shoes, and cast you aside just as easily?"

Gwenn frowned, too familiar with this argument to return a glib answer. In truth, she hated the idea of losing her autonomy, but the world could be cruel and lonely, and sometimes she longed for something simpler than the extravagant lifestyle her mother lived. Extravagant it might have been, but to Gwenn it seemed empty of anything she herself desired.

In her mind she pictured a simple room, elegantly but not lavishly furnished, and a man sitting by the fire, talking to her about the day they'd just shared. He was a faceless man for now, but someone she could trust, someone she could count on not to throw her away and abandon her, someone who would love and respect her and raise a family with her.

A silly daydream, nothing more, and one Marie would scorn.

"But... don't you ever wish to be respectable, Mama?" Gwenn said, hesitant for fear of rousing a temper best left to slumber in peace.

Marie wrinkled her lovely nose as though a bad smell had drifted in from the cool autumn evening outside the window.

"Respectable?" she repeated, sooty lashes blinking with incomprehension. "Whatever for?" She swept to her feet, heavy satin skirts swishing with the movement. "Look around you," she said, gesturing to the opulent room that was just a small part of their vast and lavish home.

An enormous bed dominated the space, draped with scarlet damask curtains restrained with thick gold ropes and ornate tassels. Priceless works of art covered the walls—all nudes—some in dubious taste. On the dressing table were endless bottles of perfume, pots containing make-up and skin creams, and a king's ransom of carelessly abandoned jewels that glinted in the soft glow of the lamps.

"What would respectability have gotten me I ask you? A dozen brats, a dull husband and the privilege of scrimping and trying to make ends meet whilst my beloved lavishes his time and money on his mistress, that's what," she said, answering her own question. Not that Gwenn had any illusions she'd been soliciting an actual response. "No, I thank you. I'll be the mistress and take the man's best hours, the times when he's in the humour to amuse and be amusing, and have him pay handsomely for the honour of spending time in my company."

"But doesn't that man own you, as he owns any woman?" Gwenn countered. "He can cast you aside like those shoes far easier than any wife, for there is no law that says he must support you."

Marie gave her a despairing glance before returning to her dressing table and placing the notorious Davenport rubies about her lovely neck. She turned this way and that, admiring the huge stones as they glittered and sparkled.

"Men do not own me, Gwenn. They pay obscene amounts of money to hire me for a time, and I'm clever enough and skilled enough to make sure they never tire of me. I move on before they are through with me, before they have time to take me for granted, and I always leave them wanting more." She swivelled on the stool before the dressing table, her dark eyes serious now. "But my time is coming to an end, though it pains me to say it. I've taught you everything I know, Gwennie. You have the skills and the beauty to become the most famous, the most exclusive courtesan that ever was. You could be one of the most powerful women in the country if you do as we planned. Think of the life you could live. Think of everything you could see and do."

Gwenn did think of it. She thought of it constantly, and the weight of her mother's expectations bore down upon her. Unlike Marie, Gwenn did not crave fame and fortune, or notoriety. She did not long for jewels and riches, or to be seen on the arms of powerful men. Her dreams were a great deal smaller and less ambitious, yet as far out of reach as if she were living in the gutter and dreaming of diamonds.

Gwenn wanted more than anything to belong somewhere. She dreamt of a comfortable home, of being able to look respectable people in the eye without cringing inwardly. She'd seen the way mothers and wives looked at Marie with a mixture of disgust and resentment. Whether Marie just did not see it or didn't care, she wasn't certain. She only knew she longed for the esteem of a man who loved her, a family she could be a real mother to, and children she could see grow and have families of their own.

How foolish she was. Her mother was a courtesan, and had groomed her to follow in her footsteps. There was nothing Gwenn didn't know about men, about how to inflame their desires, about how to make them want her, about how to please them.

Not that she had any practical experience. Marie was cleverer than the average whore and had been careful to keep her daughter hidden away from troublesome men who might ruin her plans. When Gwenn made her come out, she would *take the world by the throat and hold it for ransom,* as her mother was fond of saying, and always with a delighted smile. The beautiful, virginal daughter of the notorious Marie de Wynn could command the highest price imaginable from her first protector. Indeed, Marie foresaw a bidding war the like of which had never been seen before.

All Gwenn had to do was hand over her innocence, what little of it remained.

Panic fluttered in her throat.

Marie meant to bring Gwenn out the following season, but she intended to start things off by taking her to some of the most select parties over Christmas, to allow rumour and gossip to build excitement whilst Gwenn found her feet in society and practised her 'flirtatious arts' in a less intimidating setting. Not that Gwenn could expect vouchers for Almack's, or anything of the sort. The most respectable company would not admit such a woman as she, but Marie was currently in the keeping of the Duke of Alvermarle, and a man like that could open a great many doors.

Marie got to her feet and, though she'd seen her mother dress for grand events on a thousand different nights of her life, Gwenn still felt her breath catch at her astonishing beauty. Despite the similarities in their classical profiles, Gwenn was her mother's opposite. She was blonde where Marie was dark, her eyes a pale turquoise to Marie's impenetrable deep brown, because Gwenn favoured her father, the Marquess of Davenport. The man who had so incensed Marie with his callous behaviour when Gwenn was born that she'd stolen his wife's rubies and run off to France with the man's younger brother. *Her* rubies now, thanks to a touch of blackmail and the mention of writing her memoirs one day. The same rubies that settled over Marie's lavish bosom and would be the envy of every woman she saw tonight.

Those rubies told tales. They said that this woman was not only shockingly expensive, but exclusive, and dangerous… a combination that men seemed to find irresistible.

Gwenn doubted her mother's hopes were attainable despite her obvious confidence in Gwenn's abilities. Marie was so very sought after, even now when far younger women vied to steal her crown. There was no secret, Marie assured her, no magic formula. Yes, her looks were important, but they were not everything.

"Look at Harriet Wilson," she would say with a laugh. "She's only passably pretty, yet what a success she has made of herself with her wit and vivacity."

Charm and a liveliness of spirit, the ability to make a man laugh and forget his troubles, to make him comfortable no matter the circumstances, not to mention a deal of skill and imagination in the bedroom, these were the marks of a clever whore. Marie had imparted the secret of all these skills to her only daughter with frankness enough to make a sailor blush. Gwenn thought there was little in the world that could shock her now, though on the face of it she'd lived her life as modestly as any innocent girl of the *ton*.

Gwenn had been sixteen when her mother had opened her eyes to the ways in which a successful courtesan made her living. At first it had been simply how to flirt and be an agreeable companion, but by her eighteenth birthday she'd studied every erotic text known to man and had matters explained in greater detail by both her mother and a variety of her female friends who plied the same trade. To be fair there had been a great deal of laughter during those lessons and a female camaraderie that Gwenn had appreciated, like she'd been initiated into an exclusive club.

Compared to many girls of her ilk she'd been lucky. Many mothers forced their daughters into their world when they were far younger. Still, she'd been well aware before then of the men who'd come and gone, and that her and Marie were reliant on their *protection* and generosity. There had been those who'd thought Marie's daughter part of the package, and to her credit Marie had packed them off without a second thought, thankfully before any damage had been done. It had given Gwenn a deep distaste for her mother's life though, and she longed for something different.

Still, it seemed vice was in her blood. The de Wynn family were an infamous lot. Gwenn's grandmother had married quite respectably to a viscount, but had embarked on a scandalous affair with a handsome naval man, which ended in a crimcom that had set the *ton* alight and was still spoken of in hushed tones generations later. Marie's sister, Aunt Letty, was living openly with Lord and Lady Chalfont, and no one was quite certain which of them she was having an affair with, or perhaps it was both of them. Gwenn hadn't liked to ask, which was ridiculous as Letty was hardly shy about her affairs.

There were stories like this attached to all her relatives, and the de Wynn family were generally considered to be a "bad lot."

"It runs in the blood, darling," Aunt Letty had lamented once, when Gwenn had confided her wish to try for something more respectable. "There's no escaping it. We're sluts, every one of us," she said cheerfully. "Mama tried, the poor dear, and look where it got her. Some people are good at painting, or music, or are clever with numbers. We're good at scandal. It's a talent like any other, you see. The de Wynns can sin *par excellence.*"

She'd trilled with laughter at her little rhyme, so pleased with herself she'd had *De Wynns can sin par excellence,* engraved on a silver snuffbox and given it to her darling Chuffy, Lord Chalfont.

Gwenn sighed. She was doomed.

***

15th *December. Portman Square, London.*

Gwenn held her breath as the stair creaked beneath her foot. It was so dark she could barely make out the outlines of the furniture and had almost plummeted headlong down the stairs before grasping hold of the bannister.

It was a little after four in the morning, and the household was finally asleep. Her mother had returned not much before three and Gwenn had listened, straining her ears to divine whether her dear Mama had finally tumbled into the arms of Hypnos, seeing as Lord Alvermarle was currently rusticating in the country with his wife and children.

Now, she was certain the entire house would erupt at every creak of a floorboard. Heavens, surely her heart was beating loud enough to rouse the dead. By the time she reached the door, she trembled with the strain on her nerves, but faint heart ne'er won fair lady. Nor would it let Gwenn escape the party tomorrow night, which would introduce her to society as the successor to her mother's fabulously tarnished crown.

Gwenn had never considered herself a particularly brave creature. In fact, if she was brutally honest, it was the terror of facing the endless list of men Mama had read out to her—all of whom would be vying for position as her first "protector" —that had finally spurred her into action. Well, that and a chance conversation she had overheard between Mama's lady's maid and their housekeeper.

They were discussing a man, a viscount called Lord Cheam. To her relief, Gwenn did not recognise his name from her list of suitors, though she didn't know why. Marie had been single-minded in adding every wealthy and titled man.

Lord Cheam's governess had quit at a moment's notice, though the family were all packed and ready to set off for Scotland the next day. According to Mrs Wittington—Mama's maid—the poor viscount was at his wits' end, as the twins were the naughtiest girls ever born and he hadn't a hope of finding a replacement, having by now run through every reputable governess in London. There was certainly no hope this close to Christmas and not a chance in hell before they were due to leave. Housekeeper and maid had chortled merrily at the thought of the poor gentleman having to endure such a long voyage in the company of two seven-year-old girls who might well have been spawned by the devil himself, the little monsters were so ungovernable.

The plan, such as it was, was beautifully simple, though it relied a fair bit on the desperation of her soon-to-be employer.

Gwenn closed the door of the elegant house on Portman Square and took a deep breath, the icy air so cold it hurt her lungs. All she could hope now was that Lord Cheam didn't look too closely at her references. She hoped, in fact, that he was desperate indeed, as she hurried into the freezing night and away from her mother's plans for her future.

Chapter 2

"Wherein our hero prays for a miracle."

Sampson was desperate.

"Selina!" he exclaimed, as the child darted past him with all the speed and skill of a pickpocket raised on the streets of the Seven Dials, not like the indulged little daughter of a wealthy viscount, albeit a wretched excuse for a nobleman. Her twin sister, Susan, shrieked as he lunged for her, but evaded him with ease, hurtling after Selina and crowing with triumph as she went. They both clutched a jam tart in each sticky hand, thieved from the kitchens.

"Cook made you those for the journey, you little brats," he shouted, to no avail. "You'll have nothing to eat on the way now, so don't go complaining about being hungry."

Giggling could be heard as the she-devils ran up the stairs to the nursery, punctuated by the sound of a door slamming.

It could have been worse, he consoled himself. They'd started pilfering things in the past fortnight. It had begun with small things about the house, but yesterday, during a walk in the park, they'd lifted a lace handkerchief and—to his horror—a rather pretty enamelled fob. Heaven alone knew who owned it. His own fault for entrusting the girl's care to his twin brothers, Solomon and Sherbourne. It was like asking Lucifer to keep two fallen angels on the straight and narrow. *Bloody laughable.*

Where the girls had inherited their larcenous talents from, he wasn't sure. Yes, their father had been a black-hearted villain, and he himself was one of four adult siblings known universally as The Scandalous Brothers, so it wasn't as if the rest of their family were paragons of virtue.

The recent demise of their vile father, whilst shocking, had been a relief to all concerned, and he didn't believe the girls missed him or the disturbing atmosphere their wicked parent had created whenever he was home. What other damage his sire had done by marrying his second wife, Sampson didn't know. The girl had been young enough to be his daughter and was ill-prepared to endure his particular brand of cruelty. Heaven alone knew what effect it might have had on two innocent little girls.

His heart constricted.

Sampson had recently inherited his father's title and become Viscount Cheam, along with an estate that desperately needed his attention, a hysterical step-mother six years younger than he was, and his two seven-year-old half-sisters, who were showing every sign of going to the devil. Whilst he and his brothers had shown remarkable skill in following a similar path, their excesses ran to gambling, carousing, and debauchery, thankfully talents the girls had declined to show an interest in... yet.

This talent for thievery was new and troubling.

Sampson had decided earlier in the year it was time to drag the family back into the realms of respectability. His little sisters being crowned The Scandalous Sisters when they finally came out was too horrifying to contemplate.

Things had begun badly with the spectacular arrival of his bastard half-brother Captain Ross Moncreiffe, who had immediately challenged his father to a duel. Not that Sampson could blame him in the least. He'd been sorely tempted himself.

When the duel had taken place, his dishonourable father had tried to shoot Ross in the back and botched the job, disgracing himself—and the family—even further, and had been forced to flee to France in shame. Not content with this, five weeks ago he'd been found dead in a brothel.

Sampson, whilst not regretting in the least his father's demise, wished him to perdition for the manner in which he'd gone about it. Not that there was much chance of his father going anywhere else.

To evade the rabid interest in the latest scandal surrounding his father, and therefore the rest of the family, Sampson had leapt at an invitation from Ross to spend the Christmas holiday with him and his new wife, Freddie. The farthest reaches of rural Scotland seemed like heaven on earth at this moment. Surely, in such a remote place, the family could get a little peace and escape the humiliation and shame that the late viscount had heaped on each of their heads?

Sampson certainly hoped so. The girls' mother—never the most effective parent, though a good-natured one—had suffered some kind of nervous collapse on hearing about her husband's demise, and had returned to live with her parents, leaving her daughters in Sampson's care. He was out of his depth and he knew it. The girls needed a father, not a poor excuse for a brother whose own reputation was far from pristine. He was weary and felt unequal to the herculean task of making his family respectable again. Of course, there was only one thing that he could do that would make any real difference to how the family were viewed. He knew it, and yet his mind shied away from the idea.

Face it, you fool, he cursed himself. He would have to marry her.

Miss Agnes Crawford wasn't so bad, from what he could tell. He'd only met her a handful of times, after all. It wasn't her fault she had a rather horsey countenance, and that braying laugh… one could get used to it. She might be a kind and loving woman behind that harsh and somewhat intimidating exterior.

She really might.

Sampson swallowed down the knot that had leapt to his throat. Yes, she had seemed to be rather bossy and yes, her father appeared to be afraid of her, and yes, she *had* bullied her companion unmercifully, sending the poor little creature fleeing the room in tears… but she *was* respectable.

Indeed, there was likely not a more respectable unmarried female in the entire *ton*.

Never mind that now, he counselled himself. He had more pressing troubles. Such as, for example, the prospect of enduring a long and tedious journey to Scotland, in bad weather, with Selina and Susan… and no governess. The urge to stamp his foot and bellow *it's not fair*, as the girls would do, was becoming hard to resist.

They could not spend another day in London. What if someone had seen the girls stealing that blasted fob? How much more scandal could the family endure before the *ton* turned their backs on them altogether?

He and his brothers had always been welcome. Good-looking, eligible young men with the ability to charm the birds from the trees were generally welcome anywhere, no matter their reputations as rakes and libertines. Yet his sisters were part of this family too, and he owed it to them to clean up both his and his brothers' stained reputations. He would not have the girls feel ashamed of their family, of their blood and their heritage. Their father had been a selfish bastard, but his sons… his sons would be better than that.

Sampson looked up as his housekeeper, Mrs Sydney, bustled towards him. He mustered a smile, aware that his situation would be intolerable if not for her unflagging loyalty. His butler, Brent, had his undying gratitude too. That the two had stuck with him and his siblings, despite the dreadful way the late viscount had treated them, was beyond anything Sampson had the ability to express.

"I tried to stop them," she said with a sad shake of her head.

"Not your fault," Sampson replied with a sigh. "But I admit I'm at a loss for what to do now."

"Oh, my lord." The woman brushed a greying lock of hair from her troubled face, and sounded anxious. "I would come with you myself, only—"

"Don't you dare," Sampson said at once, horrified by the idea. "I know how much you've been looking forward to seeing your grandchildren this holiday. Besides which, you've earned a little peace. I don't think I would have survived these past weeks without you, and that's the truth."

"It's a pleasure to serve you, my lord," Mrs Sydney said, such fondness in her eyes that Sampson felt his throat tighten. Mrs Sydney had been with them since he was a boy, one of the few sources of comfort and affection any of the brothers had experienced once their beautiful mother had died.

Sampson patted her shoulder, uncertain how to show his gratitude, which ran deeper than he was equal to expressing. "Thank you, Syd," he said quietly, using the nickname they'd given her as children, hoping to convey some of what he felt.

He turned as footsteps on the stairs caught his attention, and saw his Aunt May making her way down, dressed for a long journey. His late mother's older sister was a favourite with all the siblings and had hurried to their sides, travelling up from her home in Devon the moment she'd heard the news about their father. Widowed for many years, she was a forthright woman in her sixties who made no bones about the fact she blamed his father for her beloved sister's untimely death.

"Have you found a governess for those dreadful children?" she demanded before she was halfway down.

"No, Aunt," Sampson said, watching her shake her head in dismay.

"Heaven help us then," she said as she set foot on the ground floor and began rummaging in the large carpet bag she held. A moment later she brought out a handsome silver hip flask which she thrust towards to Mrs Sydney. "Fill that to the brim with the best brandy you can lay your hands on," she instructed. "I'm going to need it."

***

It was another hour before the carriages were packed and the twins wrestled into hats, gloves, and pelisses. His youngest brother, Samuel, was late, unsurprisingly, and Sampson paced as he waited for him. Sherbourne and Solomon had elected to take themselves off to a friend's estate in the wilds of Derbyshire, and had given their sworn oath that they would behave themselves and not cause any further scandal for the duration. Sampson would have preferred them where he could keep an eye on them, but it was better than nothing.

"Morning, Sunny," Sam hollered, sticking his head around the front door. "What are we waiting for?"

"*You,* you great oaf," Sampson retorted, snatching up his hat and hurrying outside just as Aunt May ushered the squabbling twins into their carriage.

"I'm not travelling with the devil's spawn, I tell you now," Samuel said, watching the proceedings, his expression stern as Sampson walked down the front steps.

"We're taking turns," Sampson said, his tone crisp. "Aunt May said she'd get her bit over with, so she'll entertain them until we stop to eat, if she can make it. If not until we change horses or she loses her mind, whichever happens first. Then it's your turn."

"What about you?" Samuel demanded, the picture of indignation.

"I'll gladly swap with you, Sam," Sampson replied. "As by the time I get them, they'll have spent the best part of the day enclosed in a carriage."

"No, no!" Samuel said hastily as he climbed into their carriage. "I wouldn't dream of interfering with your plans. I know how you love to organise us all."

Sampson snorted and turned to speak with his butler. "Well, you have your instructions, Brent. I do hope you will take the time off we discussed though and enjoy Christmas? God knows you've earned the right."

"I'll ensure everything is just as it should be for your return," Brent replied gravely, avoiding the question.

"I know you will," Sampson said with a smile, before climbing into the carriage.

"Well, I'm looking forward to seeing Ross, but I loathe this bloody journey," Samuel said with a sigh, shifting his large frame so he could sprawl over the seat.

"At least we don't have a bad-tempered Scot bleeding all over us," Sampson retorted, referring to the last time they'd done it, after their father had attempted to shoot Ross in the back and instead hit him in the shoulder. The poor bastard had been out of his head with pain and fever, and Sampson had been terrified he'd lose his new brother before he'd even gotten to know him.

Samuel chuckled and nodded. "True enough."

They waited in silence a moment, expecting the train of family carriages, personal staff, and baggage to lumber into motion.

Sampson frowned as the carriage still hadn't moved and craned his neck to look out of the window. "What are we waiting for?"

In answer to his question, Brent opened the door again. "My lord, please forgive the delay, but there is a young woman here, requesting to speak with you urgently."

"Oh, yes?" Samuel said, a knowing tone to his voice which Sampson ignored, waving at Brent for him to continue.

"She's a governess," Brent said, the words the sweetest Sampson had ever heard in his entire life.

"Does she have references?" Sampson asked, hardly daring to hope. Damn it, even if she didn't, he'd have to risk it.

Brent handed him a neatly folded letter, which Sampson lost no time in reading.

"From the Duke of Alvermarle, no less," he said, stunned at his sudden good fortune. "It's certainly a glowing recommendation."

"For God's sake, hire her at once!" Samuel sat up straight, his voice urgent. "What are you waiting for?"

Sampson hesitated, at the very least he ought to interview her, but they were all packed and ready to go and the horses would get cold if they waited about too long, not to mention Aunt May, and....

"Hire her at once," he said to Brent.

The man's eyes widened a little.

"But m-my lord," he stammered, clearly taken aback. "She's... she's—"

"She's what?" Sampson demanded. "Does she have two heads?"

"No, my lord."

"Horns and a tail?" Samuel suggested.

"No, indeed, sir."

"What, then?" Sampson asked, eager to get this over with.

"She's very... *young*, my lord," the anxious looking butler said, frowning. "And—"

"Nonsense," Sampson said, waving his hand. "Her reference is glowing. Look, it says right here that she's 'sensible, level-headed and utterly reliable, with the good sense of a woman with much greater age and experience.'"

"Yes, my lord," Brent said doubtfully. "Only—"

"Tell her if she's willing to leave at once, I'll hire her."

"She is, my lord. She already indicated she knew of your situation."

"So much the better," Sampson said with a sigh as Brent nodded and closed the door once again. "I'm saved," he added, sitting back against the squabs and allowing himself a moment to believe that the coming weeks might actually come close to being the family Christmas he'd always hoped for.

***

Gwenn's heart thudded in her throat. She felt quite certain the elderly butler didn't believe her story for a moment. Though she'd done her best to dress in a manner she thought might be appropriate for a governess, she was aware she was probably far wide of the mark.

She had chosen her oldest and most conservative gowns to bring with her, ones her mother would have likely thrown out the window in disgust if she'd known of their existence. Her clothes at least did not scream *courtesan* like her mother's did; Marie was far too clever for that. No, Gwenn's clothes closely resembled those any proper young lady of the *ton* might wear... except the cut was just a little different, emphasising her charms with rather less subtlety than was appropriate. The butler's wide-eyed look of disbelief on seeing her had only underlined her concerns.

When the man had returned and told her Lord Cheam would hire her on the spot, she'd thought her knees might buckle with relief. Now, however, she was being hurried into a carriage where his lordship's aunt and the troublesome twin sisters awaited her and Gwenn realised she didn't have the first notion about being a governess. Not only that, but she'd have to muddle through under the watchful gaze of his aunt, with whom she'd be in close quarters for the coming hours, if not days.

If they didn't pitch her out of the carriage ten minutes down the road, it would be a miracle.

Still, part of her training to be the perfect courtesan had covered the ability to act as though one was never afraid, uncertain, or completely out of one's depth. That at least should stand her in good stead. Added to which, her mother maintained that men were little boys at heart and ought to be treated as such. They needed attention, and to be kept busy so they didn't stray. They required praise for good behaviour and constant treats, while bad behaviour was to be ignored and not remarked upon. They should also never be allowed to go hungry; a hungry man was an unreasonable one.

Though the treats her mother had taught Gwenn to reward good behaviour were clearly of a scandalous nature, the principle was sound. Sweets ought to do the trick. She'd come prepared.

"Good morning," she said brightly, hoping she sounded brisk, efficient, and governessy as she sat in the seat opposite Mrs May Bainbridge.

The woman was small and plump, aged somewhere around sixty. A still attractive older lady—in a faded rose way — her hair, obviously once bright auburn, had softened to a pale apricot streaked with white, but her blue eyes were intelligent and compelling.

She didn't look as if she missed much.

"I'm Miss Wynter," Gwenn said, giving them all a dazzling smile. "The new governess."

Mrs Bainbridge looked her up and down in silence, an expression on her face that eloquently said *if you're a governess, I'll eat my hat.*

The carriage lurched into motion at that moment. Gwenn gave a start of surprise and made a grab for the holding strap to stop herself from collapsing onto the floor in an ungainly heap of skirts. The twins, already staring at her with undisguised interest, giggled. Gwenn winked at them and settled herself more comfortably in her seat.

"How old are you, Miss Wynter?" Mrs Bainbridge asked, her tone sceptical.

"Four and twenty," Gwenn said, grateful for her mother's tuition on how to lie through her teeth without batting an eyelid.

"Really? You don't look a day over eighteen."

Gwenn adopted an expression of delight. "Oh, how kind of you to say so," she said, before turning her attention to the twins. "And how old are you, girls?"

"I'm seven," said one, her pale blonde hair tumbling in unruly waves around a sweet face with a freckled nose.

Bright blue eyes stared at Gwenn with curiosity until her identical sister elbowed her, making the child glare.

"I'm seven too, idiot," her sibling said. "We're twins."

"I think she's realised that," retorted the first twin.

Gwenn bit back a smile. "And what are your names?"

"We are Selina and Susan," said twin number two. "And there's no point in trying to tell us apart. No one can, so you needn't bother."

"I see," Gwenn said, beginning to realise what exactly she'd gotten herself into. "Nonetheless, I should like to know."

"I'm Selina," offered twin number one.

"I'm Susan," added the other.

"And is that the truth, or are you trying to set me off on the wrong foot with a lie?"

For a moment, Gwenn thought perhaps she'd surprised them, but it was quickly hidden.

"You'll have to find out, won't you?"

Gwenn studied them. Even having known they were a handful, for the children of a viscount they were shockingly rude. Their aunt had kept her mouth closed throughout the exchange, though Gwenn was aware of her scrutiny. No doubt she was being assessed.

"Oh dear," she said with a sigh. "I was hoping this would be an exciting journey and that I would make new friends along the way, but I see I was mistaken." She shook her head and looked mournful, before reaching for her travelling bag and opening it. Gwenn rustled about, making sure the girls caught glimpses of the books and interesting items she'd packed as she searched out a paper bag. She rustled it in her hand, making a show of debating her choice before pulling out a sweet and popping it into her mouth.

"It's not nice to eat sweets in front of others, if you're not going to share," said the first twin indignantly.

"I know," Gwenn said, with a grave nod. "But I don't share with rude little girls, or ones that tell fibs." She smiled at Mrs Bainbridge and leant across the carriage to her, offering her the bag. "Should you like a sweet, madam? They're lemon and honey."

Mrs Bainbridge looked at her for a long moment before allowing the faintest trace of a smile to tug at the corners of her mouth. "I believe I would, Miss Wynter. Thank you."

Gwenn allowed a minute or two to pass before saying, "Good, aren't they?" to Mrs Bainbridge. She could almost hear the twins gnashing their teeth.

"Oh, all right," twin number one said with a huff. "I'm Susan, and that's Selina, and I'm sorry we were rude to you. May we have a sweet now?"

"May we have a sweet now...?" Gwenn prompted, deciding she'd best strike whilst the iron was hot.

"May we have a sweet now, please, Miss Wynter?" the girls sing-songed in unison.

Gwenn beamed at them. "Indeed, you may."

Chapter 3

"Wherein... first impressions."

They changed horses at Barnet, an efficient and speedy process that took barely five minutes. The carriage had already swayed back into motion as Sampson sighed.

"Ought I to have checked on them, do you think?"

"Did you hear screaming?" Samuel asked, raising one eyebrow.

"No."

"There you are, then. They've not yet murdered the new governess. Best leave them be. Aunt May will abandon ship quick sharp if things go downhill."

"Yes, I suppose so," Sampson said, though he still felt vaguely uneasy.

It was most unlike him to have just hired a woman without even setting eyes on her. Though her reference *had* been impeccable, and he *was* desperate.

"Admit it, you're just dying to catch a glimpse of her," Samuel said, giving his brother a sly grin. "Do you have a secret fetish for spectacles and grey, shapeless dresses?"

Sampson returned a quelling glare. "Don't be an arse, Samuel."

"But it's what I do best," Sam said, putting his hand over his heart.

With a snort, Sampson focused his attention to the window. They changed again at St Albans, and still Aunt May didn't come running, and there were no visible or audible signs of distress....

Hopeful that perhaps he'd done the best thing after all, Sampson tipped his hat over his eyes and went to sleep.

***

Perhaps being a courtesan *wasn't* the worst job in the world?

Gwenn pondered this question after almost four hours in the twin's company as she massaged her temples against the headache that threatened. She'd already used many of the things she'd packed in her bag to keep them quiet. They'd played noughts and crosses and eaten half a bag of sweets, and were now occupied in writing an amusing poem, with each of them composing a line in turn, a game she'd enjoyed herself as a child.

She'd also read a story from *Tales from Shakespeare*, a book that rewrote the great man's work in a form suitable for younger readers, making the girls laugh by playing all the parts, deepening her voice for the male characters and putting a deal of energy into the performance. With difficulty, she repressed a surge of guilt at having taken the beautifully illustrated book when she'd left home. Alvermarle had bought it for his children, but had forgotten to take it when he'd last visited Marie, before he'd gone to spend Christmas with his family. Of course, the duke's children had been bought so much they'd hardly miss it. She doubted the man had even noticed, and Gwenn had promised herself she'd replace it when she could. Now, she could only congratulate her own foresight in coming so well prepared. Once again, she must give her mother credit for always having a detailed plan of how to keep her lover entertained.

Perhaps men really were like children? It was a question she felt unqualified to answer until she had more experience of them, but certainly her mother's rules *did* work for children, so perhaps it was reasonable to think she was onto something.

"We must be in Dunstable, we're stopping," said Mrs Bainbridge, rubbing her gloved hand over the fogged up window. "And not a moment too soon. I'm famished."

"Oh, me too," chorused the twins in unison.

Gwen couldn't help but laugh as they discarded their poems at once, pencils and papers set aside as they scurried to kneel on the seats and look outside.

"What, after eating all my sweets?" she protested. "I'm sure you couldn't eat a morsel."

"Oh, I could," Selina said... or was it Susan?

"Me too, I could eat a horse," chimed in Susan, or... well, the other one.

"No, no," Gwenn said solemnly, shaking her head. "I'm certain you could not. Not even a mouse, certainly not a horse."

"I could eat something even bigger than a horse," Susan—no, Selina—protested.

"Really?" Gwenn said, all wide eyed with astonishment. "What *is* bigger than a horse?"

"A... A tiger," Susan shouted, turning her fingers into claws and roaring at Gwenn.

"My, how fierce you are," Gwenn replied. "Though I think there is more meat on a horse than a tiger."

"A whale!" Susan crowed. "I could eat a whale."

Gwenn laughed and set about gathering the discarded pencils and papers before handing the girls their bonnets and gloves. "Well, I'm sure you won't be eating anything at all, unless you look like young ladies who need feeding and not tigers who must be chased away."

The girls took their bonnets and gloves but made no move to put them on.

"Come along, girls," she chided, eager to get out of the blasted carriage. By now she was so desperate for the necessary she felt she might burst. "Put your bonnets and gloves on. If Lord Cheam sees you both looking like hoydens, he'll dismiss me before my first day is over."

Somewhat to her surprise, the girls exchanged glances and did as she told them without protest. Gwenn glanced at Mrs Bainbridge as she drew on her own gloves, to see an approving smile.

"I don't know what your game is, Miss Wynter," the lady said quietly, "but I've never seen the girls take to anyone like they have to you."

Years of practise at keeping her expression carefully blank was the only thing that saved Gwenn from the blush that ought to have stained her face.

"Game?" she replied, her tone cool. "I'm sure I don't know what you mean."

Mrs Bainbridge quirked one eyebrow. "Credit me with a little intelligence, girl," she retorted. "But you handle the girls better than any of the insipid creatures who've had charge of them these past months, so I'll keep my thoughts to myself. I warn you, though: these two will be the least of your troubles."

Before Gwenn could enquire what the lady meant by that, the carriage door had opened and the steps let down. The girls leapt out with a joyful shriek of relief and ran out into the yard.

"Girls!" Gwenn called in dismay, watching them run off toward a sweet black puppy that barked and wagged its tail at them, sensing a game in the offing. "Oh, drat it, you little devils."

With no other option, Gwenn hurried after them.

***

"You're still in one piece, then?" Samuel quipped as they sought out Aunt May. "All arms and legs accounted for? What about mental faculties? Any left?"

"A few, you dreadful creature," Aunt May replied with dignity. "Though I must give credit to the new governess for that. She's a marvel."

Sampson felt his chest ease, as though he'd been holding his breath since they'd left London and hadn't even realised it.

"Where is she?" Samuel asked, staring about the bustling yard.

"She's gone after the girls. Naturally, they ran off at speed the second their feet touched the ground after all morning cooped up. She'll round them up, I don't doubt."

At that moment, Aunt May's lady's maid appeared with a twin clasped firmly in each hand.

"Where is Miss Wynter?" Aunt May asked her maid, who opened her mouth to speak, but Selina beat her to it.

"She's using the necessary," she said, in the clear, bright tones that only a child possessed, with the ability to carry halfway across the yard.

Susan snickered.

"Girls!" Aunt May remonstrated, glaring at them. "Young ladies never refer to such— Oh, never mind. Come inside at once."

Aunt May moved off, but the girls fought free of the maid and each ran to Sampson, clutching a leg each.

"Thank you for our new governess, Sunny," they said, beaming at him with such obvious delight that he couldn't help but return the expression.

It was so good to see them smiling again. For all the glee they derived from their mischievousness, Sampson had feared unhappiness fuelled their bad behaviour. Whoever this new governess was, he would ensure she stayed even if he had to pay her a king's ransom to do so. If the girls were happy, it was worth every penny. If she could make them behave, too... so much the better.

"Yes, well, just don't chase this one away, brats," he scolded, tugging their blonde curls before they ran off after Aunt May. "For I'll make sure the next one makes you do nothing but sums, and gives you slugs for tea."

Sampson's lips twitched as he caught the look in Samuel's eyes. He shrugged, knowing Sam adored the girls every bit as much as he did. Even his dastardly twin brothers were putty in their hands.

"Coming?" Sam asked him as he headed towards the inn.

"In a moment. I must just stretch my legs before I sit down again."

Sam nodded and Sampson strode down the lane, enjoying the ability to move after hours in the cramped carriage. The air was cold but sweet, weak sunshine penetrating the thick clouds overhead. He took a deep breath and let it out again, trying to release some of the pent up tension that had made his chest tight for what seemed an eternity.

His breath clouded about him and he allowed himself a moment to believe he wasn't making such a hash of things as he feared. The girls were excited to meet their new brother, though explaining how and why they had a brother they'd not known about had tested him sorely. Damn his bloody father. Sampson had taken the cowardly route and fudged an answer together which had left them confused but accepting.

At least Ross was a good man. A little rough around the edges, perhaps, and Sampson dreaded to think what kind of bad language and habits the girls might learn from him, but he was family. He wanted his sisters to know what that was, what it meant. He wanted to see them enjoy a Christmas with presents and games and silliness, not the stilted, brittle affair it had always been when his father lived, with everyone on tenterhooks, waiting for everything to go to hell.

The chill of the December day was making itself felt through his coat, and Sampson turned on his heel, heading back to the smart red brick building that was The Sugar Loaf. It stood, proud and elegant, on the road that the Romans had dubbed Watling Street, and was a popular stopping place. Knowing this, and with his usual meticulous planning, Sampson had written some days previously to secure one of the private rooms. He hurried through the door now, grateful for the warmer temperature inside. Having been here several times before, he made his way down a narrow corridor that skirted the public rooms, towards the private dining room.

A door opened at the far end of the corridor and Sampson looked up, expecting to see a serving maid or perhaps the inn keeper come to greet him… and all the breath rushed from his lungs.

There were certain moments in his life that Sampson would never forget. Some of them were happy memories, like the time he'd taken Samuel fishing as a boy, and the look on his face when he'd hooked a bigger trout than Sampson for the first time. Sam had idolised him when they were children, and the pride in his eyes as he'd shown his prize to his big brother had been a moment that had etched itself into Sampson's heart.

The moment he'd truly understood what kind of man his father was had been another. There had been a scandal, as ever, and Sampson had known instinctively that the vile story was true. The realisation that Sampson could never talk of his father with pride and respect like the other boys did was a painful one, but he'd survived it.

The first time he'd seen his twin sisters, so tiny and pink and fragile, had also been an unforgettable moment in his life. He'd fallen for them at once, despite not having the slightest notion what to do with such helpless little babies, too terrified to even pick them up for fear of damaging them. When he'd seen them, he'd made himself a promise to protect them from their father as best he could, and to ensure they had a happy life, untarnished by their wretched sire, no matter what he must do to achieve it.

His half-brother Ross, striding defiantly into their lives just a few months ago and challenging his father to a duel... that one would stick, too.

Those memories marked significant moments in his life, moments that had changed him, for better or worse. Sampson's heart gave several uneven thuds in his chest before righting itself, and he knew, knew without a doubt, that this was one of those moments.

Karma. It was a Sanskrit word, and he knew its meaning well enough, but he'd never felt the impact of it before, the sense of inevitability, of fate bringing two people together in this moment, though whether as a blessing or punishment for past deeds he neither knew nor cared.

He'd never seen such a beautiful woman in all his life.

She was slender, but with generous curves in all the right places. Her hair, which had been wrestled into a harsh style, scraped back from her face and secured in a tight chignon, was gold. There was no other word, it *was* gold and lustrous, and he suspected it had a tendency to curl as a few unruly locks had escaped the fierce restraints and framed her face in guinea gold tendrils, and her face....

Her face....

She turned at that moment, and he forgot how to breathe.

Her eyes were turquoise, a delicate, elusive colour somewhere between a pale blue and a delicate green, and thickly outlined with darker gold lashes.

Though his wits had been scattered, he recognised the spark of interest in her expression as she looked at him, and the way her eyes widened a little. What he was not prepared for was the slow, lingering perusal of his person. Her intent gaze travelled over him, from head to toe and back again, assessing. Sampson had never been regarded with such undisguised interest by a lady, and she did *appear* to be a lady. Heat rushed over him and he was totally discomposed by the realisation he was blushing.

Him. *Blushing?*

Good heavens.

He wondered if she liked what she saw.

Though it was bold and rude and utterly inappropriate, Sampson had to know who she was.

At once.

"Forgive me," he said, noting that his voice sounded odd, a little scratchy and not quite as it ought. "I didn't mean to startle you."

Not that he had startled her, quite the reverse, but it was all he could think of to say.

Please don't be married. Please don't be married.

Her chest rose and fell, and she licked her lips, a movement that his eyes devoured whilst every masculine part of him longed for the right to do the same himself.

"I was not startled," she said, and her voice was soft and cultured, melodic. "But if you would excuse me, I have become a little lost. My party will be missing me."

"I should think they will," Sampson said with feeling, before she could turn away, as was clearly her intention, before adding, "Miss...?" with a gently probing tone that must be unmistakable.

What the devil had gotten into him? A gentleman did not speak to a young woman he'd not been introduced to. Yet he could hardly follow her and ask her father, brother, *husband*... for an introduction, and he felt as if he might run mad if he never discovered her name.

The slightest curve touched her lush mouth before she turned away from him.

"Good day to you, sir."

She moved back towards the door she'd entered through and all Sampson could think of was that if she left he might never see her again, might never know the name of the heavenly creature before him, because surely she was no mortal woman. It was not possible.

She was fate. His fate. Karma.

Don't let her go, you damned fool!

He didn't think, he acted.

"Wait!"

She started a little as he closed the distance between them and put his hand on the door.

"At least let me escort you back to your... husband?"

Something that might have been amusement, or perhaps even regret, flickered in her eyes.

"I don't think that would be appropriate."

Sampson stared down at her, the terrible knowledge searing his chest that her face would haunt him for the rest of his days.

"Please," he said, startled by the quality of his own voice, the desperation.

He didn't even know what he was asking for. He was acting like the worst kind of fool. If she wanted to go, he should let her leave and not utter a word of protest. Yet his chest ached with the certainty that it was regret in her eyes. He was sure of it.

"Wynter," she said, her voice hesitant, as though she knew she ought not speak it. "Miss Wynter."

Sampson let out a breath that was not entirely steady.

"Miss Wynter," he repeated, his relief at knowing both her name and that she was unmarried so overwhelming he could do nothing but smile at her, compounding his idiotic behaviour.

He was about to make some utterly nauseating comment about her being more properly named Summer, for the light she brought to the world, when two things happened at once.

Wynter?

The name suddenly struck him as familiar. As he was pondering this, the door flew open, and he snatched the hand away that had been holding it. Selina and Susan burst through it in their usual elephantine manner, and each of them grabbed at the poor woman's hand, trying to tow her through the door she had been about to leave by.

"There you are!" Susan said, tugging at her. "We've been looking everywhere."

"Were you lost?" Selina added.

"Indeed, I was a little," Miss Wynter said, smiling at them.

The effect of that smile was devastating, and for a moment Sampson could not get his faculties back in working order.

"No, she wasn't," Susan said, gesturing to Sampson. "Look, Sunny is with her."

"S-Sunny?" Miss Wynter stammered, staring at each twin in turn before turning her accusing gaze on him. "You know this gentleman?"

"Of course," Susan piped up. "That's our big brother, Sampson. Now that Papa's dead he's the viscount. You must call him Lord Cheam."

Wynter.

Miss Wynter.

The governess.

Sampson felt hot and cold all at once. He'd just acted like a lovesick puppy....

Over the governess?

Despite feeling like a prize gudgeon, Sampson's heart constricted as he saw all trace of warmth, interest, or amusement seep from her beautiful face, along with all the colour.

"Lord Cheam," she said, his title crisp and as well starched as his cravat, her demeanour now every bit as icy as her name. "Do forgive me for blundering about the inn. I'm afraid, as the girls surmised, I was lost. I am your new governess, as you have no doubt deduced. Please excuse us, the girls ought to wash up before eating."

A moment later and she'd gone, and Sampson was left alone.

Discombobulated.

Now there was a word.

Sampson liked words. He'd been particularly taken with that one as a boy but had never had cause to use it. He used it now, mentally at least.

He was certainly discombobulated, not to mention addled, shaken, thrown, and undone.

What the devil had just happened?

Chapter 4

"Wherein the brothers know trouble when they see it."

Oh my. Oh my. Oh my.

"Are you all right, Miss Wynter?" Susan asked, screwing up her pretty freckled nose.

"Quite all right," Gwenn said, though that was a big, fat lie. "Why should I not be all right?"

Because your insides have melted into a puddle, that's why, you ninny.

"I don't know," Susan said, giving Gwenn a hard look as she guided them back to the private parlour. "You went a funny colour when I introduced you to Sunny. All white and pasty. Didn't you like him?"

Like him? *Like* him?

"Of course she *liked* him," Selina said, tutting and shaking her head. "All the ladies like Sunny. In fact, they *luurve* him. I heard two of the maids talking and they said it's because he's so big and handsome and rich and could charm the birds from the trees, and also because he has such a large pego."

"Susan!" Gwenn exclaimed, shocked despite her own upbringing.

"That's Selina," Susan said, shaking her head with a sigh.

Gwenn rolled her eyes and spoke in the cool, crisp tone she had decided would best suit her role as governess. "Whichever of you is which, that is not a conversation for young ladies."

34

"Isn't it?" Selina asked, delicate blonde eyebrows drawing together.

"No," Gwenn said, a little gentler now as she tried to compose herself. "At least...."

She paused, realising how unfair it was that girls of their ilk were kept in such ignorance about men and sex, and even their own bodies. Marie had always raged about it and, on this, Gwenn felt she had a point.

"You may discuss such subjects with me or with your sister, but only if you are quite certain we are alone, and no one can overhear us. You must never, *ever* say such things before anyone else or they'll... they'll get quite the wrong impression about you."

To her relief, both Selina and Susan seemed to accept this, though Susan was quick to clarify.

"And you'll answer us truthfully, if we ask you a question that makes everyone else go red in the face and talk too loudly about something totally different?"

Gwenn bit back a smile. "I will. I promise, but only if you swear to hide such knowledge. If your brothers or Aunt May discover what I've told you, I'll likely be dismissed on the spot."

"We'll not breathe a word of it," Selina said, her expression solemn.

"Not ever," Susan agreed. "We want you to stay forever."

Sincerity shone in their bright blue eyes and Gwenn came a little unglued as she remembered an identical pair that had stared at her with such undisguised lust just moments ago.

"Come along, girls," she said, all brisk and governessy again, though she felt nothing like a governess inside as her inner harlot seemed to be fighting to get out. "Let's go and eat."

She took their hands and tried to batten down the commotion inside her. Never in her life had she had such a reaction to a man.

Admittedly, she'd not met that many, as Marie had been careful with her, but sometimes her mother had allowed her strictly supervised outings and to attend a few quiet dinner parties. It was laughable how carefully chaperoned she'd been, really, but Gwenn's physical innocence was a commodity that would fetch a vast price and there could be no question of doubt as to its veracity.

One look at Viscount Cheam and Gwenn had known how futile her flight from her fate had been. Aunt Letty had been right. It was in the blood. Suddenly every lesson she'd been taught about how to please a man flashed into her mind, and she'd wanted to try every one of them... with him.

On him.

Under him.

No.

No. No. *No.*

Lord Cheam was her employer, for now at least. She had no intention of staying with the family for long. It was clear enough that the life of a governess was not for her, though she liked the girls, dreadful as they were. Besides which as soon as they returned to London Marie would track her down with ease. Somehow, though, she had to find a respectable way of living. She had a small fortune in jewels hidden in her baggage; she simply needed to find herself a companion, a widowed lady or a respectable woman fallen on hard times... then she could set up home and live quietly and try to find herself a kind husband, that faceless man who sat with her by the fire and talked about the day with her.

For now, she just needed to escape London and her mother, and disappear. Once she was safely married, she could get in touch with her family and hope they would forgive her for the loss of all their dreams for her.

Until then, she had to keep Lord Cheam at bay. She recognised the look in his eyes well enough, and now she completely understood Mrs Bainbridge's wry comment.

These two are going to be the least of your troubles.

Oh, good grief.

***

By the time he'd found the private parlour, Sampson had gotten himself under some semblance of control. This appeared to be a complete waste of effort, however, as the moment Miss Wynter entered the room, he unravelled all over again.

Sampson, unused to being so... discombobulated, did what most men did when in turmoil and vacillated between silence and truculent ill humour. She was the governess, he told himself. He could *not* touch the governess. He couldn't marry her, and he certainly couldn't have an affair with her. His goal was respectability, and either of those things would only add to the family's notoriety. It was no great difficulty, he assured himself. He'd lusted over women before; it wasn't the first time and it would not be the last. He would simply put her from his mind and treat her as he had all the other governesses.

Liar, liar, liar, crowed a jaunty voice in his head.

He was doomed.

Sampson's temper was not helped on viewing Samuel's face when he got his first look at the new governess.

He looked just like Sampson must have looked himself, as if he'd been struck in the head with a heavy, blunt object. The temptation to do just that to his brother was tantalising. Sampson settled for kicking him under the table. Hard.

"Stop gawking," he muttered as Samuel tore his stunned green gaze from the vision and back to Sampson.

"B-But...." he stammered.

37

"I know," Sampson said, his mouth set in a grim line, ignoring his aunt's obvious amusement with rigid determination.

They ate their meal, Sampson eating his so fast in a bid to get out of the room he knew he'd have indigestion for the rest of the day, and Samuel repeatedly stopping with a forkful of pie suspended halfway between his plate and his mouth to gaze upon the unholy temptation that had been thrust into their midst. His shins would be black and blue by the time he got back in the carriage, that was for certain.

No wonder Lord Alvermarle had given Miss Wynter such a glowing recommendation, even though she couldn't have worked with them for long, she was too young. No doubt his wife would have made his life a living hell if he'd not gotten her out of the house at once.

The twins babbled merrily but to his consternation they behaved themselves, complying at once when Miss Wynter gently reprimanded them for raising their voices or speaking with their mouths full. He couldn't dismiss her, not when she was so obviously just what the girls needed. That would have been a relief, to get her out of his life and his mind, and....

He jolted with a muttered curse as Samuel kicked him in the shin. Sampson tore his gaze away from the wretched woman to glare at his brother.

Hell's bells.

***

Gwenn did her utmost to concentrate on her meal. The Sugar Loaf was famous for its lark pie, which was indeed delicious, though she could not help but feel regret for all the tiny birds. Dunstable was also famous for larks, the poor little things caught with nets by the thousands on Dunstable Downs. All at once her appetite deserted her, and she pushed her plate away.

To her relief, the girls chattered nonstop, their merry conversation needing little input from her, which was just as well.

She was horribly aware of the striking man at the other end of the table, and all the ways in which he could destroy her plans and her peace of mind.

His brother, Samuel Pelham, was every bit as handsome, the similarity between them obvious even without the red hair that screamed their kinship. His eyes were green, not blue, however, though she recognised the gleam of interest when they settled on her easily enough. Strangely, her reaction to him was not the puddle of goo, knee-trembling response that Lord Cheam had instigated in an instant, which was odd, as there was little to choose between them in looks. Yet she had only to sneak a glance at the viscount for her insides to quiver and her thoughts to stray to all things wicked in the most outrageous manner.

There was only one way to survive the coming weeks, she realised. She must rebuff any interest from that quarter with her iciest, most governessy conduct. Any attempt at flirtation would be nipped in the bud, any flattery or teasing behaviour mercilessly stamped upon with a few frigid set downs. She would treat him with a frosty politeness that barely remained on the right side of contempt. Sadly, she was aware that some men craved such treatment—another of her mother's lessons in being a talented whore. Marie had trained her to recognise such traits and play to them, but she saw nothing in Lord Cheam that suggested he enjoyed being dominated or treated like dirt.

To her relief, the meal was finally over and everyone hurried back to their respective carriages to continue the journey. At least she would only see him at mealtimes for the duration of their journey to Scotland. Once there, she would stay away from any family time where possible and make sure to keep the girls thoroughly occupied and out of mischief every other moment. That would keep her thoroughly occupied and out of mischief too, with a bit of luck.

Despite her intention to stop her thoughts from lingering on the man, she could not help but wonder why his name hadn't appeared on her mother's list. He was titled and wealthy and, from what the girls had let slip, he liked the ladies. She refused to contemplate what else they'd implied, though heat uncoiled low in her belly all the same. Well, anyway, his being a one for the ladies had been clear enough, the man had *seasoned rake* practically stamped on his forehead. So did his brother, come to that.

So, a sulky little voice in her head persisted, why had Lord Cheam not appeared on the list? Gwenn had never even heard of him, though she was not allowed to read the scandal sheets as yet. Marie said it would be her job to keep up with all the gossip and tattle once she had selected a protector, but for now she must appear innocent of such worldly scandal.

Gah!

What a laugh.

Personally Gwenn thought Marie preferred to keep her in ignorance of the people who inhabited the world she was to enter to keep a greater level of control over her future. She knew her mother would accept nothing less than a marquess for her first lover, but she'd added plenty of lesser titles not to mention wealthy merchants to the list, simply because the more interest there was, the higher it would drive her price.

Had Lord Cheam not been asked, or had he declined?

She was far too interested in the answer for her own good.

By the time they reached the Saracen's Head in Towcester, Gwenn was exhausted. The girls were bright and funny, but they needed constant attention on the journey or they would begin squabbling and getting fractious; it took every bit of Gwenn's ingenuity to keep them fully occupied. Once she'd handed them into the care of their nursemaid, who would get them washed and ready for bed, she retreated to her room and collapsed onto the mattress with a groan.

What had she done?

With a wistful sigh she thought of what her day might have been if she'd not been so reckless. Dress fittings, shopping, and filling her leisure time with playing piano and reading or painting. Ironically, she was technically well qualified to be a governess, having had a rigid education. Whilst it behoved a whore to hide her cleverness with some men, others relished a conversation with a woman who could speak eloquently and with wit, and who could follow a discussion about politics. A wise courtesan would use the information she gleaned to further her own interests, whether financially or socially, and making the best use of that information required a lively mind and a good understanding of the world and how it worked.

Of course, a governess was also supposed to look to her charges' moral education. Here things got a little foggy, but Gwenn had already decided to do what she felt best by the girls for the short time she would be with them. Young women ought not be thrust into the world like lambs led to the lion's den, without the slightest idea of what life was about. So, whilst the girls were young, though she'd not force information upon them, if they asked any indelicate questions, she would respond with as much frankness as she felt appropriate, and to the devil with the consequences.

***

The next morning, Sampson climbed into the carriage feeling just as fractious and irritable as he had the day before. Worse. He'd slept badly, his dreams infested with heated visions of a certain gorgeous governess whom he couldn't seem to get off his mind. He didn't doubt the fact his perverse libido had decided that, now she was totally off limits, she was even more desirable than before... if that were even possible.

No matter how often—or how severely—he told himself she was *off limits*, for more reasons than he could even number, the moment she entered the room he felt like a hound that had caught the unmistakable scent of a fox. He practically quivered with the urge to hunt her down and melt the frosty expression that settled on her lovely face whenever she looked at him, until the warmth and amusement returned to her eyes. Sampson knew he hadn't imagined that warmth, or the spark of interest. He had not.

He was aware of Samuel's scrutiny as he sat down in the carriage opposite him, but ignored it. He was not in the mood for conversation.

This ought to be obvious to his youngest brother too, but when had that ever stopped him?

"If she's a governess, I'm a pirate."

"You *are* a pirate, or at least you must have been in a past life," Sampson remarked, though the comment sparked his interest all the same. "Why do you say that?"

If there was one thing Samuel had a talent for, it was unearthing secrets. He even made a living as an investigator, and had done so ever since their father had cut him off financially and thrown him out of the house. Though Samuel had done it purely to infuriate the late viscount, Sampson had been none too pleased either, and regularly pleaded with Sam to return to the fold and stop being so bloody obstinate. Their father was dead, and Sampson could well afford to keep his brother, but Sam would have none of it. He liked his work and was bloody good at it.

Samuel snorted and rolled his eyes. "Good lord, Sunny, look at her. When was the last time you saw a governess who looked like that? Not to mention her clothes. They might be last season's, but they'd have cost an arm and a leg."

Sampson frowned and leant across the carriage.

"What are you saying? Why would she pretend to be a governess if she's not? It's hardly a position a woman aspires to, is it?"

"Of course not," Sam said impatiently. "She's hiding."

Sampson sat up in alarm, all his protective instincts bristling at once.

"Hiding from who?"

"How the devil should I know?"

"Well, you seem to have all the answers," Sampson snapped, folding his arms.

Sam shrugged. "I'm only telling you what is blatantly obvious to anyone with half a brain in his head, but as you're only using the tiny brain in your britches, I suppose it's not surprising you didn't figure it out."

"Oh, like you didn't spend every mealtime gazing at her like a blasted lovesick mooncalf!"

"I did not!"

"Liar!"

Sampson snapped his mouth shut as he realised they sounded like a pair of five-year-olds in need of a spanking from their governess. Then he imagined himself telling the governess that turnabout was fair play and his vision went blurry and he got hot all over. Sampson muttered, cursing himself roundly for that image which would be imprinted on his brain for the rest of the day, if not eternity.

There was a taut silence.

"It's either a man, or a scandal caused by a man. Whether or not she's responsible in any way is impossible to know. A woman who looks like that is going to have men behaving like idiots at every turn." Samuel broke off to give Sampson a pointed look which he ignored. "I know one thing. She's trouble, whether she means to be or not."

"We'll have to get rid of her," Sampson said with a groan.

"Well, you can tell the girls," Samuel retorted, shaking his head. "They think she's the sun and the moon and the stars, and I can't blame them. She has the knack of conversing with them, of making everything interesting. I've never seen anyone wrap the two of them about their finger like she can. It's remarkable."

Sampson swallowed down the observation that she could wrap him about her finger whenever she liked. It was obvious Samuel had concluded as much already and felt the same way. The idea of Samuel laying a finger on the woman made Sampson want to stamp his foot and rage that *he'd seen her first.*

Bloody hell.

What was it about her that made him act like a spoilt boy?

His brother was right about one thing. Miss Wynter was trouble, and she would have to go.

Chapter 5

"Wherein Gwenn discovers she's not the only scandal in town."

"The Scandalous *what?*" Gwenn said in alarm, as two sets of identical blue eyes blinked at her in amusement.

They'd stopped at Market Harborough to change horses and Mrs Bainbridge—who had insisted that Gwenn now refer to her as Aunt May, as everyone else did—had taken the opportunity to use the conveniences. Taking advantage of the moment, Gwenn had probed a little about their family, too curious not to discover more.

Why hadn't Lord Cheam been on her list?

"The Scandalous Brothers," Susan repeated, grinning at her. "Didn't you know? I thought everyone knew."

"Our family is wicked," Selina added with a sigh.

"Bad blood," Susan added cheerfully, though as Gwenn studied her a frown puckered her forehead and she looked troubled.

"What nonsense," Gwenn replied, startled, even though she'd had similar thoughts about her own bloodline.

"It's not nonsense," Selina said, and Gwenn felt her heart constrict at the sadness in the girl's eyes. "Our father was a bad, bad man."

"He did terrible, wicked things," Susan added, her voice little more than a whisper. "And he's gone to hell. Sunny thinks we don't know. He tries to keep things from us, but we've listened to them talking when they think we've gone to bed, so we know it's true."

The girls shared a glance and shuffled a little closer together, but then Selina brightened, turning a dazzling smile upon Gwenn. "But *we* shan't go to the devil now, or to hell, because you've come, and you can stop us."

Gwenn gaped at them.

"No one else could," Susan added with a sigh and a blithe wave of her hand. "Because they made us so cross that we *felt* like going to the devil, but you don't. So, as long as you stay, we ought to be fine."

"But if you leave, *we're doomed.*"

The two girls spoke the words *we're doomed* in unison, which was creepy enough, but with such a gothic interpretation that all the hairs on the back of Gwenn's neck stood on end.

Those blue eyes stared at her, all guileless innocence, and she realised far too late that she was in way over her head.

***

By the time they made the inn at Derby that evening, Gwenn was frozen. The weather had taken a turn for the worse somewhere around Loughborough, and the temperature had plummeted. Though the hot bricks beneath their feet had been replaced whenever they stopped to change horses, her toes felt like tiny blocks of ice and she was certain she'd never be warm again.

Dinner had been excellent, and hot too, but somehow the chill in her bones had not diminished. Gwenn shut her chamber door and prayed the sheets weren't damp and the bed had been warmed. She was looking forward to climbing under layers of blankets and thawing herself out when she realised she'd left her shawl in the private parlour downstairs. It was made of the finest cashmere, and was the warmest one she had. She didn't dare leave such a valuable item lying about in the inn. One never knew how honest the staff, or the other patrons were. Not wanting to risk losing it, she hurried back down the stairs to the where the family had dined earlier.

Mr Pelham, Lord Cheam's younger brother, turned as she walked in and she started in surprise.

"Oh, I beg your pardon. I thought everyone had gone to bed," she said, hesitating in the doorway. "I just came to get my shawl."

"Here you go," he said, taking it from the chair beside the fire and handing it to her. "I was going to have one of the serving girls run it up to you. I was just having a nightcap. I can't seem to get warm tonight." He gestured to the glass in his hand. "It's doing the trick, too," he added, giving her a grin that made him look like a naughty schoolboy. "Would you like a drop?"

Gwenn opened her mouth to refuse, knowing she ought not, but a drop of cognac might be just the thing to warm her up and send her to sleep.

"It's excellent stuff," Mr Pelham coaxed. "Here, try for yourself."

Without awaiting an answer, he poured a drop out and handed it to her.

Gwenn took the glass from him and cupped it in her palm, warming the liquor within for a moment before lifting it to her nose. "Mmmm," she said, smiling a little. "That does smell good."

She swirled it around the glass, inhaling the heady scent again before taking a sip and closing her eyes with a sigh of pleasure.

"Lovely," she said, savouring the complex flavours. It really was a superb vintage and just the thing to chase away the chill. "Vanilla and apricot, and a hint of…." Gwenn frowned, trying to place what it was she could taste. "Oh, of course, hazelnut!"

She laughed as she opened her eyes and looked to Mr Pelham. He was staring at her with undisguised interest.

"You have quite the refined palate, Miss Wynter."

Too late, Gwenn realised she'd been carried away with her enthusiasm. It was second nature to her to savour a fine liquor or wine, but what was acceptable in a whore was hardly the thing for a respectable woman. A governess would probably never even have tasted cognac before, let alone be a connoisseur. Hurriedly, she set the glass down.

"Not really," she said briskly. "I was only guessing. I once saw my father taste in such a way; I merely copied what I remember him doing."

It wasn't entirely a lie. It hadn't been her father, but her mother's lover, the Duke of Alvermarle, and she hadn't merely watched. The duke had spent a great deal of time with her, teaching her how to appreciate both wine and cognac, and how to tell quality. He'd also taught her how to prepare a cigar. She could smoke one, too, though she didn't enjoy them, but some men liked to see such things, so....

"Oh, don't go. You've not finished your drink, and it would be a pity to waste it," Mr Pelham urged.

Gwenn sent the glass a longing look. It had been extremely good.

"Sacrilege, in fact," he pressed, grinning.

"Well, for just a moment," she said, though she remained where she was by the door. She'd left it ajar, so it was all perfectly respectable, she assured herself.

Taking up the glass again, she took another sip and felt the liquor easing into her bones and threading through her blood, warming and relaxing as it went and creating a little glow of heat in her belly. She enjoyed the sensation as her thoughts drifted and she wondered what her mother was doing, and just how furious she was. Would she send out a search party for her? Perhaps she'd contact Alvermarle? The thought made Gwenn shiver despite the warming qualities of the cognac.

"The duke must have been sorry to see you go?" Mr Pelham said, his words coinciding so closely with her thoughts she jolted with alarm.

"W-What?"

"Your last employer," Mr Pelham said mildly, though there was a glint of curiosity in his eyes. "The Duke of Alvermarle, was it not?"

"Oh," Gwenn said, composing herself and cursing her own stupidity. "Yes, indeed, but it was only ever a temporary posting. He is a f-friend of my mother's, and agreed to let me try my hand with his children before I found myself a permanent situation. A recommendation from a duke can open a lot of doors."

Marie had always told her that, if one must lie, it was best to stick as close to the truth as possible. Yes, there was a chance that Mr Pelham might speak with the duke if they were acquainted and such an enquiry *could* lead her mother back to Gwenn, but by then she would be long gone, so it was a minor risk.

"That was good of him," Mr Pelham said lightly, a little too lightly perhaps. "Though if he was your mother's friend, one wonders that he could not help you in other ways?"

Gwenn stiffened, aware now that Mr Pelham was probing as to why she'd not been saved from the ignominy of working for a living. "My family do not need or require charity, sir," she said, her voice cool. "I accepted his offer to work for him and I did a good job. To be beholden to him in any other way would be most improper, as I am sure you are aware."

"Please forgive me, Miss Wynter," Mr Pelham said, his manner soothing, though there was still something in his eyes that disturbed her. "I assure you, I meant no disrespect, but to be frank, it is unusual to see such a young and stunningly beautiful woman in the role of governess. Most families would not employ you, you know. Any wife with an ounce of sense would want you far away from any husband."

His gaze held hers, a glimmer of challenge there.

"Yet you mean no disrespect?" she repeated, glaring at him.

Mr Pelham laughed, shaking his head. "I'm sorry, Miss Wynter. My manners are appalling, I know, but truly, I did not mean it as an insult, just a truth of which we are all well aware. You cannot expect me to believe you are ignorant of the effect you have on men?"

"I am a respectable woman," Gwenn snapped, furious at the fact it was a lie, furious that she couldn't seem to outrun the path fate had laid out for her. She knew well enough that he was quite correct. "You cannot hold me responsible for—"

"What the devil is going on here?"

Gwenn swung around in the voice's direction to discover Lord Cheam standing close behind her and glaring at his brother.

"Sam?" he asked, a warning note to his voice.

"Sampson," Mr Pelham replied, using the same deep tone, though his expression was alight with mischief. "Miss Wynter has just been schooling me on the finer points of this cognac. Try some. It really is excellent."

Gwenn narrowed her eyes at him, tossed back the last of the drink without blinking and stalked from the room. At least, she tried to stalk... but the imposing figure of Lord Cheam blocked the exit.

"Excuse me, my lord," she said, with as much ice as she could muster with the cognac threading fire through her veins. "I just came to retrieve my shawl. I will leave you and Mr Pelham to enjoy your evening."

"It seems you got more than the shawl," he replied, matching her frigid tone. "I hope the cognac warmed you sufficiently?"

Despite his chilly demeanour, Gwenn could hear the unspoken invitation, the desire to find other ways to warm her. The fool was jealous of her being alone with his brother. Men. They were so bloody predictable.

50

"Indeed, my lord. I feared I would take a chill, having been so cold all day," she said briskly. "A medicinal tot of brandy is just the thing to ward off such problems. I should hate to delay your journey by falling ill."

Lord Cheam stared at her, his blue eyes searching hers for a long moment and she forced herself not to turn away from him. Curse the man, why did he have to look like a burnished pagan idol with all that red hair gleaming in the firelight? She wondered if the hair elsewhere on his person was the same shade and then scolded herself for even considering the question. At least she was brazen enough not to blush, though his gaze was so intent she had the sudden and forceful desire to do something, to establish just who had the power here. She need only to speak a flirtatious word in a low, breathless voice, or to lick her lips, slowly and sensually, and she'd see his eyes darken, see the look he'd worn the first day they'd met—the hunger.

That was what Marie would do, what she'd taught Gwenn to do, but it was not the life she wanted for herself. She wanted a husband, a settled life, not a string of lovers and constant uncertainty, and so she kept her expression cool and aloof. She was saving herself for her wedding night. If she would give herself away for anything less, she might as well go home and accept the highest bidder.

"If you would excuse me," she repeated, with a little more force this time.

"Of course, Miss Wynter," Lord Cheam said, scrupulously polite as he stepped aside for her.

Gwenn hurried away and didn't breathe again until she'd closed her chamber door.

***

Sampson glowered at his brother. "What the hell are you playing at?"

"Playing at?" Sam repeated, the picture of innocence. "Whatever do you mean?"

Ignoring the question on principle—his bloody brother knew exactly what he meant—Sampson snatched up the decanter and poured himself a large measure. His reaction on discovering Miss Wynter alone with his brother had not pleased him.

"She's off limits, Sam," he growled, taking a mouthful of his drink.

"Oh, but, Sampson," he said, laughing a little as he shook his head. "You've never seen such an unholy temptation as Miss Wynter savouring a fine cognac. My word, when she closed her eyes and licked her lips…." He let out a low whistle. "She knew what she was doing," he added, winking at Sampson and giving him the strong desire to knock the glass from his brother's hand. "Vanilla and apricot," he said with a smirk. "With a hint of hazelnut."

To his chagrin, Sampson discovered that was exactly what he could taste too. His eyes widened.

"Who the devil is she?" he demanded, his annoyance with his brother dissipating as his curiosity grew. She was like no woman he'd ever met before. Samuel was right about her being wonderful with the girls, that was obvious. It was also clear that she genuinely liked them. Her rapport with them was easy and in no way forced. What kind of woman could befriend his little sisters and keep them in order, and down a glass of cognac without so much as blinking, let alone point out all the finer details of its quality? What else could she do? He almost shivered at the possibilities his mind conjured. Damn it. She was a conundrum, and one he was increasingly interested in unravelling.

"I don't know who she is," Sam replied with a sigh. "But I think I might just marry her. It will be a world of fun trying to find out."

Though Sampson was fairly certain his brother was joking, the words set off an unpleasant reaction inside his chest.

"You'll stay away from her, or I'll make you sorry you were born," he said, even though he knew, *knew*, this was not the way to handle Samuel. "I told you, she's off limits, and I meant it."

"You mean, you want me to leave the field open for my big brother?" Sam retorted, shaking his head. "Oh, no, Sunny. No, I think not."

"No," Sampson ground out, though he rather feared it was exactly what he did mean. "I mean she's off limits, to both of us. You said yourself, she's trouble. We'll have to keep her on until we return from Scotland, but that's it. She must go."

Samuel snorted. "You play the respectable nobleman if you want. I'm not passing up a woman like that, not even for you."

"Damn it, Sam," Sampson cursed, putting down his glass with a little too much force. "I'm not playing at this. We've all got to be bloody respectable. In ten years or so our sisters will be looking for husbands. What kind of match will they make if they're kin to The Scandalous Brothers? They'll be ruined before they even come out. You know we couldn't get vouchers for Almack's if our lives depended on it. That must change, Sam, it *must*."

His brother stared at him, considering. "I know things have to change, Sampson," he said, but that doesn't mean we have to change who we are. I'll do my best for the girls, I swear, but I won't be someone I'm not, and it would be a disservice to them if I tried. I don't give a damn if they marry a title or make a brilliant match. I only care that they're happy. If the bloody *ton* can't see what marvellous girls they are, then they don't deserve them. They can marry outside of it. There are plenty of self-made men with far more character and worth that some of the noble fools we meet."

"You can't be serious?" Sampson said, horrified. "You'd have them looked down on and sneered at, ostracised by their own kind?"

Samuel sighed and upended his glass, draining it in one large swallow. "I'm not going out of my way to make it happen, you fool, and there's plenty of time. I only mean that there is a world outside of the upper ten thousand, and you ought not tie yourself in knots worrying so."

Sampson stared at him in disbelief and Samuel rolled his eyes.

"For God's sake, have another drink and relax. You'll never sleep if you don't calm down. Speaking of... I'm off to bed. G'night, brother dear. Sweet dreams."

Sampson glowered as Sam gave him a wink and left him alone.

Cursing, Sampson decided his brother had a point about one thing, and poured himself another drink.

Chapter 6

"Wherein Gwenn tests her charms."

"What do you think of our new governess?" Sampson asked his aunt as they took a few minutes to stroll in the chilly morning sunshine.

They'd stopped at Ashbourne on the southern edge of the Peak District to change horses and, although they'd not been going long, she had requested a moment to stretch her legs.

"She's a marvel with the girls," she replied, watching the woman herself on the other side of the road as she said something that made the twins roar with laughter.

Miss Wynter grinned at them, a mischievous glint to her expression. That naughty smile lit up her face and made Sampson's heart flutter. Wait, *flutter?* He stiffened as he recognised the danger. Bloody hell.

"Yes," he said, though his agreement sounded terse and impatient. "But what about *her?* Do you think she's everything she seems? Is she respectable?"

His aunt glanced up at him, searching his face. For a moment, he thought he saw her lips twitch with amusement. "She has a recommendation from the Duke of Alvermarle, dear. How much more respectable do you want her to be?"

"Yes, I know, but—"

"I suppose you believe a woman who looks like that cannot be respectable?"

There was an edge to the question and Sampson frowned.

"No, I…." he began, but then he wondered if her question had merit.

A woman who looked like that would never be short of male attention. Even if she didn't have a penny to her name, a woman of such extraordinary beauty could catch herself a wealthy husband with ease, though it wasn't just her looks that could make a man lose his grasp on reason. There was something about her that called to a forbidden corner of his soul. It was reckless and wild, and he didn't approve of it, in either of them, not when he was trying so hard to move the family out of their father's shadow.

She didn't even move like most respectable women. There was an awareness of her own body in the way she swayed her hips, the way she lifted a morsel of food to her mouth and chewed, something innately sensual that no innocent miss he'd ever come across possessed. Why would a woman like that be a governess, unless she was running away from something, as Samuel had suggested?

"Perhaps," he conceded, dragging his unwilling mind back to the question. "But when was the last time you saw a governess who looked like that?"

Aunt May shrugged. "Perhaps her family has fallen on hard times. Perhaps her parents were trying to force her into a bad marriage. Who knows?"

The protective instinct that had beset him when Sam had suggested she was running away rose again. The desire to protect his sisters warred with the desire to protect Miss Wynter from anything that might take that mischievous smile from her face and was at once understandable and terrifying. Sampson tried to rationalise it. After all, she was in his employ; of course he would protect her, as he would protect Mrs Sydney or any of his staff.

It wasn't the same, and he knew it.

"You could talk to her," his aunt suggested, though the words were a little faint as she'd turned her head away from him. "Get to know her. Then she might confide in you. If you're that curious to know the truth."

He could, Sampson thought. He could get to know her, which would mean spending time with her, naturally. If he was friendly to her, she might tell him her secrets, she might....

Visions of Miss Wynter gazing at him with gratitude for having eased her mind of troubles filled his imagination. In the picture she stared up at him and smiled, and lifted her mouth, inviting him....

Bloody hell's bells and damn me for a fool.

"I don't think that's appropriate," Sampson said, unnerved by the rasp in his voice and the longing for everything he'd just imagined.

What was wrong with him? He wasn't the kind of man to fall apart and make a cake of himself over a pretty face, not even a beautiful one. What was it about Miss Wynter that made him want to act the fool?

Aunt May sighed. "No, I don't suppose it is," she said, something in the words that made him turn to look at her, but her face was expressionless.

"You could do it, though," Sampson said. "You're with her all day in the carriage. *You* could find out about her." He watched his aunt's face darken. "You like her." He wished it hadn't sounded so much like an accusation. "You think there's something odd about her, too, but you like her, so you don't want to know."

She glared at him and tutted. "I do like her, and I think life is hard enough for a young woman alone in the world, without people poking and prying into her private life. If I saw anything that suggested she was ill-suited to looking after my nieces, I would be the first person to ring alarm bells, but I do not see that. I see a lively and well-educated woman who has wit enough to keep those girls under control without squashing their spirits."

Sampson felt a surge of guilt as he considered this. "I just don't want this family embroiled in any further scandal," he said, wondering if that was the only reason Miss Wynter unnerved him so.

Of course it wasn't.

It was not comfortable to be around a woman he desired so badly when she was off limits. Especially not when that woman had his little sisters in her charge. He didn't want to behave badly, but he suspected Miss Wynter was going to sorely test his willpower. Yet, everything his aunt had said was true. Why should Miss Wynter lose a position, she was well suited for simply because she was beautiful? He was an educated man, a gentleman, not an animal. Yes, he wanted her, but he could keep his trousers buttoned and his mind off her. *He could.* Besides which, she'd been every bit as frosty as her name implied when they interacted. It wasn't as if she was interested in him, and he'd certainly not force his attentions where they were not welcome.

Despite his best intentions, his mind returned to those first few seconds in the corridor of The Sugar Loaf, and the interest that had gleamed in her eyes, the lingering way she had surveyed his person, her gaze taking him in with shameless approval.

"I will not spy for you, Sampson," his aunt said, recalling him to the conversation. "However, if I believe that the young lady is in any way ill-suited to her position, you may rest assured I shall let you know."

Sampson let out a breath. He could hardly ask for more than that. "Thank you, Aunt."

***

For Gwenn, the day passed in much the same way as the previous one, keeping the girls entertained over the long and tedious journey.

She began to spend some time quizzing them to see what, if anything, they'd been taught to date. When they responded with correct answers, she would reward them by playing a game for a while before returning to their lessons. Since the disturbing revelation of their belief they'd risked going to hell, Gwenn had made a point of telling them how very good they were, and praising them for their politeness and anything that resembled appropriate behaviour. When they were rude or a little naughty, she'd simply give them a mild look of surprise and say nothing at all. Often, they begged her forgiveness a short time later, and Gwenn would hug them and tell them it was quite all right, everyone behaved badly at times, even her—though she'd bitten her lip a little at that understatement.

Somewhat to her surprise, the sisters responded to her words, and their behaviour improved perceptibly. Oh, they were still high-spirited and probably too loud for any other governess to take a pride in, but Gwenn didn't care a jot about that. She had no desire to crush their spirits; they'd need that vivacity to survive a male-dominated world.

To her relief, the girls were every bit as bright as they appeared, and despite having chased away several governesses they seemed to have learned something in the process. Better yet, she often saw approval in Aunt May's eyes, and was gratified by the occasional murmur of congratulation.

They stopped in the market town of Leek in Staffordshire to stretch their legs and eat a hot meal. During this time, Gwenn attended to the girls and scrupulously ignored the brothers, especially Lord Cheam. At least, she made a show of acting as if he were not there. She was all too aware of his presence at the table. It was the hardest thing not to allow her gaze to stray and admire the breadth of his shoulders and the gleam of that thick, red hair. Her fingers itched with the desire to touch it and her wicked nature was only too easily led into thoughts of the kind any respectable young lady ought to be incapable of. She scolded herself for being so weak willed and concentrated on her meal, and the twins.

Macclesfield and Stockport came and went during the afternoon, and they arrived for their overnight stop in Manchester. The inn they were staying at was charming and the staff were attentive. The Black Bull was set away from the main thoroughfare where one would be awoken at all hours of the night by the comings and goings of travellers, and catered instead to the more well-to-do visitor. One thing she would say for Lord Cheam, he had meticulously arranged this journey. Aunt May had explained that her eldest nephew did not like surprises, and everything in life had to be planned and arranged in advance. That he had undertaken to do this himself, rather than have a steward or secretary arrange it for him was surprising, and Gwenn had commented as much.

"His father was a rather disreputable figure, to put it mildly, and an unreliable one," Aunt May confided to her when they'd had a moment alone. "At a young age, Sampson decided it was better to rely on himself if anything was to get done in the manner it ought. He's certainly the most serious of the brothers, not that his reputation would suggest as much. In his youth he was every bit as capable of kicking up a lark as the other three and, as you know, reputations once established are hard to change. In reality, he's sobered a great deal in recent years. Indeed, I think his worry for the family has extinguished much of his spark, which is terribly sad."

Gwenn thought it sad too and couldn't help but consider just how easy it would be to chase away the lines of strain and worry she could see about his eyes. *Not your job*, she reminded herself, snapping her attention back to Aunt May, who was certainly probing for information. She was a clever woman, and not a little devious, inviting Gwenn to trust in her by confiding in Gwenn first, though the information she offered would be obvious enough to anyone in close contact with the family and half a brain, so she wasn't giving as much away as it appeared.

Gwenn wondered if Lord Cheam had put her up to it, for it was apparent he was mighty suspicious of her, as was his brother.

So, she trod with care and gave as much real information as she dared whilst keeping the details vague.

Yes, her father was still living, but they were not close as her parents were estranged. Her mother had raised her alone, but they were not divorced—this was a misdirection rather than a lie, bearing in mind they'd never actually been married. She had been given a comprehensive education at her mother's insistence, as that lady knew her daughter would be forced to earn her keep, as she was unlikely to marry—not being often in the company of the kind of men who would make a respectable offer. She'd had a sheltered upbringing and knew no one among the *ton*.

All *fairly* accurate.

By the time Gwenn had danced in and out of the truth of her own story and avoided any outright lies, she had a blinding headache. Thankfully, Aunt May recognised her fatigue and sent her off for a lie down before dinner.

A short nap restored her enough that she felt guilty at having shirked her duties and hurried downstairs early. No doubt the girls had foisted themselves on one of the poor maids, who would have enough to do without keeping the two of them entertained. They'd be bound to get themselves into mischief if left alone too long.

As Gwenn rushed down the stairs and turned towards the private rooms, she heard an unmistakably familiar voice close behind her. With her heart beating in her throat, she turned and gasped as she saw the profile of a man she knew all too well.

Charles Lawrence, or more formally, the Earl of Wychwood, was deep in conversation with another fellow she did not recognise. She recognised Lord Wychwood well enough, though; he was high on her mother's list of suitors. A man in his prime, he was handsome, outrageously wealthy, and had a reputation for high living and generosity. He was also one of the few men who had already met Gwenn, as he was a close friend of the Duke of

Alvermarle. His interest in her had been marked, and there was no question of him bidding high if he ever got the opportunity.

Oh, no.

Oh, no, no, no.

Panicked, Gwenn ran for the first available door and hurried through it, closing it just as the earl turned in her direction. She let out a shaky sigh of relief and wondered how long she'd have to hide before the wretched man went on his way. Pushing away from the door, she turned, and her heart dropped to her boots as she saw Lord Cheam staring at her in outrage, as well he might. She had just burst in on him in a private parlour, without invitation.

Oh, this was bad.

Gwenn swallowed and put her chin up, meeting his furious gaze.

She could hardly tell him the truth of why she'd rushed in here, and she could still hear the earl's deep voice from the other side of the door. If he saw her, she was sunk. She'd just have to brazen it out and pray the earl would go about his business sooner rather than later. Distracting Lord Cheam for the next ten minutes ought not be a difficult thing to do. How she could best distract him was obvious enough, and made her heart thud a little too hard and too fast. She ignored it.

"Forgive me for disturbing you, my lord," she said, making her voice low and breathy as she lowered her gaze. "I did not realise you were in here... alone."

"Did you not?" he replied, an unmistakable edge to his voice. "Well, you do now."

"Yes," she admitted, and allowed her gaze to fall to his mouth. She licked her lips and almost smiled as she saw his eyes darken as they noted the movement. Too easy. Gwenn averted her eyes as though her reaction to him embarrassed her. "Forgive me, I ought not to... I won't disturb you any longer."

She did not have to pretend reluctance at the thought of removing herself from the room. Though it was a risk, she turned to leave, her heart thudding in case she had misread the situation, but as her hand touched the doorknob, he spoke again.

"Wait."

She almost sagged with relief. Thank heavens.

"Would you like a drink?"

Gwenn glanced over her shoulder at him, giving him an expression somewhere between uncertainty and pleasure. "It's really not appropriate," she said, with obvious regret.

"The family will be down shortly," he said, the words still gruff but less icy than they'd been before. "There's no harm."

"If you're quite sure."

She met his gaze head on and did not look away. A long moment passed as the surrounding atmosphere smouldered. He stared at her and she suspected his breathing picked up, though she could not be sure.

She smiled as he cleared his throat and turned away to pour another drink.

"It's a very tolerable claret," he said, and she hid her smile as he held out the glass.

Gwenn walked towards him, aware of the quality of his gaze as she moved. Despite her not wanting the life her mother led, she was not averse to enjoying the look in a handsome man's eyes. There was pleasure in being found desirable, especially by this man, and she did not think the worse of Marie for relishing her lifestyle, she only knew that it was not what she wanted. Yet, in this moment, there was a certain appeal, an acknowledgment of her own power.

Lord Cheam watched her as she moved, like a lion watching a gazelle. Gwenn took the glass from his hands, careful to ensure her fingers brushed his as she did so. Had he shivered?

"I understand you are something of a connoisseur," he remarked, not sounding particularly pleased at the knowledge.

No doubt it was a strike against her in the *things that did not add up* column. She didn't question that he was keeping a list. He was that sort of man.

"Oh, no," she said, lowering her gaze and wishing she had the ability to blush. Still, she could act the ingenue as well as any little innocent. "Only I have a remarkably clever tongue." Gwenn glanced back at him in time to see his eyes widen in shock. "It seems to be able to divine any number of flavours," she added, guileless as she took a dainty sip of the wine. She closed her eyes, licking her lips with slow deliberation as she savoured it. He was right, of course, it wasn't at all bad.

"Lovely. From the Medoc?" she asked, smiling a little.

Lord Cheam nodded at her but didn't reply. She wasn't sure he could.

When at last he spoke, the question didn't entirely surprise her.

"Who are you?"

He sounded somewhat breathless and Gwenn widened her eyes at him.

"Why, Lord Cheam, I am Miss Wynter, your governess."

He set down his glass and closed the distance between them. Gwenn's heart skipped about a little at his proximity, the desire to reach up and coil her arms about his neck hard to resist. Oh, he was dangerous. A man like this could ruin all her plans if she didn't tread with care. All at once this was a hazardous game. If not for the fact she could still hear bloody Wychwood gabbing, she'd have picked up her skirts and run. As it was, she'd come this far.

"You're no governess."

Her mother had instructed her that the ability to cry at will was a useful one to cultivate. It was also one to be used with great care, as no man enjoyed keeping company with a watering pot. Now, however, she felt the situation called for desperate measures to stop the fellow sacking her and having done with it.

Gwenn forced herself to remember a cat she'd had as a child, and the depths of her sorrow when it had died. As the grief-stricken emotion rose in her chest others followed unbidden. She remembered the home she'd left behind and the reasons why she'd run, she remembered her hopes and dreams for the future, and how futile they likely were. She remembered the fact she was alone in this adventure. Her eyes filled easily enough, and she saw the look of horror in Lord Cheam's as he noted her distress.

"Have... Have my services n-not been adequate, my lord?" she stammered, discovering she wasn't entirely acting, as the thought of being dismissed had her nerves leaping with anxiety. "I had hoped that... that the girls were happy in m-my care, but if that is not the case—"

"*No*! I mean, yes, yes the girls are very happy," Lord Cheam said in a rush.

"But if you have doubts about me...." Gwenn tilted her head up to him and one tear slid down her cheek.

"Oh, lord, Miss Wynter, please...." He stepped closer, too close, and reached out, wiping the tear away with his thumb, his big hand cupping her face. "Don't cry," he said, his voice soft. "Please, don't cry."

Gwenn gasped, and she was unsure if that shaky intake of breath in response to his hands on her had been fake or genuine as his touch made her knees tremble. Her mouth parted a little, and she stared up at him, into eyes of dark blue, and suddenly, it was no game, hazardous or otherwise. She didn't give a damn if Wychwood was outside or not. All she could think of was that he

Emma V. Leech

would kiss her, and she wanted it. More than anything. She wanted to lean into him, into that strength and warmth.

His hand still cupped her face, and she closed her eyes, turning into it. Gwenn heard his breath catch, felt him move closer, and then heard the door swing open.

Chapter 7

"Wherein Sampson has a narrow escape."

Sampson leapt away from Miss Wynter just as the doorknob turned. He spun around, snatched up his glass and stared down at the fire as he tried to get his breathing under control.

Daring a quick look, he saw his Aunt May and the twins enter the room. His aunt gave him a rather sharp glance, but when he stole a glimpse of Miss Wynter, she looked as composed and demure as ever. He'd moved away from her before his aunt could have seen anything, he assured himself.

Anything like him making improper advances towards the bloody governess!

Hell and damnation.

What had gotten into him? One minute he was demanding she explain herself and the next... the next....

He'd made her cry, and the anguish in her eyes had struck a pain deep in his heart. Only the worst kind of brute could feel nothing in the light of that beautiful face marred by tears. It was like... like kicking a kitten!

He'd just wanted, no—*needed*—to make it better. Except then he'd touched her and that had been a mistake, a terrible, *terrible* mistake. Desire still thrummed under his skin.

Though he didn't believe for a moment that she was a real governess, she *was* doing a wonderful job with the girls. His sisters were happy, he could see that, and they were behaving themselves. Well, they were as close to behaving themselves as they ever were, and that was miracle enough in the short time she'd been with them. More than that, though, she needed this position.

Sampson wasn't sure what he'd seen in her eyes, but there had been uncertainty there, vulnerability... and desire. Oh, yes. There had been desire, and the knowledge of her desire for him would plague him without cease for as long as she remained with them.

Bloody, bloody hell. He was a fool. If he'd only kept his distance as he'd planned, but then she'd burst into the room and closed the door, as if she was running from something. Sampson frowned as he recalled her expression in the moments before she'd seen him. She'd looked... afraid.

"I'll see what's keeping Samuel," he said, setting down his glass once more and hurrying outside before his aunt could stop him.

There was no one in the corridor now, but he could hear Sam, and followed the sound of his brother's voice.

"Sampson, look who I found," Samuel exclaimed as Sampson drew closer to see him in conversation with Lord Wychwood. "I just came down the stairs this minute and there he was! He'd almost made it out the door but I caught him."

"Well met, Pelham," Lord Wychwood said, holding out his hand. His face fell. "Oh, but no, it's Cheam now, isn't it?"

Sampson nodded with a grimace and shook Wychwood's hand. The name had been associated with his father for so long that it felt tainted, as if the taint had been transferred to him after his father's death.

"I'd say I was sorry for your loss, but...."

Samuel snorted as Wychwood trailed off, looking awkward. "No one is sorry, believe me. Least of all us. It's the only decent thing the bastard ever did, though he couldn't even die decently."

"Sam," Sampson snapped, glowering.

Not that he disagreed, but he hated their dirty linen being aired with such ease. He knew damn well everyone was talking about it, but he didn't have to like it.

"Are you staying here?" Sampson asked the earl. "We're about to dine, if you would care to join us?"

"Ah, I'd love to, but I have a prior engagement," Wychwood said with regret. "I was just leaving when Sam here caught me. I'll be here for a few days, though, if you're about?"

Sampson shook his head. "No, we're on our way to Scotland for Christmas to stay with family. We'll be off early, I'm afraid."

"Ah, yes. Captain Moncreiffe, your new half-brother. I spoke to a chap that served with him not so long ago. He said Moncreiffe was something to behold in battle. Brave man."

"Sounds like Ross," Samuel said with a grin. "All brawn and belligerence."

Sampson rolled his eyes. "He's a very decent fellow. As well you know, ingrate," he said to Sam. "Unlike some of my brothers."

Sam gave an unrepentant smirk and bid the earl a good evening, before following Sampson back to the private dining room.

***

After dinner, Sampson and his brother remained in the dining room, sharing a nightcap. Try as he might, Sampson could not get his idiotic brain to think of anything else but Miss Wynter and the almost kiss. Every time he thought of it—which was every second since it hadn't quite happened—he felt a shiver of desire rush over him. He saw the sweep of golden lashes as her eyes closed and she lifted her face to him like a sunflower towards a summer sky. Her lips had looked soft and lush and....

"What's wrong with you?"

Sampson jolted and felt a surge of guilt. Damn him. He was thinking lewd thoughts about the blasted governess. *Again.*

He tugged at his cravat, trying to loosen it. "Nothing," he replied, aware that such a terse reply rather indicated it was a lie.

"What happened, did Miss Wynter reject your advances?"

If he'd have stopped to think about it, he'd have remembered that Samuel was a rather good investigator, the kind of man who could wheedle the truth from a fellow without him even knowing it was happening. Samuel knew damn well that suggesting his big brother could not do something was almost guaranteed to get a rise out of him.

Sampson placed his foot firmly in the trap.

"No, she did not reject them," he growled, and then cursed himself as he fell into a deep hole.

"I see," Samuel replied, with the faintest lift of one eyebrow.

"Nothing happened," Sampson said, annoyed with himself for having to say that, for having revealed that, and with Sam for being as irritating as ever. Blast him.

"Ah, so she *did* reject you," Sam said with a satisfied smile. "What a pity. Never mind, old fellow. I think she prefers me anyway. I shall have to try my luck."

"Damned if you will!" Sampson snapped, sitting up ramrod straight and glaring at his brother. "She did not reject me. I already said that. She practically issued an invitation."

"Oh, come on, Sunny. If she was so mad for you, why did nothing happen? You can't have it both ways," Samuel drawled, staring at him over the top of his glass.

Sampson huffed and decided he may as well get it over with. Perhaps if he confessed, he'd feel ashamed of himself and do better... or perhaps he was staking a claim, because the idea of Samuel trying his luck made him want to throw things. "Because we were interrupted, you dolt. Aunt May and the girls burst through the door."

"Oh, Sunny," his brother said, giving a sad shake of his head. "You never tried to seduce her in the parlour before dinner? When you knew you would be interrupted? And you call me a dolt," he added, indignation all over his face.

"I didn't *try* to seduce her," Sampson ground out. "I didn't even mean to seduce her, it... it just—"

"It just happened?" Samuel finished for him with a sceptical lift of one eyebrow.

"I know!" Sampson retorted, feeling like an idiot. "I didn't make a move, I'm sure I didn't. Not at first, anyway. I don't know how she did it, but she did. I had every intention of treating her with the utmost respect, well, like ice in all honesty, I really did, but... but she's like... like *catnip*."

"Well, you're certainly doing a fine impression of a ginger tom," Samuel said, his green eyes glittering with amusement.

"One thing I know, she's no governess," Sampson grumbled, pressing his glass against his temple.

"I already told you that," Samuel said. "Though, whatever she is, she's the best governess we've ever had. Lord, if I'd had a governess like that, I'd have worked a damn sight harder, I can tell you." He sighed wistfully.

"You haven't had a governess since you were five, when you went sent to school like the rest of us."

"Don't spoil my daydreams." Samuel glowered at him.

"There will be no daydreaming about Miss Wynter."

"You said nothing happened. If that's the case, she's not made a definitive choice."

"Dammit, Sam," Sampson said, sitting forward again. "She's in our employ, under our protection. I thought you didn't want to be the kind of man our father was?"

Samuel narrowed his eyes at him. "Oh, that was low, Sunny," he muttered. "I'd rather die than be the man my father was, and you bloody well know it, but that doesn't mean I have to be a damned saint. I will not seduce her or pretend I'm offering anything I'm not, and I'm certainly not going to force her. I'll only flirt a little. If she wants me, she's of age and can make her own decisions who she takes to her bed. I doubt I'd be the first. None of us need you to nanny us, no matter what you think."

Sampson got to his feet, staring down at his brother. He tried hard to tamp down the irrational anger that was clawing at his chest, but his words were still harder than he'd allowed for.

"You'll leave Miss Wynter be, Samuel."

Sam stood too, the brothers toe–to–toe. "What, so you can have her to yourself, you mean?"

"No, I don't mean!" Sampson said, hoping he wasn't lying to both himself and his brother. "We must stay out of her company as far as possible. I shall chaperone you and, by all means, you chaperone me. Miss Wynter deserves more than the two of us bickering over who will have her, no matter who or what she is."

He watched as Sam studied his face and then let out a sigh. "God, you're annoying, Sunny. Why must you be such a bloody killjoy?"

Sampson shrugged. "I'm trying to be better than he was, Sam, that's all. I'm not saying I'm any good at it, but I have to try."

Samuel stomped to the fire, glowered at it for a moment and then straightened. "Fine," he said. "But if I find you so much as looking in her direction all bets are off."

"Fine," Sampson agreed. At least under his brother's scrutiny he'd be forced to behave himself.

"Ugh, I'm going to bed," Sam said with a huff, and left Sampson alone.

Sampson stared at the fire and crouched down to put another log on, the heat of the flames making his face burn. *I doubt I'd be the first.* The words circled in Sampson's head. He could see why his brother thought it. There were occasions, like the almost kiss earlier, when it seemed Miss Wynter was a great deal more knowing than one might expect of an unmarried young woman. She had a past, that much was clear, but was it a *past*?

None of your business, he told himself. Perhaps Miss Wynter was trying to make a new and respectable life for herself, just like he was. He could admire and understand that. As long as that past in no way tainted his sisters, he ought to allow her the privacy and the opportunity to move on. Yet, there had been something in her expression in the fleeting moment before she'd closed her eyes and lifted her face towards his. It had caught at his heart and made him wonder if he was wrong, for she'd looked like an innocent girl, her eyes full of hope and anticipation for her first kiss.

The image stayed with him, burrowing into some tender part of his soul that he'd left unprotected. Try as he might, he could not shake it off. She was young and lovely, and he thought perhaps she needed protecting, needed someone to care for her—needed him. No, no. She did not need him as anything but her employer, he amended. He urged his thoughts to reroute themselves but it was no good. Miss Wynter was an enigma, and the more he glimpsed of the puzzle the more he wanted to unravel it. He wanted to do as his aunt had suggested and get to know her, to discover what she was running from and to make it all right. Not to get her into bed, but to take that anxious, vulnerable look from her eyes.

Impossible.

If there was one thing he knew, it was that Miss Wynter could ruin all his plans as easily as he could ruin her. There was only one answer, and that was to keep as far away from her as possible.

***

Gwenn lay in her bed and tried to sleep. She ought to be asleep already. Her eyes were heavy, and she'd been longing for her bed this past hour, yet sleep eluded her.

Sampson Pelham, drat the man, was all she could think of.

Lust. That's what it was. She knew that, had heard her mother warning against acting on it when good sense told you otherwise. Many a fine courtesan had thrown it all away when she'd lost her head over a man. It started as lust, and sometimes that was all it was, and—her mother had counselled—a good tumble was all it took to rid yourself of the need for the object of your desire. Sometimes, but not always. Women were too often ruled by their hearts, and a clever whore understood and avoided such instincts. Lust and desire could all too easily become liking, and regard and even love, and love… that was dangerous for a woman in such a position.

Gwenn's mother had loved the Marquess of Davenport, so much that she'd grown careless and born him a daughter. Marie had known Davenport did not treat his by-blows kindly and would quickly tire of her if she fell pregnant, but fate had other plans. Marie had held his attention throughout her confinement. Indeed, the marquess had been a devoted lover, until Marie had needed a little time to devote to her newborn babe. He'd immediately begun an affair with one of Marie's rivals… and broken her heart. Gwenn had heard the story often. An illustration of men's loyalty and love.

Marie had retaliated, of course, and in style. The marquess had allowed her to borrow his wife's ruby parure to wear to a private dinner, which Marie had given in the months before her confinement, but he neglected to get them back. More fool him. Marie had decided they would do nicely in compensation for her heartbreak. She took them and her daughter, and seduced Davenport's younger brother on the way out. They'd run to Italy and had a lovely time until Napoleon had made a nuisance of himself and Marie had judged it safer to return to England and find a new and more powerful protector.

That was what lust did for you, Marie had told her. It got you a bellyful of trouble and a broken heart. *Use your head, girl, and leave other parts of your anatomy for business.* It wasn't as if you had to choose an ugly man and get no pleasure from life. Desire and lust were fine, so long as they weren't the kinds that threatened to overwhelm reason and good sense, the kinds you needed to run from as soon as you recognised them, before it was too late, for they would lead you to nothing but ruin.

Gwenn remembered the moment she'd realised Lord Cheam meant to kiss her, and shivered with longing. With dismay, she suspected that this was exactly the kind of thing her mother had warned her about.

If only he was a bad man, it wouldn't be so difficult, but she knew he was trying hard to look after his family. She'd watched him with his sisters when he wasn't aware of her doing so, and it was clear from his demonstrative manner that he adored them, and that the feeling was mutual. Yet whilst Mr Pelham had kept the teasing, affectionate role of big brother, Lord Cheam had become a de facto parent. She wondered if he resented it, resented having the role of father forced upon him on top of all the other responsibilities his feckless parent had heaped on him by leading such a dissolute life and dying in a brothel?

Aunt May had confided that the girls had begun stealing things, and that was why he'd leapt at the invitation from his half-brother to get them out of London. It accounted for the worry she saw in his eyes when he looked at the girls. Aunt May said he was desperate to rid himself and his brothers of their infamous title, though Gwenn could not help but wonder how well he'd earned his share of it. He was trying his best, though, that was clear. She knew how badly he desired her, that had been obvious from the first, but he'd tried to keep things cool and formal between them, he'd been doing well too, until she'd spoiled it. Guilt rose in her chest as she remembered how she'd manipulated him, seducing him with her whore's tricks when he would have treated her quite as he ought, given the opportunity.

Yet, he'd not grabbed and helped himself as many a man in his position would have. He'd been tender—oh, and the look in his eyes when he'd begged her not to cry—that had been the look of a man who'd fight dragons if he had to. Gwenn sighed and then cursed herself for being a thousand times a fool. Was she stupid enough to think Lord Cheam would marry a governess? *Pffft!* What if he did and then discovered he'd saddled himself with the illegitimate daughter of a nobleman and a courtesan? The scandal would humiliate him, and his family, and he'd despise her for it.

No.

No, there were no happy ever afters with Lord Cheam. A position as his mistress would be all he'd offer her, and that would not do. He could only ever be her Marquess of Davenport, and she doubted she'd get away with a splendid set of rubies to ease her aching heart.

The only thing she could do was keep her head and her distance, and then get as far away from him as possible.

Chapter 8

"Wherein a scheming younger brother makes mischief."

"My turn," Susan said with a grin. She was sitting beside Gwenn, her sister opposite them, next to Aunt May, as the carriage rumbled on. "Let me see…. Oh, I have it! There once was a lady from Kendal," she began, before grinning at Selina to take over the next line.

Selina frowned and then giggled. "Whose beauty could make a man tremble!"

Gwenn clapped her approval at the clever rhyme. The girls loved this game and were very witty with words.

"So, she bought a new hat…."

"And adorned it with cats…."

"…because it looked so ornamental!"

The twins snickered and elbowed each other, pleased with themselves.

"Very imaginative," Gwenn said with an admiring nod. "Now, Susan, how do you spell ornamental?"

Susan began carefully sounding out the letters, her pretty nose screwed up in concentration. Gwenn listened, glancing to see how Aunt May had enjoyed the poem. The older lady usually roared with laughter when the girls said something funny, but she'd been quiet this past half hour.

"Excellent, Susan, well done," she said, as the girl beamed at her. She turned back to their aunt. "Mrs Bainbridge? Are you quite well?"

Gwenn hoped she hadn't caught a chill. Though they were all bundled up in travelling cloaks and blankets, and Lord Cheam ensured the hot bricks were replaced and hot drinks delivered to the carriage whenever they changed horses, the cold got into one's bones after a long day.

"Aunt May," the lady corrected with a smile, though her eyes looked heavy and her face was pale. "And quite all right, just a bit of a headache."

"Oh, I'm so sorry. Girls, we must keep the noise down, your auntie is not feeling well."

"Oh, don't fuss," Aunt May objected. "The girls were having a lovely time, and it's so nice to hear. They've been stifled for too long."

Gwenn searched through her bag and found the illustrated book of Shakespeare's tales.

"Read quietly," she instructed them.

"Yes, Miss Wynter," they said, with startling obedience.

Selina changed places to sit next to her sister and the two of them settled back together to look at the book. *Quietly.* Gwenn blinked and wondered at the fact she was rather good at this governessing business. Who would have thought it? Her mother would be so surprised. No. Strike that. Her mother would be apoplectic. She'd not think on it. Instead, she rummaged about in her bag again until she found the small bottle of lavender oil that she always carried.

"Give me your hands," she said to Aunt May. The old lady did so, and Gwenn put a drop onto each wrist and rubbed it in with slow, even strokes. Then she put another drop on her own fingers and touched it to the lady's temples, repeating the slow massaging technique.

"Oh, that's lovely," Aunt May said with a sigh. "You have magic fingers."

"Thank you," Gwenn said with a small smile, wondering what the sweet old lady would think if she knew just how detailed her instruction in the art of massage had been.

She'd probably suffer a breakdown, but not before throwing Gwenn out of the carriage with a cry of disgust.

Best not mention that, then.

The carriage rattled ever onwards and Aunt May at least seemed to be sleeping peacefully, though how she managed it, Gwenn had no idea.

"Miss Wynter?"

Gwenn looked down to Susan who was looking up at her, her blue eyes troubled.

"Yes, Susan."

"Was our father evil?"

Gwenn opened and closed her mouth before remembering her training and schooling her expression into something placid and unruffled.

"Well," she began, trying to figure out what on earth to say to that question. "I'm afraid I didn't know your father, so it isn't my place to say."

"He did horrible things, though," the girl said, her voice little more than a whisper.

"Really horrible," echoed Selina, looking around her sister.

They looked so terribly young and fragile that Gwenn's heart felt squeezed, and she put her arms about Susan's shoulders and gestured for Selina to come and sit on her other side. She gathered them both close.

"Whatever your father did or did not do, is not something you need worry about," she said firmly. "His sins are not your sins, and never let anyone make you believe they are. You are lovely, good-hearted, clever girls. This is quite obvious to me, even after such a short acquaintance. What's more, your brothers are also good people, are they not?"

"Oh, yes," the girls said in unison. "They're nothing like Papa was, even though people say they are scandalous."

"Oh, well." Gwenn waved this away impatiently. "Some of the nicest people can be scandalous, you know," she said, rather aware that she ought not say such things to two impressionable young girls, but really, she couldn't abide them feeling they were wicked or their family tainted. "It doesn't signify."

"Really?" They both brightened and Gwenn smiled, hugging them both tighter. "I think you are both perfectly wonderful and the best travelling companions I've ever had, so there."

This won her a tight hug in return from each sister, and it was a long time before Gwenn could clear the lump from her throat to speak again.

***

The journey was interminable today as the weather closed in around them, shrouding the countryside from view and obliterating any landmarks. Middle Hulton, Cholley, Preston, and Garstang had all come and gone in a grey haze as they headed for Lancaster and their overnight stop. It seemed an age since they'd eaten, and Gwenn handed around her dwindling bag of sweets before taking one herself to ease the clamour in her belly. The temperature had dropped further, and it was all but dark, the landscape beyond the windows nothing more than blurry shapes in the gloom.

By the time they reached Lancaster, the girls and Mrs Bainbridge were dozing, their aunt snoring softly as the carriage drew to a halt. The Inn at Whitwell was a welcome sight on such a night. Situated close to the River Hodder, the ancient manor house was a handsome and sturdy building with mullioned windows and enough chimneys to suggest there were fires aplenty to huddle about. The scent of dinner coiled invitingly from the front door, and Gwenn roused the twins and ushered them inside with instructions to wait, before returning for Aunt May.

"Come along," she said, as she gently woke her travelling companion. "We'll get you inside, and your maid will arrange a nice hot bath and supper in bed. A good night's sleep will do you the world of good."

Gwenn regarded Aunt May's weary expression with misgiving and swept into action, quite forgetting she was the governess. The staff, all of whom were fond of Aunt May, and rightly so, leapt to do her bidding. Soon, all the delights of a hot bath, a warm bed, and supper on a tray had been delivered as promised and Gwenn left Aunt May to enjoy a bit of peace, pleased to see the colour returning to the lady's cheeks.

As she closed the door on Aunt May's room, she found Lord Cheam waiting for her and stilled. They'd done very well to avoid each other until now, each acting just as if the other did not exist whenever they were forced to share the same space.

"Is my aunt unwell?" he asked, his blue eyes full of concern.

Drat the man, why did he have to be so lovely and caring?

"A little fatigued, I think," Gwenn replied, holding on tight to her starchy governess persona. "I feared she had caught a chill, but I think a good night's rest will do her the world of good. Indeed, all of us. I shall arrange for the girls to have supper in their rooms tonight, too."

"And what of you, Miss Wynter?"

"I shall eat with my charges, naturally," she said, a little too quickly, glaring at him.

Whatever did the man think she was suggesting?

"Oh, no...." he said at once, appalled. "I did not mean to imply... I only meant to enquire if you were well." Anxiety clouded his face and once again she saw the strain about his eyes. "I wonder if perhaps this journey was a good idea? The weather has closed in and we've a way to go yet. It's only that the girls were so excited to see Captain Moncreiffe and visit a real castle, and I was so desperate to get them out of London before...." He stiffened, standing a little straighter. "Forgive me, Miss Wynter, I am detaining you. Thank you for your kindness to my aunt. It is much appreciated."

He began to turn away and Gwenn's heart went out to him, this man who was trying to be a father to two little girls he clearly adored, and to look after his family.

"I'm sure this visit is just what the family needs, Lord Cheam. A chance to be together and away from society. Your aunt is just a little tired. She looks much better already, I assure you. Please, do not worry so. The journey has been most wonderfully arranged, and we have all been grateful for your thoughtfulness."

A little of the tension about his eyes eased.

"Thank you, Miss Wynter," he said softly. "Good night."

"Good night, my lord," she said, and watched as he retreated down the corridor and out of sight. "Sweet dreams," she added under her breath with a sigh.

***

Sam watched his older brother as he stared into his cup of coffee at breakfast the next morning. Since taking the title, Sampson had aged about a hundred years, the poor bastard. Oh, not that he looked a deal different. He hadn't gone grey overnight or become stooped, or anything like that, but one could practically see the weight he was lugging about on his shoulders.

82

When he'd suggested the trip to Scotland, Sam had leapt at the idea. Not only to get the girls away from London and their newfound ability for pilfering, but to get Sampson away too. Their new half-brother, Ross, was a no-nonsense kind of fellow who called a spade a spade—if you were lucky. Samuel was hoping Ross might succeed where he had failed. Not that he didn't understand what Sampson was trying to do, but worrying himself into an early grave wasn't the answer, and neither was trying to make his brothers into something they weren't.

Sam knew his occupation as an investigator was hardly respectable for the son of a viscount, but he had a talent for it, and now and then he did some good too. He felt useful and valued in a way he'd never done before. Certainly, his father hadn't valued him, or any of them. Even Sampson, his heir, had been a disappointment. The late Lord Cheam had tried to mould his eldest son in his own image, but Sampson was too decent, too inherently good to bend to someone as corrupt as their father. He'd suffered for it, too, but he'd never broken. Sampson had protected them all as best he could, their mother too, while she lived. Once she'd gone, he had gone a little wild—they all had, hence their infamous title—but Sampson had still been the one to bring them back when they'd risked going too far. He'd been the one to remind them that life wasn't so bad, that their father could not taint everything they touched merely by being their father.

Samuel wondered if his big brother had forgotten that fact himself.

Then their father had married again and there had been another soul to protect, swiftly followed by two little girls, so innocent and fragile it had made Samuel's heart hurt whenever he'd considered the vile creature who'd fathered them. He knew Sampson felt it too.

He saw the way Sampson winced whenever his title was used. Lord Cheam had been synonymous with wickedness and vice for so long that the mantle sat heavy.

As Samuel scrutinised his brother he saw him stiffen, saw the immediate flare of interest in his eyes, the way his whole countenance came to life... at the exact same moment Miss Wynter's voice drifted in through the half-open door of the parlour.

Samuel hid a smile. An affair with Miss Wynter was just what his brother needed. Hell, from what he'd seen of the woman, she was what any man needed. Though he admitted to an interest himself—he did have a pulse—most of what he'd said to Sampson had been to get a reaction from him. He'd gotten one, too. Sampson was smitten, whether or not he wanted to admit it.

To his knowledge, Sampson hadn't had an affair in over a year, perhaps longer. He'd been discreet about such things since the girls had been born, but he'd often confided in Samuel when he had. Sam had never seen his brother react to a woman like he did to Miss Wynter, and though Sam still had reservations about her, he found he liked her. Whatever she was running from, and she *was* running, her affection for the girls was genuine, her care of Aunt May had shown a kind nature, and the way she dealt with the staff implied she was a woman who knew how to run a household. He would have said she was a lady, except she wasn't. Miss Wynter was no green miss. She knew something of the world, and she knew a deal about men and how to manage them, too, which made her a puzzle.

Had she been some man's mistress? It seemed the most logical answer. Perhaps her lover had turned her out, but what man in his right mind would do so? It was possible the man had been cruel or possessive and she'd run from him... more likely, perhaps. Well, either way, Sam thought the two of them would deal admirably together. Sampson would protect her from whatever she was running from, as was his nature, and Miss Wynter would take that pinched look from his brother's face. If the fool had an ounce of sense, he'd marry her and have done with it.

Only, Sampson would do nothing as scandalous as marry a woman he had half a chance of caring for. No, he must save the entire family single handed and resign himself to a loveless marriage just so they could all be respectable. *Gah!* What rot. The man was an idiot. An idiot with a heart of gold, yes, but an idiot all the same.

Samuel and Sampson rose as Aunt May came down, smiling and far perkier than she had been last night.

"Good morning, Aunt," they both greeted her.

"Good morning, boys," she said, her usual cheerful self and addressing them the same way she had done when they were small boys.

"I'm glad to see you looking so much better," Sampson said to her with a smile. "We were worried for you."

"Oh, no need. Miss Wynter is a marvel," she said blithely, watching Sampson as his attention drifted back to the hallway, from where the soft sound of Miss Wynter's laughter emanated. "Do you know she not only entertained the girls all day yesterday, she taught them, too? I don't even think they knew it was happening, and then she still has the kindness and energy to see to my comfort. Why some clever young man hasn't snatched the girl up and married her, I cannot fathom."

"Yes, yes, excellent," Sampson murmured, clearly not having attended a word she'd said. "Would you excuse me?" he said, getting to his feet and hurrying from the room.

Aunt May watched Sampson go, an arrested expression on her face. She turned back to Samuel, her eyebrows raised. He grinned at her and a conspiratorial light entered her eyes.

"If only we could get them alone together," she whispered, reaching for a slice of toast. "Without harming Miss Wynter's reputation, of course," she added. "The poor girl, I feel like she's looking for something. She'd make a wonderful wife and mother, but I fear what will happen to her if she carries on this course.

Some man will take advantage of her sooner or later. She's canny for one so young, but life is lonely for a single woman, and that will lead her into some unworthy fellow's arms, no doubt."

"Oh, but Sampson would never see her come to any harm," Samuel objected, though having an affair with her was perhaps not the best way of ensuring that.

Aunt May paused in the buttering of her toast and pulled a face. "I'm not speaking of your brother! If you think her intention is to stay in this post for long, you're not the investigator I took you for, Samuel." She shook her head at him. "No, she'll be off again soon enough, though—I flatter us, perhaps—I think it will pain her to do so. It will certainly break the girls' hearts. I dread to think what we shall do with them when she goes."

The idea made Sam's heart ache, but he realised his aunt was right. He'd not thought that far ahead, but if Miss Wynter was running, she'd keep moving for fear of being discovered. Their route to Scotland was a handy way to get out of London fast. What if she didn't wish to return? No. No, that could not happen. His sisters needed her. Hell, Sampson needed her.

She must stay.

His gaze returned to his aunt.

"What?" she asked, alarmed by his expression.

"Eat quickly," he said. "No, better yet, take it with you."

"Samuel!" she said in outrage, as he snatched up her carefully buttered toast and wrapped it in a napkin.

"Aunt, your headache has returned," he said gravely. "And the last thing you need is to spend an entire day in the company of the girls."

Chapter 9

"Wherein… the difference between catastrophe and safe arrival."

Gwenn bit back a chuckle as her charges hurried down the stairs to her.

"Sorry, Miss Wynter. Susan overslept," Selina said, her voice loud enough to carry to all corners of the inn.

"So did you," Susan retorted, elbowing her sister.

"It's quite all right, there's no need to thunder down like a herd of elephants," Gwenn said, shaking her head at them. "You are elegant young ladies, not wildebeests."

"I'd prefer to be a wildebeest," Selina said with a sigh. "They don't have to worry about keeping their pinafores clean and brushing their hair."

Gwenn tugged one of the girl's blonde curls and returned a sympathetic expression. "Yes, I can see the appeal, but no doubt wildebeest have a deal of rules to abide by, too. I believe they must travel great distances when they migrate. Imagine all that walking."

Selina pulled a face. "Perhaps not a wildebeest," she conceded. "I'll be a pony instead." She neighed and pawed at the ground with her foot and Gwenn couldn't help but laugh.

"And a very fine pony you would be too, but do you think you might return to being a young lady long enough to eat breakfast? After all, ponies only get hay and an occasional carrot, not sausages."

"Sausages!" the girls exclaimed in unison. "Why ever didn't you say so?"

They turned to run for the breakfast parlour and barrelled straight into Lord Cheam.

"Morning, Sunny," they said, pushing past him. "There are sausages for breakfast!"

"Girls!" Gwenn called after them in dismay. "Not ponies, wildebeest nor elephants. *Young ladies.*"

The girls slowed enough to grin, and then gave quite creditable curtsies before walking away in a more civilised manner.

Gwenn sighed.

"You're doing a marvellous job with them," Lord Cheam said, surprising her with the compliment.

"Oh, well, they're lovely girls," Gwenn said, trying to ignore the way his words made her feel as if she'd done something worthwhile, and the way the sunlight slanting through the open window gleamed on his red hair. "They're full of life and imagination. They just need to be kept busy and reminded how good they are."

Lord Cheam frowned at that, his blue eyes crinkling with concern. "Reminded how good they are?" he repeated.

Gwenn nodded. "Yes, I...." She hesitated as a maid bustled down the corridor and bobbed a curtsey before carrying on up the stairs. "Perhaps we ought not talk here?"

Lord Cheam understood her at once. "Would you care for a stroll before breakfast? It's cold, but the sun is shining this morning."

"Certainly, if it won't delay our departure? I know how keen you are to get to Scotland before the weather worsens."

He returned a smile that had the strangest effect on her knees, which seemed all at once a little wobbly.

"A few minutes ought not make the difference between safe arrival and catastrophe. Fetch your cloak. I will wait for you."

Gwenn complied at once, scolding herself for being so eager to be alone in his company when she'd promised herself to stay away from him. *I only want to speak to him about the girls, that's all,* she told herself.

That was a big fat lie.

She knew it would upset them when she left, though, and it was important that Lord Cheam understand what to expect and how to deal with them.

That was true, at least.

From what the twins had told her of their previous governesses, they'd been strict and humourless women who used discipline as a weapon and fear of punishment to enforce good behaviour. The girls were too clever and far too stubborn to bend to such tactics. The stricter the governess and the harder the punishment, the more they rebelled against it. Perhaps they felt they deserved the punishments and so pushed for more. Either way, the worse they behaved the more they feared they were wicked, and that they were following in their father's footsteps. Their brother needed to know this.

Huddled in her cloak, Gwenn peeked in at the breakfast parlour to see both girls were happily tucking into a mountain of sausages and egg, and went to meet Lord Cheam.

She wasn't certain if she was relieved or disappointed when he didn't offer her his arm, but walked at a respectful distance beside her.

"Please explain your concerns, Miss Wynter," he said once they were out of earshot of the inn and its comings and goings.

"I only want to describe what I have observed of Susan and Selina, and what I have learned from speaking to them. Only... I must speak frankly, and I fear—"

"Miss Wynter. You will not offend me if you have the best interests of the girls at heart. They are my priority. I well know that this family is not... that I'm not...."

There was such guilt in his eyes as he spoke that Gwenn acted without thinking, reaching out and placing her hand on his arm. "Lord Cheam. The girls are loved and cherished by both you and your brother. That is obvious to anyone. That your aunt has been so insistent on accompanying you only shows that your extended family is also supportive. No one can hold you responsible for the actions of your father, any more than they could hold the girls responsible. But you, as an adult, must know this. Susan and Selina do not."

Lord Cheam, whose gaze had been riveted on the sight of her fingers upon his sleeve, looked up at that.

"They think they are responsible?" he said, his auburn brows tugging together.

"Not exactly," Gwenn said, shaking her head. "But the last few governesses they've had have been strict disciplinarians."

"They were out of control, Miss Wynter." He ran a hand through his hair so it stood up at odd angles, betraying his anxiety. "I didn't know what else to do. They were abominably rude and refused to do as they were told...."

Though she knew it was a mistake, Gwenn could not help herself. The poor man looked so guilt ridden. So this time she took hold of his hand within both of hers.

"Of course you didn't know what to do. I know you did not have a good relationship with your father, and neither did the twins, but... they were still grieving, as you were too, and you had the world upon your shoulders. This is not your fault. I'm only trying to explain that those governesses, as well meaning as they may have been, made the girls feel as though they were bad, wicked children. Susan and Selina heard you and your brothers speaking of their father being a devil, of him going to hell, and they thought that was where they were bound too because they were bad like him."

"*What?*"

Gwenn hated herself for saying it as she saw his response. It was as if she'd struck him and the blow had winded him. They came to the river, and he stood staring down at the water, and at the mist that swirled over the surface.

"I can't believe they thought such a thing," he said, never taking his eyes from the water as it slid past, rushing towards its fate. "They've always been such happy girls, despite everything. I thought I'd protected them from it, from him."

"You did," she said, squeezing his fingers before forcing herself to let them go. "But they hear gossip all the same and, if things aren't explained to them, they aren't past creeping out of bed and eavesdropping on the adults."

"You've made them happy again," he said, turning to look at her, such gratitude in his eyes that her heart skipped about in her chest like a mad rabbit.

"Oh, I-I…. Well, it really wasn't difficult. They just needed a bit of reassurance, that's all, but I wanted you to know, so that you understood. They need to be told they are good girls. They need to know that even good girls do naughty things now and then, and it doesn't mean they're wicked. We're all human, we all make mistakes, that doesn't make them evil, or mean they will go to hell."

He was staring at her, such obvious admiration in his eyes she felt a blush rise to her cheeks. Good Lord! Blushing? *Her?* She thought she'd lost the ability years ago. Yet she felt undeserving of that look. It had been given to her under false pretences. He might have figured out she wasn't really a governess, but he didn't know she'd been trained to be the finest courtesan London had ever seen. If he knew that, he'd get her out of the girls' company so fast her head would spin. She'd do well to remember that. Except it was hard to remember anything, think of anything, when the poor man looked so in need of someone to hold him, to smooth the anxiety from his brow and kiss him until he smiled again.

Oh, she wanted to make him smile.

Oh, she was in such trouble.

"I think perhaps we all need reminding we're only human now and again, Miss Wynter," he said, such warmth in those words that the cold morning disappeared, and she basked in the heat of them. "What a good thing we have you around to take the weight from our shoulders."

Gwenn's breath caught. There was a look in his eyes that told her he wanted to kiss her, to pull her into his arms and hold her tight until she did all the things she'd just been considering and made him smile again. Alarm bells sounded in her head and she reminded herself of all the reasons she could not have him. She could feel the pull of temptation, desire rising beneath her skin, and she knew she ought to be afraid. She ought to keep her distance. He was her Marquess of Davenport, and there would be no rubies to take the sting from losing him. There weren't rubies enough in the world to ease the pain of losing a man like that.

No.

Run now, you fool. Run while you have the chance.

She took a step backwards and forced a cool smile to her lips.

"Well, I'm sure I'm not deserving of such praise, or such responsibility. I only wished you to understand the girls so when you next sought a governess for them you would choose with a greater knowledge of what you need."

"Another governess?" He stared at her. "You're... leaving us?"

"Oh, not at once," she said, turning away from him, away from the shock and disappointment in his eyes, and keeping her voice light. "I shall remain with you for the duration of the holidays of course, and for as long as it takes to seek another to replace me if you desire it. Indeed, I should be happy to assist if you wish it."

That was something she could do for him at least. For the girls.

"But so soon?"

Gwenn steeled herself against the words. She wanted to tell him she'd stay if he asked her to, but it was stupid, and she was not stupid. Foolish, perhaps—to hope for a future far away from the glittering glamour her mother had promised was within her grasp—but not stupid.

"Oh, I know we had no time to discuss it, such was the urgency of your situation, but it was only ever a temporary position for me," she said, forcing herself to sound as though it wasn't a wrench to her heart to leave them when she was just beginning to do some good. "You desperately needed my services, and I was at a loose end for the Christmas period, so it was mutually beneficial. For the future, however, I have… I have other commitments."

"Other commitments," he echoed, returning his gaze to the river. His voice was low, and he sounded weary. "Yes, of course. I understand."

The tight little lines were visible about his eyes again, and Gwenn clenched her fists against the urge to reach for him. "It's for the best," she said, her voice softer now. At once she wished the words back, wished she had in no way alluded to what had almost passed between them.

He looked at her then, the full force of those vivid blue eyes settling on her.

"Is it?" he asked, as though he wanted an answer at once, and then he laughed and shook his head. "Yes," he said, and it was a decisive sound. "Yes, of course it is." She watched as he straightened, his expression hardening, though his tone was light enough. "We'd best return to the inn before the girls run out of sausages."

Gwenn nodded and turned to follow him and then paused, frowning. "Aren't... Aren't those your carriages?" she asked, as the glossy back conveyance that bore the crest of Viscount Cheam left the yard and took to the road at a smart clip. Behind it followed the carriage that carried his valet and the ladies' maids, and yet another that held the bulk of their luggage.

"Yes, they bloody well are!" he said, quickening his pace. "What the devil is going on?"

***

Sampson cursed as he stared down at the hastily scribbled note in his hand. According to his brother, Aunt May had suffered a relapse and couldn't face a day in the carriage with her nieces. They would go on ahead and meet up in Carlisle where they were due to stop for the night.

What the hell were they playing at? Aunt May had seemed in fine fettle when she'd come down to breakfast this morning and, if she'd wanted to travel with them, there was room enough without leaving him behind. No, it was too smoky by half. This was Samuel's work, no doubt, but why? Why would he throw Sampson into close quarters with Miss Wynter, with only the girls to chaperone, when he was so clearly interested in her himself? It made no sense.

Whatever the reason, it was a disaster. He'd been so close to kissing her down by the river.

Miss Wynter's insight into what the girls had been feeling and her evident concern for their welfare, for *his* welfare, had touched him deeply. Her beauty, combined with an understanding of human nature, and such compassion.... She took his breath away. He felt as if everything was just as it ought to be when he was with her, as though holding her in his arms could chase away all his troubles and make everything right. Nonsense, of course, yet when she was before him it didn't seem like nonsense; it seemed natural and obvious and damn near irresistible.

Thank God she'd had wit enough to keep things on a professional basis. She might be young, but she had more prudence than he possessed to put a halt to such a disastrous move. Though why she had when she'd so clearly invited his advances before….

She'd come to her senses, that was all. She desired him, but she knew it was impossible. He desired her and he knew it was impossible. He sought to avoid scandal and to secure the girls' future, and the disparity in their positions made any honourable solution out of the question. They both knew it. Therefore, they must part company. It was for the best.

Just as she had said.

It was.

Yet his heart felt heavy, and not just for himself. The girls would be crushed.

Now, however, he would have to share the confines of a closed carriage with her for hours on end, and he would kill bloody Samuel when he got to Carlisle… if he didn't go mad in the meantime. Anger rose in his chest. His brother was a menace. No doubt Sam thought an affair with Miss Wynter would do him good, never stopping to think whether such a thing would be good for Miss Wynter.

Now, instead of them both taking care to keep clear of temptation, they would be forced to face it head on. Irritation simmered beneath his skin and he held onto it. If he was angry and irritated, he'd be bad company and Miss Wynter would not be tempted to hold his hand or touch his sleeve as she had this morning. Both incidents, slight as they were, had sent desire slamming through him, proving to him just how catastrophic this was. His earlier words to her came back to haunt him.

A few minutes ought not make the difference between safe arrival and catastrophe.

Sometimes he thought the Almighty had a twisted sense of humour.

Chapter 10

"Wherein temptation triumphs."

Lord Cheam was in a foul temper. It was obvious from the
rigid set of his shoulders. Not that he'd been in any way rude or
irritable with either her or the girls, he'd simply tipped his hat over
his eyes and feigned sleep from the moment they'd left the inn.

Gwenn couldn't blame him for feigning sleep or being
irritable. She suspected that today's little arrangement had not been
accidental, but she could not understand what was to be gained by
it. Aunt May had professed herself quite recovered when Gwenn
had seen her in the upstairs corridor, and a sudden relapse seemed
unlikely, if not impossible. Yet, why sneak off like they had? Aunt
May could very well have shared the carriage with both Lord
Cheam and Mr Pelham and left Gwenn with the children. Indeed, it
would be normal to do so.

It made no sense.

They could not be hoping to promote a romance with a woman
so below Lord Cheam's standing, and she could not believe Aunt
May would approve of an affair. The woman had too much regard
for Gwenn for that. Didn't she? Was she just a dispensable servant
who would serve to put a smile on Lord Cheam's face until he
grew tired of her? Surely not.

No. She refused to believe that.

They changed horses at Burton and Lord Cheam didn't so
much as blink. Hot bricks were delivered as usual, along with
steaming cups of chocolate, his meticulous planning needing no
further input. Kendal came and went with the same outcome and a
repeat of the girls' poem. Gwenn thought perhaps Lord Cheam's
lips twitched as they recited it, but she couldn't be certain.

The carriage moved on once more and everyone subsided into a weary silence. Gwenn fought against the temptation to stare longingly at the girls' big brother and forced herself to watch the scenery. The sunny morning had given way to a grim afternoon, and the sky was a stark white and rather threatening. They stopped briefly in Shap for a meal, which was adequate rather than the excellent repasts they'd enjoyed to date. Gwenn and the girls made the most of a warm fire and a private parlour whilst Lord Cheam ate in the public rooms after making some excuse about seeing someone he knew.

On they went again, with Lord Cheam once more retreating behind the safety of closed eyelids, until they changed horses at Penrith before the final leg of the journey to Carlisle. He spent the next hours glowering out of the window at scenery which appeared to glower back at him. A few solitary flakes of snow drifted about, buffeted on the wind over the barren landscape, and Gwenn regarded them with misgiving.

After an hour of unexpected peace, Gwenn studied Susan, who had curled up with her head against the squabs and was staring out of the window. Selina sat beside Gwenn, looking at the pictures in the book of Shakespeare's tales. It occurred to her then that both girls were unusually quiet.

"Susan, are you well?" she asked, noting the girl looked rather wan.

"My head hurts," she admitted, a little tearful. "And my throat is all scratchy."

"Oh, dear," Gwenn said in dismay before turning to Selina.

"My throat's sore, too," the girl said, closing her book and rubbing her eyes.

"What is it?"

They all looked around, a little startled by the deep voice after so many hours of silence.

"I think the girls are coming down with colds," she said, taking off her glove and putting her hand to Selina's forehead. "Certainly a little feverish."

"What can I do?" Lord Cheam asked at once.

"Nothing, my lord," Gwenn said. "Though if you could contrive not to fall ill yourself, I should appreciate it."

"I'll do my best," he replied, looking between the girls with concern. "We ought to be in Carlisle shortly. I think hot baths and an early bed for both of you."

The girls groaned and huffed but made no further complaint, which was telling enough.

The Blacksmith's Arms in Faugh, on the outskirts of Carlisle, was a pretty whitewashed building and a welcome sight. As soon as they got through the door, Lord Cheam began barking instructions and had the staff scurrying back and forth fetching hot water and warming beds, whilst Gwenn oversaw the brewing of some willow bark tea.

Once the girls were tucked up in bed and looking much better for all the fuss they'd received, one thing became apparent. Mr Pelham and Aunt May were not here.

Gwenn hurried downstairs to find Lord Cheam and discover what was going on.

She found him staring moodily into the fire in the private parlour.

"I understand there is no sign of Mr Pelham and Mrs Bainbridge?" she said, as he looked up at her, his expression grim.

Silently, he handed her a note. Gwenn took it from him and read.

We've made excellent time and are reliably informed that snow is coming so will push on to Gretna Green. See you there. Sam.

"I can hardly turn the girls out of bed to catch them up," he said as she handed the note back to him.

"No, of course not," she agreed, watching as he crumpled the paper and threw it into the fire. "Well, it's no matter. We shall meet up tomorrow instead. Perhaps they'll wait for us?"

He snorted at that and her suspicions that this was some kind of plan in action grew. Perhaps his brother was just trying to annoy him? It was certainly working. Brothers played such tricks on each other, she knew. Perhaps this was normal. She could only imagine how irritated he was to find himself without a valet or even a maid to care for the girls. Not that Gwenn minded. She was happy to see to them… especially as doing so would keep her busy, and keep her mind off Lord Cheam.

Well, it would keep her busy, anyway.

"I did not realise we were passing through Gretna Green," she said with a smile, trying to lighten the atmosphere a little. "I shall be fascinated to see it."

"There's nothing to see," he muttered, glowering down at the flames in the hearth, where the paper was nothing but ash. "It's an unremarkable village, and we shan't be stopping other than to change horses."

"Well," she said, aware that he was in a prickly mood, and that the two of them spending an evening alone together would not be sensible under any circumstances. "The girls are looking much happier and should benefit from a good night's sleep. I will leave you to your evening."

"Where are you going?" he asked, lifting his head, his expression fierce.

Away from temptation, she thought, but pasted what she hoped was a reassuring smile to her lips. "I shall eat with the inn's staff," she said, moving towards the door. "It is quite acceptable for me to join the family when I am supervising the children, but I should not dream of imposing—"

"You're not imposing," he said, looking affronted. "And you cannot eat with the other servants. It wouldn't be at all the thing. You're a lady, not a servant. What's more, they should feel uncomfortable if a lady were to join them. I don't want their meal disrupted."

Gwenn felt the stir of something uncomfortable squirm in her chest at his words. *You're a lady.* Oh, no, she certainly was not a lady. If he knew the truth of her he'd be horrified at just how far from a lady she was. She accepted that the staff would find her presence irksome, however, though she thought he could have softened his words a little. It was never pleasant to realise one was unwelcome, no matter the circumstances.

"Very well. I do not wish to cause any discomfort. I shall eat in my room tonight," she said with a brisk nod. "Good evening, Lord Cheam."

"Wait."

Gwenn paused, frustrated as it seemed like the same scene would keep repeating itself over and over, with her trying to escape her fate and him forever putting temptation in her way.

"Don't go," he let out a breath and ran a hand through his thick hair, drawing her attention to the coppery red glints that caught the firelight. "I'm sorry I've been in such a wretched mood all evening, but... I should be glad of your company, if you would be so good as to join me?"

Gwenn stared at him. It would be so easy to stay, to share a meal and some wine, to talk and allow the man to charm her and lull her into a closeness that could only lead them both to disaster. She shook her head.

"Forgive me, but I think it best if I retire for the evening."

"Why?" he asked, a flicker of irritation and what might have been hurt glinting in those blue eyes. "We are in the middle of nowhere and everyone is far too occupied to pay us any mind. I promise you I'm not so very untrustworthy. You can leave the door ajar if you believe my motives to be suspect."

Oh, it wasn't only him she didn't trust. Gwenn knew well how it would end if she stayed and it mattered little who started it. They couldn't be alone together, and he damn well knew it. There was only one thing for it, she supposed.

"I do not believe you to be underhand, my lord, and I know you think your intentions are sincere, but your judgement is unsound. It is clear that you are smitten with me and, no matter your intentions, being alone with me is dangerous to us both."

"*Smitten?*" He gaped at her, outrage in every line of his body. "I am no such thing!" he said, his shoulders taut as he stood and faced her. "I'm not some green boy to be led about by the nose."

She smiled at that, amused by his indignation, at his refusal to own what was blatantly obvious. Some devil in her soul urged her to taunt him, to shatter the arrogant pretence of his indifference to her, when she'd have done better to have used his anger as an excuse to leave.

"Ah, but I could lead you anywhere I wished, my lord, should I choose to do so."

"What nonsense." He turned away from her and she suspected it was to hide a flush of colour, though whether from anger or embarrassment she could not be certain. He leaned on the mantle, scowling at the flames again. "I will allow that you are a remarkably beautiful woman, but I'm not so feeble-minded as that."

Gwenn snorted and his head turned sharply in her direction.

"You think otherwise?"

"I think if you use your head, that is quite correct," she allowed, prepared to be magnanimous. "The problem with men is that—when roused—they think with other parts of their anatomy."

"You seem to know a lot about the subject," he said, his eyes narrowing. "For a gently bred lady."

"*You* said I was a lady," she reminded him. "I did not. I am only trying to save us both from a situation we would be unwise to entertain."

He stared at her, such a look that would have searched out every dark corner of her soul, every secret, if only he could. Gwenn returned his gaze, outwardly placid. A good courtesan was never flustered, unless she wished to appear so. In truth, she shrank under that piercing scrutiny, wishing she was the lady he'd suggested she was. She ought not have admitted that she wasn't, for it threatened her position here. What if he dismissed her? But it was too late now.

"What are you, then, if not a lady? Not a governess."

There was suspicion in the question, and his brow furrowed as he stared at her, trying to figure her out.

The tension in the room prickled between them and Gwenn wished she'd just pretended a headache. She could have avoided all this easily enough, but something in her had wanted to provoke him. Perhaps it was the unfairness of it, of being born who she was instead of a young woman who could have smiled at him and accepted a stolen kiss, safe knowing that Lord Cheam would never insult her by taking advantage, that he would offer for her. He was a gentleman, the kind who abided by society's rules, and she was a lady. Therefore, he would marry her.

Perhaps he was that gentleman, but she wasn't that lady. She was the daughter of a courtesan and her noble lover—the rules did not apply.

"I am not here to cause you or your family the slightest trouble, my lord," she said after a tense silence. "I have already told you of my intention to move on after the Christmas holiday. If you prefer I do so sooner, I will of course comply."

She turned away again, but he stopped her once more.

"No, Miss Wynter, I don't wish you to leave, either your position or this room." He sounded frustrated and perplexed, but his face softened, and she knew he would try to cajole the truth from her along with her company. If she allowed it he'd say, *come, come, Miss Wynter, we are being foolish. Two adults can enjoy a convivial evening together with no dramatic consequences, surely...* or something of the sort. If he believed that, he was a fool. Perhaps another two adults, but not the two of them.

"That is not your choice to make, my lord," she said, her voice firm. "On either count, and you are not thinking clearly."

"On account of me being besotted with you, I suppose," he said with a snort. He folded his arms, his expression contemptuous.

"Yes," Gwenn replied gently, needing him to accept the truth but not wanting to aggravate him further.

"What rot."

Damn him!

"You deny it still?" She lifted one eyebrow. Heavens, the man was stubborn. "When it is so blatantly obvious?"

He glowered at her, his posture so stiff that the muscles in his arms flexed, straining at the close-fitting sleeves of his coat. "I do deny it. Oh, I don't pretend that you are not a beautiful woman, I already said as much. That doesn't mean I cannot control myself for the time it takes for us to eat a meal together, or for the rest of this journey, or for however long you choose to remain with us. I'm not so easily led as you may suppose, nor so easily tempted."

"You think not?" she said, her lips twitching. Lord he was handsome, and so deliciously indignant. The desire to prove him wrong was too tantalising now. She need only make her point, after all, and then he'd realise his mistake and allow her to keep her distance. He'd send her away if he had an ounce of sense. "You try to kiss me at every opportunity. I think you'd not last until the entrée arrives."

He stilled at that, at the challenge he must have seen in her eyes.

"Then, you will dine with me, Miss Wynter," he said, all stiff and formal.

Gwenn licked her lips as she considered this. The desire to rattle his composure and muss up his impeccable person was beyond anything she'd ever known. She looked up at him from under her lashes.

"If... that's what you want," she said, her voice low.

"It is." He gave a brisk nod and moved to the fireplace to ring for service. A few moments later a maid appeared. "You may serve."

"Very good, my lord," the girl said and hurried away.

He turned back to her, his expression smug. "Your time is running out."

Gwenn laughed and leaned against the wall, one finger trailing along the neckline of her gown. It was not an especially revealing gown, but far too immodest for a governess. "It's not my time that is running out, but yours. If you wish to kiss me before she returns, you must make haste."

He grew very still.

"Isn't that what you want?" she asked, staring at him. "To kiss me? To hold me against you... don't you want to put your hands on me?" Gwenn laid her palms upon her thighs and swept them slowly upwards, caressing her curves as she went until she cupped her own breasts, lifting them up as though she would offer them to him. "Or perhaps your mouth?" she suggested with a mischievous quirk of her lips.

She watched his Adam's apple bob as he swallowed, saw the way his chest rose and fell and how his fists clenched. The look in his eyes made her own breathing quicken, desire coiling in her belly and making the place between her thighs throb with wanting. The poor fool hadn't stopped to consider that she might goad him.

"Come to me, my lord," she said, the words low and sultry. "I want to feel your hands on me."

She smiled, aware of the power she held over him, aware of how badly he wanted to do as she asked. His eyes had darkened, his expression fierce as he battled against his own desire, knowing he'd lose, because he wanted to lose, no matter what he told himself. He knew all the reasons why it was right to refuse her, to refuse himself, but that didn't change the fact that giving in would be delicious. It only made it ever more tempting.

They jolted as the maid reappeared with a jug and wine glasses, followed by another maid and a male servant, both hauling a heavy tray loaded with plates and covered dishes. Lord Cheam turned away to stare at the fire and Gwenn took a moment to compose herself too, as the staff arranged their dinner for them. She was hot and flustered and out of control. What the devil had she been thinking? Never mind Lord Cheam thinking with his nether regions! Had she run mad? What if the maid hadn't appeared and brought him to his senses?

You bloody fool, Gwenn, and after everything Marie taught you, too.

She was an idiot, and she'd best take herself off to bed before she had any more bright ideas.

"Will there be anything else, my lord?" asked the maid, once the table had been set to her satisfaction.

"No," Lord Cheam replied, never taking his eyes from the fire. "Leave us and don't come back until I call."

Gwenn felt a prickle of alarm shiver down her spine, and the moment the door closed she prepared to run.

"You win, my lord. I underestimated... *oh!*"

"No," he said, pulling her into his arms. He'd crossed the room so fast there'd been no time to escape. "You win. You're right, right about all of it. I am smitten, besotted, infatuated, whatever you want to call it. I can't think of anything but kissing you. Though I think perhaps I'm not alone. You are not a bystander in this, are you? You want me too."

Gwenn stiffened in his arms, her hands braced on his biceps, feeling the powerful shift of the muscles beneath her fingertips. She opened her mouth to deny it, to give him a set down, to demand he let her go... but she didn't. Instead, she stared up into his eyes, so blue they ought to be cold as an ocean, but they were the salt blue of a driftwood fire, blazing like an inferno.

"Yes," she said, helpless to deny it.

His mouth came down on hers before she could think to say another word, before she could remind him of all the reasons this was a bad, bad idea, and then all those reasons disappeared. They seemed as insubstantial as soap bubbles when faced with the fierce desire that rose inside her at his touch.

She was hesitant at first, overwhelmed by the heat and size of him as he engulfed her smaller frame, but his lips were soft and surprisingly gentle. She'd expected to be devoured, claimed and taken to the floor like the whore her mother had taught her to be, such was the ferocity of his declaration, but he held her as if she was precious, kissed her as if she was to be savoured and treated gently, like she was the well-bred lady she wished she was. That he did so, even knowing she was not—hadn't she told him so? — touched her. It made dangerous emotions rise in her chest, too, made her want things she could never have.

He teased her lips apart, coaxing her to open to him and toying with her tongue. Gwenn sighed, sinking into his embrace and delighted with his kiss, learning the way of it with him. He was every bit as delicious as she'd imagined, and instantly addictive. She wanted more, wanted all of it, all of him, and wasn't that beyond foolish? Nonetheless she clung to him, discovering the taste of him, and how to receive his kiss, how to explore in return.

For all that Gwenn had an explicit knowledge of what to expect, how to behave, and what a man wanted from her, in terms of practical experience she had little. Her mother had sheltered her deliberately, not from any sense of propriety, but to ensure she didn't devalue herself with an ill-advised love affair.

Not that there was any difficulty in following his lead.

She sighed with pleasure and his arms tightened about her, one hand dropping to her hip and pulling her flush against him. His arousal was evident, blatant, and she pressed closer, wanting and needing a prowling, living thing inside of her. She wanted with a hunger that surprised her, despite her mother's teachings. She'd thought she knew what desire was, how it felt, how it could overpower reason and good sense, but what she thought she'd understood and what she felt now were the difference between the gentle waves upon the shore on a summer's day, and the ferocity of a winter storm that battered the coastline and tore away defences.

Though she knew she risked everything, she could not tear herself from his arms, from his kiss. She felt cherished and safe and, though she knew it was an illusion, it was such a beautiful one that she wanted to live every last moment of it.

His mouth left hers at last and he stared down at her, breathing hard as one hand cupped her face.

"Tell me who you really are," he said, stroking her cheek with his thumb. He kissed her forehead, her nose, the corner of her mouth, so tenderly her throat tightened. "Give me the truth and tell me what it is you are running from. Let me help you."

That, she reflected, was likely the only thing that could have brought her to her senses, and out of his arms. She pushed out of his embrace, alarmed to discover her knees did not feel equal to the task of keeping her upright.

"There is no point," she said, relieved that he hadn't fought to hold on to her but had released her at once.

Everywhere she trembled, torn between the desire to throw herself back into his arms and to run away from him before he discovered the truth. She could not bear to see the disgust in his eyes when he realised what kind of woman he had been so desperate for, not when he'd treated her so tenderly.

"There is no future for us," she said, the words hard and bleak, for how else could they sound? "Nothing that wouldn't end with a scandal of the kind you want to avoid at all costs."

She put distance between them and smoothed down her dress, striving to find some measure of calm.

Fool. Fool. You bloody fool.

"Perhaps if you explained," he said, his manner so gentle and coaxing she wanted to scream at him for being kind to her. Hadn't she shown what kind of woman she was? Didn't he realise a nice young lady would not have invited him to touch her with such a lewd invitation?

"There is nothing to explain," she snapped, the effort of will to stop herself from crying making her brittle and angry. "I'm not for you. I'll not be your mistress and I'm so far from a suitable bride you'd not even wish to speak with me if you knew the truth. There is nothing more to be said, no future for us, nothing to be done except to stay far away from each other until this journey is at its end. I will part company with you as soon as you reach your destination. It is for the best."

She dared to look at him, a little stunned to discover her words had neither made him angry nor shocked him. He stood with one hand braced on the back of a chair and she wondered if perhaps he was as shaken as she was.

"Perhaps you're right," he said, never taking his eyes off her. "But I think you might confide in me all the same. I would help you, if you'd let me. If there is someone who is pursuing you, if you are in some kind of trouble…. I'm not an ogre, Miss Wynter, I…. Lord, I don't even know your name. Can't you trust me with that much?"

Gwenn closed her eyes and forced herself to shake her head.

"No," she said, as the last vestiges of her willpower began to fray. If she stayed here any longer the temptation to run back into his arms and pretend he could make everything all right would be too hard to resist. "If you'll excuse me, Lord Cheam. I'm very tired."

"Don't go," he pleaded, moving towards her though he made no move to stop her leaving. "Please, Miss Wynter, you've not even eaten." Gwenn heard his protests but only ran faster for the door and snatched it open. She didn't turn back, didn't wait to hear any further pleas to allow him to help. She didn't stop until she reached her room and slammed the door shut, turning the key and leaning back against it with her chest heaving and tears pricking at her eyes.

"Oh, Marie," she said, blinking them back. "I should have listened. How cross you will be when you discover what a fool I am."

She laughed, though it was not in the least a happy sound, and the bitterness of it echoed around the empty room until she gave up, threw herself on the bed, and sobbed.

Chapter 11

"Wherein fate falls gently from the skies."

Sampson stared at the door Miss Wynter had fled through. With a hand that was not entirely steady, he raked at his hair, and then sat down at the table before his knees gave out. Something momentous had happened, and he was shaken by it, changed by it. From the first moment he'd seen her, he'd been certain it was fate throwing them together, though he'd not admit that to another living soul for he knew precisely how outrageous it sounded. It *was* outrageous. He was a man who read science journals and kept up with innovations, always keen to discover the newest discovery, not some whimsical old lady who believed in fairies and put a saucer of milk out for the little people. Yet he'd never felt such a connection to another human being before, such a desire—no, *a need*—to be in their company.

It made no sense, he knew it didn't, but the sensation persisted. She wasn't a lady, she'd said as much; she'd implied that he'd not want to know her if he knew the truth of her past, but he did want to know her, the past be damned. Perhaps she was ruined, perhaps there had been a scandal, or a failed love affair. Perhaps there was a child… but no, she'd never leave her child. He'd not believe that after the care she took with his sisters.

Besides which, there was that kiss, bold and unashamedly wanting yet surprisingly unpractised. The way she'd touched herself, inviting him to do the same, the way she'd spoken, it all suggested a woman who'd had lovers and knew how to drive a man mad with desire. She'd accomplished it with ease, hadn't she?

Yet that kiss had been eager and… strangely innocent. It made no sense. She made no sense. What was she was running from?

There was something, something she was ashamed of, or believed he would be ashamed of.

Sampson had wanted to explain to her, to promise her he didn't care, didn't care about the past. He only cared that she trust him with it. Perhaps he didn't want to think of her having had a lover, certainly didn't want to imagine it, but he was not the kind of man to condemn her for it.

She had a kind and loving nature, that much was certain. Perhaps she'd been taken advantage of. Except then he remembered her bold perusal of his person when they'd first met, the way her lingering gaze had looked him over, head to toe and back again. He remembered the sight of her just moments earlier, touching herself to inflame him, such a blatant invitation. Perhaps a passionate affair gone wrong, then, for she *was* passionate. She'd been ablaze in his arms, clinging to him, inviting him to keep taking, and he'd wanted to badly, but he'd wanted to know her even more.

Maybe he'd been selfish, but he'd known then that her kisses weren't enough, her body wasn't enough. He wanted it all. He wanted her secrets and her fears and her past and all of it, and God damn him, but he was a fool because she was right. It wasn't in his future, *she* wasn't in his future. If she was right, and she'd bring him scandal, then he needed to stay away, stay clear, as she'd warned him to do. The girls were his priority. He owed them a future free of the taint their father had bestowed upon them, and he could not be so cruel as to make them ever more notorious as a family.

This had to end before it began, for it could only bring them misery.

So, tomorrow he must continue this farce, continue to pretend that Miss Wynter was not in the carriage, that his entire being was not attuned to her every move, every word she spoke. He must pretend he didn't ache to reach across the carriage and haul her into his arms, but that she was nothing more than the governess, and therefore beneath his notice.

Cursing, he reached for the wine and poured himself a glass, downed it, and poured another. The third he drank a little slower. Hangovers and long carriage journeys did not make comfortable bed fellows, as he knew to his cost. By God, but he would have Samuel's hide when he caught up with him.

Sampson stared at the covered dishes on the table and his stomach rebelled at the thought of eating but he forced himself to dish out a serving all the same. Staring down at the plate with little enthusiasm, he picked up his knife and fork and then set them down again and strode to the door, calling for the inn keeper or someone to attend him.

The maid appeared once more.

"Have something taken up to Miss Wynter," he instructed. "She was feeling unwell and has retired early, but she has eaten no supper. If you would prepare something suitable?"

"Of course, my lord. I'll see to it at once."

Sampson nodded his thanks, and the woman bobbed a curtsey and hurried off. With a sigh, he returned his attention to his meal and the long and sleepless night that was bound to follow.

***

Gwenn told herself that she was relieved when Lord Cheam greeted her with cool civility the next morning. He'd taken her words to heart and realised she'd spoken true. Now they could get this interminable journey over with and, as soon as may be, she'd be on her way. It appeared his half-brother lived in the wilds of Scotland and far from civilisation, however, so that might present some challenges. All the better, she assured herself. A challenge was just the thing to keep her occupied instead of pining for something she'd known she couldn't have from the outset.

Honestly, if she'd known she could be such a peahen as to have her head turned by the first handsome man who paid her any attention, she might as well have allowed Marie to sell her to the highest bidder. She could at least have fallen in love with a wealthy duke who would have been generous when he grew tired of her. Better that than the temptation to throw herself at Lord Cheam, and for what? A night of passion and a lifetime of regrets?

No, indeed.

Wait….

Fallen in love with?

No, she scolded herself soundly. She certainly *had not* fallen in love with him. Gwenn had never believed in love at first sight, and she wasn't about to believe that a few heated gazes, some insults, a few soft words, a carriage ride and an embrace….

Not just *an* embrace.

Very well.

A knee-trembling, breath-stealing, soul-shattering embrace, on top of the few other shared incidences, was not enough to send her head over ears in love. She was an idiot, but even *she* wasn't that great a ninny.

Thankfully, Selina and Susan appeared before she could spend any more time considering just how great a ninny she was, which was just as well.

"How are you feeling, girls?" she asked as they sat down to breakfast.

"Better," Susan said, and sneezed.

"Fine," Selina added, sniffing and wiping her nose on her sleeve.

"Selina!" Gwenn exclaimed, hurriedly producing a handkerchief and thrusting it at her.

"Sorry," Selina muttered before blowing her nose, hard. She offered Gwenn the hanky back.

"No, no, dear," Gwenn said, her lip curling as she waved the offending item away. "You keep it." She looked from one to the other and put a hand to each of their foreheads. "No fever, that's good."

"It's just a head cold," Susan said, sniffing. "We're fine, really."

"Are you sure?" Gwenn asked. "I'm certain your brother would delay until you feel better, if you think the journey will be too much for you."

"Ugh, no," Susan said in disgust. "There's nothing to do here and my bed was lumpy."

"And the chimney smoked," Selina grumbled. "We'll be fine."

Thank heavens, Gwenn thought. Being stuck here with Lord Cheam would be the worst kind of torture. She'd been overwhelmed with relief when she'd looked out this morning and not seen a scrap of snow on the ground.

Liar.

"Well, come along, then. A hearty breakfast will do you the world of good, and we'll get some extra blankets, so you'll be as snug as a bug in a rug for the journey."

The girls laughed.

"Are there sausages?" Susan asked hopefully, taking her hand.

Gwenn smiled at her and squeezed her fingers. "Why don't we find out?"

***

As Lord Cheam had suggested, Gretna Green was underwhelming. The girls were mad with the desire to see the blacksmith's shop but were told in no uncertain terms that there was not time.

"Oh, but Sunny, please?" Susan pleaded, but was met with stony silence.

"You and Miss Wynter could get married," Selina added with a wistful sigh.

"Selina!" Lord Cheam snapped at her. "You will keep such inappropriate comments to yourself."

Selina's lip trembled a little, but she put up her chin and folded her arms, turning her back on her brother to stare out of the window.

Gwenn held back a sigh and tried to soften the blow by surreptitiously offering Selina a sweet. The girl gave her a faint smile and accepted it, leaning her head on Gwenn's arm.

The weather was worsening, and snow drifted from above once more. Only tiny flakes for the moment, but the sky was a dirty white and the temperature had plummeted. Even though they were buried beneath thick travelling cloaks and blankets, with hot bricks at their feet, as the day wore on it was hard to keep warm. The girls sat either side of Gwenn now, huddling closer for warmth and she cuddled them to her, trying not to notice the growing concern on Lord Cheam's face as he watched the weather.

By the time they changed horses at Ecclefechan the snow had stopped, though a thin covering had settled over the hills beyond the window, and Gwenn was certain it had grown colder still. The terrain was becoming ever more challenging, and she feared the roads would soon be too bad to continue. For the moment they pressed on, though it was slow going and they changed horses more often as much of the way was steep and the beasts tired quickly.

When they stopped at the Beattoch Bridge Inn, the snow began again and Lord Cheam would not allow them to linger. Their overnight stop was a good many miles distant yet.

Gwenn did her best to entertain the girls, as much to keep herself occupied instead of fretting over the fat snowflakes falling in slow, graceful tumbles outside the window. It appeared they would be stuck with her a while yet, so she tried to act as a governess might and to teach them a little French and Italian and read another of the Shakespeare tales. It had been awkward at first, with Lord Cheam there too, but it seemed he really was sleeping now, and soon she was too caught up in the story to care if he was listening or not. Now and then she glanced out of the window as the weather worsened and spared a thought for the poor coachmen and the horses, exposed at they were.

Having exhausted her own talents and the girls themselves, the three of them were dozing when Lord Cheam's voice roused them.

"We'll not make it." He sounded resigned as he stared out at the dazzling white, his jaw tight. "I can't ask them to go on any further in this," he added. "Besides which, if we don't stop soon, we risk getting stuck."

Gwenn nodded her understanding, though her heart sank at the idea of being snowed in with Lord Cheam. "I'm sure the girls would welcome a warm fire and something to eat," she said, doing her best to sound cheerful for their sakes.

"Oh, yes, please," Susan said, before punctuating that with a lusty sneeze.

"We ought not have pressed on," Lord Cheam said, and she could almost hear him cursing himself. "It'll have done the children no good to be frozen all day."

"We're fine, Sunny," Selina said gamely, before snatching up her handkerchief and sneezing louder than her sister.

Lord Cheam sighed.

"You had no way of knowing the weather would close in so quickly," Gwenn said, hoping to soothe him.

"Yes, I did," he replied. "My brother's note said as much, but I thought he was just making mischief in order to get us—" He snapped his jaw shut, but Gwenn's concerns that Mr Pelham had thrown them together on purpose were obviously not so far from the mark. "And I wanted to catch them up," he finished stiffly.

"Well, never mind," Gwenn said, smiling at the girls. "We shall consider it an adventure, stuck in the wilds of the snowy highlands."

"Can we build a snowman?" Susan asked, her blue eyes wide with excitement.

Gwenn laughed. "Not whilst you both have such a cold, I think, but when you are feeling better, I shall insist upon it. We shall build the biggest snowman Scotland has ever seen."

"Sunny must help us, though," Selina said, grinning at her big brother. "He makes the best snowmen."

"Oh, yes, he does. You must help us, Sunny," Susan said, turning pleading eyes on him.

Lord Cheam frowned and looked uncomfortable as he glanced at Gwenn. She could not help but tease him a little.

"I can believe it," she said. "He looks like an expert snowman builder."

Despite his obvious anxiety, he gave a begrudging huff of laughter.

"Of course I'll help," he said, before turning his attention back to the increasingly white scenery outside.

They gave up in Crawford, though John Coachman and his fellow driver urged them to try for Abington, much to Gwenn's surprise, as they must be frozen to the bone. Lord Cheam was adamant, however.

"No, my sisters are cold and need to rest in the warm and I fear we might not make it to Abington in this." He gestured to the skies and the steady fall of white flakes that settled in silence around them. "Besides, there aren't any other guests staying here, and they've plenty of room for us. The inn at Abington is half the size, and for all we know they're full. No, we'll stay. See to the horses."

Gwenn watched the head coachman turn to his companion, and they exchanged a wary glance before doffing their hats and doing as the viscount bid.

"I thought they'd be relieved to stop," she said to Lord Cheam, once Susan and Selina had been hustled inside.

He rolled his eyes and lowered his voice. "We stayed here a few months ago and poor John had a bit of a turn. Swears he saw a ghost."

Gwenn's eyes widened with alarm. "No!" She gasped, horrified.

Lord Cheam, the wretch, seemed amused by her appalled expression. "Oh, yes," he said, smiling a little now. "Apparently, this place is notorious. It has three ghosts. It appears John saw the apparition of a young woman. She was the daughter of one of the former proprietors and had the misfortune to be run down by a carriage on the street there. She haunts the stables."

As he spoke Gwenn found her hand moving to her throat, and she swallowed her alarm, telling herself that Lord Cheam was only teasing, and she would not be bird-witted enough to let him see how unsettled she was.

"Well, no doubt it is an amusing tale to frighten travellers with," she said, her voice fainter than she would have liked. "I expect it leads them into spending more on strong spirits than they might have otherwise done."

Gwenn turned away from him and hurried to find her charges and get them settled in the warm as soon as may be. Anything to keep her mind from ghosts. She'd been terrified of such night-time spectres since a child, and hated the dark. The idea that the inn was teeming with the damn things and that now they were stuck here... well, of all the rotten luck.

***

Sampson watched Miss Wynter hurry away and allowed himself a small smile. It was shameful of him to have tormented her so, but she'd been tormenting him all day with her scent and her voice and her beauty so close to him. It seemed only fair. The more time he spent in her company the more he wanted to know her. She was funny and affectionate with the girls, and remarkably clever. His aunt had been right; his sisters enjoyed her company so much, half the time they didn't even know they were being taught something.

She'd discussed Shakespeare with them after having read one of the stories. The reading had been marvellous, with Miss Wynter taking on all the voices as though she were acting each part in turn. The girls giggled and snickered at the funny bits, sometimes making Miss Wynter dissolve into laughter too, and good Lord, what a sound that was. It had hit him square in the chest and made him want to join in. It had been the hardest thing to not laugh, and instead continue feigning sleep, but he'd been as riveted by the story and her telling of it as his sisters had. Then she'd helped them make up silly rhymes, testing their grammar and spelling, and later she'd spoken to them in both French and Italian with an authentic and lilting accent he'd found utterly beguiling, and which suggested an impressive fluency.

Sampson had stolen glances at them from under the brim of his hat, pride bursting in his chest as Susan and Selina strove to imitate her. When she praised their efforts, their cheeks flushed with pride and Sampson's throat ached. He'd been so worried for them. When each governess had followed the last with disapproving scowls and warnings that the girls were either wicked or mentally impaired, he'd been beside himself. Not that he'd believed anything of the sort, but he'd been frantic that they were out of control, and he'd not had the first idea of how to keep them from disaster. When they'd begun stealing things, too, he'd been at the end of his tether, but Miss Wynter had swept in and made everything all right.

That she'd been the one to tell the girls they were good and in no danger of going to hell made guilt sit heavy in his chest. He'd been so busy protecting them from their father he'd not considered that they would have overheard rumours and gossip from other quarters. He'd not wanted to speak of that foul tyrant in their presence. Now he realised that, by pretending the monster hadn't existed, he'd only made things worse. He must try to be a little more open with them and make them understand that they could come to him, and speak with him about anything that troubled them. At least they had Miss Wynter to turn to now... except they didn't.

Miss Wynter was leaving, sooner rather than later.

The idea made his chest tighten, and he tried to breathe, to dislodge the sensation but it wouldn't budge. It would devastate the girls when they found out. That was the only reason he was so troubled by her departure, he assured himself. Sampson knew it was a lie, but he forced himself to accept it. They had no future together, not if he wanted the girls to emerge from under the dark reputation that surrounded the family. They came first, not what he wanted. If not for them, perhaps things could have been different. His brothers were all grown men, after all. If his sisters were older and married, it would not signify so much. Then he could have pursued Miss Wynter, society be damned, and seen where this fascination for her might lead. He could have courted her and coaxed the truth of her past from her.

He could have married her and had that vivacious laugh all to himself... instead of worrying that it would haunt his dreams for the rest of his days.

Chapter 12

"Wherein ghosts of the past make trouble for the future."

Gwenn lay in bed, rigid, her eyes squeezed shut.

"Stop being such an utter ninny," she scolded herself. "There are no such things as ghosts."

She repeated the phrase to herself until she heard a creak outside her bedroom door and stifled a whimper. There was a brief murmur of voices, and then another creak as the footsteps moved away.

"Idiot," she muttered into the darkness, forcing herself to open her eyes. It was no use. She would not get a wink of sleep. Cursing, she fumbled with the tinderbox until she'd lit a candle, and then wrapped herself in her dressing gown and shoved her feet into slippers before searching out her cashmere shawl and draping that about her shoulders too. The only way she would get any sleep at all was by doing exactly what she'd suggested earlier and finding some strong spirits. The kind that didn't go bump in the night.

Gwenn muttered to herself about unscrupulous innkeepers all the way down the stairs. At least they were the only guests staying here, so she'd not risk running into strangers on her night time expedition. Keeping her eyes on the floor, Gwenn prayed she'd see nothing more extraordinary than her rather extravagantly embroidered slippers. She was concentrating so hard on not looking where she was going that she almost screamed the place down when she walked straight into a very solid body.

"Hush!" Lord Cheam hissed, smacking his palm over her mouth.

Gwenn stared at him in outrage as he hurriedly removed his hand.

"I beg your pardon," he said, immediately contrite and taking a step away from her. "But I thought you were about to scream."

"I was," she snapped. "You scared me half to death!"

"Well, it's not my fault you weren't looking where you were going."

There was reproach in his eyes and he folded his arms, scowling at her.

"I was trying not to see a ghost," she shot back at him, and then bit her lip as she realised how daft that sounded. To her chagrin, she saw his lips curve upwards.

"Really?" he said, with a tremor of mirth.

"Really," she retorted, feeling like an idiot.

"I do beg your pardon once again, Miss Wynter," he said, apparently striving for gravity, but his lips kept quirking at the corners and ruining it. "If I'd known how lively an imagination you have, I would never have mentioned it."

"Them," she replied tersely. "You said there were three."

"So I did." He seemed to have given up on trying to look sincere, and was grinning at her.

"It's not funny," she said with a huff. "I can't sleep."

"Oh." He really did look remorseful now. "Is that why you're prowling about down here?"

Gwenn nodded. "I thought a little tot of something might help."

He nodded and gestured for her to follow him. "I've found the very thing," he said, leading her into a private parlour where a fire still glowed in the hearth. He lifted a bottle in her direction. "Captain Moncreiffe was good enough to introduce me to the terrible pleasure of whisky when I stayed with him."

"I thought it was illegal?" Gwenn said, watching as he poured a generous measure into each of two glasses.

"It is." He chuckled. "You don't think that would stop any self-respecting Scotsman, do you? I had to pay the innkeeper a pretty penny, but it's good stuff. Good enough to help you sleep without being troubled by ghoulies and ghosties," he added with an unrepentant glint in his eyes as he handed her a glass.

"Don't mock," she chided him. "It's all your fault."

"I know, and I *am* sorry."

"No, you're not. You think it's hilarious." She gave a dignified sniff and saw him struggle to keep a straight face. Though she knew she was a fool, she was too happy in his company to scold him anymore and laughed a little. "Oh, stop trying to look so chastised. I know it's ridiculous, but I can't seem to help it. I've always been somewhat afraid of the dark and...." She shrugged and gave a rueful shake of her head. "I'm an idiot."

"No," he said, his voice too warm, too soft. "You're certainly not that. You're clever and kind and funny, and my sisters adore you." He paused and his words sank into her bones, into her heart, warming her like no praise of her beauty had ever done. "It will break their hearts when you leave us."

Gwenn stared at him and proved him utterly wrong about her intelligence by willing him to add *and mine too*, which he wouldn't, of course.

There, see, a complete idiot.

"I wish you wouldn't leave," he said, the words stunning her.

He just doesn't want his sisters unhappy you fool, she told herself, but he wasn't done.

"I don't want you to go. I know I should urge you to do just that but… I want you to stay."

"You ought not say such things," she said, turning away from him.

"I know."

She sipped at the whisky, feeling her eyes water and her breath vanish as it lit a trail of fire down her throat and then warmth unfurled in her belly, easing into her blood. *Goodness.* Rather taken with the sensation, she took another sip. The silence stretched between them and she wished he'd say something. Anything.

"Why are you afraid of the dark?" he asked.

Gwenn shrugged, relieved he'd done as she wished. "I don't know. I suppose because my mother was rarely home at night, or if she was, she was… occupied. We never seemed to keep staff for very long when I was a girl and, if I woke from a bad dream, I was never sure who would come to me. Some of them were lovely, others… less so."

"Less so in what way?" he asked at once, the enquiry sharp edged.

She smiled, touched by his unease. "Oh, nothing sinister. Just some poor impatient maid, torn from her sleep and resentful for it, or sometimes they were unused to children and uncaring. I was far too sensitive to sharp words back then. I grew out of it."

"Have you received so many sharp words in your life?" he asked, too much concern in the question. "To have gotten used to them."

She clutched the glass a little tighter, fighting the urge to sink into the warmth in his voice, to allow the intimacy he offered her so unthinkingly. Why should he think about it? She was only the governess and he a powerful lord. No, that was unfair, and she knew it. He wasn't the kind of man to ruin a woman and leave her to her fate. At least she hoped not. Either way, it didn't change the fact that she ought not be here.

"Oh, not so many," she said, striving to lighten her tone. She took another, larger sip of the whisky and then raised the glass to him. "You're right, this is rather good."

"How do you know the Duke of Alvermarle?"

The question knocked her off balance, and she jolted. For a moment she stared down into the amber liquid while she worked to steady herself. "I worked for him," she said, the words stiff and given after too long a pause.

"No," he said at once, shaking his head. "You are not and have never been a governess, which is strange as you're the best we've ever had, and we've had a few," he added wryly. "But that reference of yours bore the man's seal. So, either he wrote it as a favour, or you were close enough to him to have access to it."

Gwenn's heart beat in her throat. If she'd not been so damned stupid, she could have been asleep and not here, getting herself into trouble. She took a deep breath, fighting for calm. What did it matter now, anyway? It wasn't as if she was staying, and he'd already guessed she wasn't what she seemed.

"Were you his mistress?"

She let out a little huff of laughter. Of course he would think that. Gwenn shrugged. Why not let him believe it? Perhaps he'd not want another man's cast off and would leave her be. Her chest tightened uncomfortably, but she forced the word out. "Yes."

He studied her for a long time and then shook his head.

"You're lying."

For a moment she was too stunned to speak. How could he know that? She was a damned good liar; even Marie said so. It was him, dammit. Everything about him unsettled her and made her act the fool. "Why would I lie about such a thing?"

"I don't know," he said, moving a little closer to her. "But it's a lie all the same."

Gwenn stiffened, sensing danger and increased the distance between them.

"Don't be a fool." The words were hard, the bored, imperious tone that her mother used when her adoring suitors—the ones that couldn't afford her—wore on her patience.

"Oh, I'd have likely believed it, before you kissed me."

The blush stung her cheeks, and she felt a flash of indignation that he'd managed it a second time after everything she'd learned. He made her feel like an innocent girl, which was so laughable she wanted to cry.

"What do you mean?" she demanded, mortified. "What was wrong with my kiss?"

There was a low sound, a gentle huff of amusement, and he closed the distance between them. Gwenn was caught with the fire close behind her and the over-furnished room holding her barricaded with nowhere to run. He reached out and touched her heated cheek with the back of his hand, such a tender caress that her breath hitched.

"There wasn't a damn thing wrong with it," he said, such a fierce exclamation she blinked in surprise. "It was perfect, you are perfect—"

"I certainly am not," she objected, speaking over him, unsettled by such ridiculous praise.

"You are perfectly wonderful," he finished, sounding amused. "But that was your first kiss. Which begs the question, why would you pretend to have been another man's lover?"

His hands settled on her waist and the warmth of them burned through her dressing gown and nightdress. The desire to have them on her bare skin was so fierce she ached all over with longing.

"It was not my first kiss," she retorted, wishing she didn't want his hands on her so badly. It would be so much better if she could push them away and stalk off with an angry toss of her head, but she wanted his touch with such desperation she could not bring herself to do it.

He tilted his head to one side, studying her, before returning a crooked grin.

"Ah, your second, then."

"No," she muttered, irritated.

"My word, well, if it was your third, I can only believe you've been kissing green boys who knew no better than to peck at your lips." He lifted a hand to her cheek, his thumb tracing her lower lip with a barely there touch. "I think I can do better," he whispered.

That was so accurate an assessment she could say nothing in retaliation. It was the reason Marie had guarded her so fiercely. Those stolen kisses had been sweet and clumsy, but Marie would take no chances once she'd discovered the truth from a maid who had tattled on Gwenn. Marie was determined that her daughter would be a beguiling melange of explicit knowledge and physical innocence. Because of it, her price would be the highest ever seen in London, perhaps in the world. The memory pressed down on Gwenn, reminding her of all the reasons she ought not be alone with a man she was in danger of caring for.

No rubies, Gwennie, they're not worth a broken heart. They only take the sting from humiliation.

Her heart thundered as he lowered his mouth to hers.

"We've been here before," she said, turning her head away and refusing his kiss though she ached for it. "You know it's hopeless. We both know it."

"I know," he said, lowering his head to touch his forehead to hers.

It was some consolation that he sounded as anguished as she felt. Gwenn closed her eyes, wishing she had the strength to move away, to put some distance between them, but she was drawn to him by some invisible force she didn't understand. Like some stupid moth burning its wings over and over again, but never learning the danger.

He let out a heavy sigh, his hands tightening on her waist. "I keep telling myself to stay away. I know I ought to. I know all the reasons. I repeat them, over and over again, but...."

Hope burned inside her, which was ridiculous. She ought not hope his resolution should crumble.

"*But?*" she repeated, breathless with desire, looking up at him with anticipation.

"But I can't—"

He stopped, gazing down at her before cursing, low and angry, and then he pulled her into his arms. She went eagerly, like a stupid rabbit leaping into a poacher's snare and welcoming the savage arms that proclaimed her fate. Gwenn coiled her arms about his neck, pulling his head down and pressing closer to him.

Oh, heaven have mercy, but she wanted him.

***

She was in his arms.

Triumph blazed through him like a spark chasing a line of gunpowder, triumph and exhilaration, and something terribly like joy.

Her desire scalded him, sending his own need raging hotter as she clung to him, snatched at him, her hands in his hair, pushing his coat from his shoulders, tugging his shirt from his waistband. Yet he understood, for he felt this all-encompassing madness too, the desperation to touch her, to have her close, closer, as close as they could get.

He tugged at the tie holding her dressing gown closed and stripped it from her as she pushed him backwards. His legs hit an overstuffed armchair and he sat heavily. Dazed, he watched as she hitched her nightgown, a wicked confection of almost transparent fabric trimmed with lace and ribbons. It was ill-suited for either a Scottish winter or a governess, and it made Sampson smile, helpless with delight until she came to him, straddling him and chasing away the breath in his lungs.

He shifted forward and tugged her closer until his cock nestled against her sex. Even with several layers of fabric between them the contact was electric, and he moaned, smothering the sound in her neck as she clung to him. When she moved, rubbing herself against him, he knew he was lost. This was fate. Karma. Inevitable. They'd tried to fight it, but fate had other plans for them, and he was glad. In this perfect moment, this woman filled his senses. She was everything he'd ever dreamed of; a woman he could talk to, clever and funny and caring, challenging too. Clever and caring enough to understand what his sisters had needed, sweet enough to explain it to him without making him feel guilty for not having understood. She made him laugh, made him ache with wanting, made him feel like his soul would unravel if he couldn't keep her near him.

"I don't know your name," he said, and it sounded like a tragedy, the longing in his voice so raw he almost flinched. Yet it was true, he needed her name, needed every intimacy she would grant him, every part of her that only a lover would have.

She laughed a little, a wonderful breathy sound that fluttered over his mouth. "Gwenn," she said, sliding her hands from his shoulders to his neck.

"Gwendoline?" he guessed, his smile faltering as she hesitated.

If he hadn't been so focused on her he wouldn't have noticed, it was so fleeting.

"Yes," she said, and he didn't know why he doubted the answer, but then she kissed him and he didn't care.

"Gwenn," he said, grasping her hips and rocking against her.

"Yes, my lord." Her words shivered over him, a seductive murmur against his ear.

"Sampson," he corrected. "My name is Sampson."

She gasped as he slid his hands under the frilly nightgown and touched the warm silk of her skin.

"Ah, but you like being my lord," she said, the words sleek like a purring cat. "My lord, *mon seigneur, mio signore,* my master." She punctuated each title with a little press of her hips against his cock as her hands fisted in his hair, and Sampson feared he'd spend as the words rocked through him. A moan tore from his throat and she laughed. "Ah, yes, master. You like that one?"

"Yes," he admitted. "But I have no power here. I'm at your mercy, love."

He reached up, sliding his hands under her nightgown and cupping her breasts, squeezing and plumping the soft mounds as her head tipped back on a satin sigh of pleasure. He pinched and rolled the tight little buds beneath his fingers and she shivered at his touch.

"Oh, God, Gwenn," he said, beside himself with need for her.

She shifted back and reached between them, fumbling at the buttons on the fall of his trousers before moving away from him. He almost protested as she backed up until she sank to her knees before him and his brain ground to a halt. She couldn't possibly....

Hazy with desire, he watched in stunned silence as she freed his cock and wrapped her slender fingers about him. A shocked exclamation tore from his lips as he fought not to climax at once, overcome by the exquisite touch, but too desperate to know what she'd do next to allow it.

Sampson held his breath as she smiled up at him, a naughty, impossibly knowing smile from a woman who'd barely been kissed. He hadn't been wrong about that, he was certain but…. She slid her thumb over the slit, gathering the moisture there and spreading it as his breathing sped. Oh Lord. Never looking away from him she blew, gently, the cool air shivering across his overheated skin and making gooseflesh prickle over him. Any ability to think, to speak, to do anything other than gaze at her, bewitched and spellbound, was long gone. All that remained was the choked sound that burst from him as she leaned in and licked him in one, bold swipe, from root to tip.

Sampson closed his eyes and submitted, enslaved by her touch, by the clever hands that caressed and stroked and squeezed and the velvety warmth of her mouth that made him believe he might die from pleasure.

It was an embarrassingly short time later that he cried out, fighting to muffle the sounds of his ecstasy as he came hard and fast.

Sampson was only dimly aware of the world around him as the waves of his climax ebbed and he blinked, trying to focus on his surroundings, which seemed blurred and indistinct. Slowly, the world returned, and his gaze settled on Gwenn. She sat back, a little away from him, and her eyes seemed wide and frightened, watchful, as though she didn't know what to expect from him now.

"Christ," he said with a quavering laugh that didn't sound as if it belonged to him at all.

Gwenn flinched, and he frowned, reaching for her.

"Love?" he said, tugging her closer as she hesitated before returning to his lap.

She curled against him, pressing her face to his neck as though she was too embarrassed to look at him. Sampson held her tightly, too shaken by the whole experience to question her. He stroked her back, bewildered by her and wishing she would trust him enough to explain, but he'd not earned her trust. She was in a tenuous position, a woman in his employ, and he'd coaxed her into this relationship even though she'd warned him how it would end. His heart ached, the desperate desire to keep her safe, to keep her with him, overwhelming any other argument.

"Gwenn," he said, trying to turn and look at her but she hid her face from him. "Gwenn, did I... did I do something wrong, or frighten you?"

She laughed at that, but it wasn't an especially happy sound.

"You did nothing wrong," she said, the words a little muffled.

"Then what is it?" he asked, hating that she seemed to regret what had passed between them. "Do you despise me for making this happen?"

"No!"

She shook her head, and Sampson couldn't bear for her to hide from him, so he shifted about and took her chin gently in his hand, tilting it up to meet his eyes.

"Then what, love? I don't understand. That was... I don't even have words for what that was," he said with a rueful smile. "I only know I want to make you feel that way too, but I'm afraid you wish this had never happened."

"You liked it, then?" she asked, the words hesitant.

Sampson's mouth fell open and it took him a moment to reply. "I'm not sure you need ask that, love."

A smile tugged at one corner of her lips before falling away again. "But...."

"But?" he urged gently.

"You don't mind that... that I knew how?"

He let out a breath of relief and slumped in the chair, taking her with him. "Oh, good Lord," he said, closing his eyes for a moment. When they opened again she was watching him, those pale turquoise eyes intent with interest. "No, love, I can't say I mind." His lips quirked in a smile, but she didn't look entirely reassured.

"Gwenn, your answer won't change anything at all, you have my word, but... have you... Did you ever...?"

She shook her head, and though he'd been telling the truth, he was honest enough to admit he was pleased he'd been the first, even though it puzzled him.

"I believe you," he said, seeing the relief in her eyes. "Though, in that case, how ever did you learn...?"

The blush that stained her cheeks was so sudden and so marked that he sat a little straighter.

"Gwenn," he said, tightening his hold on her. "I don't know what will happen, where this will lead us, but I promise I won't let you down. Won't you trust me, just a little?"

He watched as she drew in a deep breath and let it out again. "Don't ask me questions, Sampson," she said, the words quiet as she touched his cheek with her fingers, tracing the line of his jaw. "Just promise me one thing."

"Anything," he said, meaning it.

"When it ends... when you finally accept how impossible it is... don't give me rubies."

He blinked, not understanding her. When this overwhelming need threatened to consume him, the very idea of ending anything was beyond his comprehension. As he opened his mouth to protest, to demand to know what she meant, she pressed a finger to his lips, silencing him.

"Didn't you say something about making me feel that way too?" she murmured, the question rioting through him.

"Yes," he said, the single word rough with desire. "Oh, yes." He pulled her close and kissed her hard, and they both froze at the creak of footsteps on the stairs.

"Damnation," he cursed as they both held their breath. The footsteps paused for a moment and followed the faint murmur of voices as they continued down the stairs. Sampson cursed again, low and filthy this time. Damn him, why hadn't he taken her to his bedroom, where they were in no danger of being disturbed or discovered?

He rose quickly and straightened his clothing as Gwenn tugged on her dressing gown. He grasped her hand, urging her behind the heavy brocade curtains that were closed against the freezing night outside. Thankfully they were long, pooling on the floor, and Sampson tugged them shut just as the door swung open.

"There, see, nae ghosties nor ghoulies," said an exasperated voice. "Really, Callum, you're nae a wee laddie anymore to be firt of the dark."

Sampson pulled Gwenn closer against him. It was bloody freezing with the cold of the snowy night seeping through the glass at their backs, trapped with them behind the thick material of the curtains.

"I ain't firt," returned an indignant voice. "I'm tellin' ye, I heard a strange and eerie sound, moanin' and a-groanin' it were, pure gave me the willies an' all."

Biting his lip, Sampson held Gwenn closer, thinking she was shivering with the cold until he glanced down. The moonlight glimmering on the snow outside lit her beautiful face with a strange silvery light, making her look like some unearthly creature come to steal him away from the mortal world. As he gazed at her, he realised she was not trembling from cold, but from the effort of not laughing. Her eyes glimmered with mischief and he grinned at her, pressing a finger to her lips as something in his heart shifted. The realisation settled in his soul that he would never forget this moment—or this woman—for as long as he lived. He wanted her, wanted her badly, and not simply for more of what had been so rudely interrupted. The smile that played at her lips was his, and he wanted to keep it for himself. He wanted all of her smiles and the sound of her laughter, both the joyous, carefree sound she made when she was with the girls, and that wicked, filthy chuckle that had made his blood stir when she'd laughed and called him her master—and God, wasn't that a joke.

He was every bit as besotted as she'd accused him of being, and he didn't care.

Once Callum was reassured that there wasn't a new ghost in residence at the inn, the door closed again, and Sampson let out a breath of relief. That had been close, and he owed Gwenn better than a furtive tumble in the parlour of some bloody inn.

She was smiling at him, and the sight of it made the strangest sensation fill his chest, pushing at his ribs until he felt he could not contain it. Too unsettled to voice such feelings, he kissed her instead.

"I think we'd best get you back to your room," he said, though he hoped she could hear the regret in his voice. "But don't think I've forgotten what I said. I'll make it up to you."

There was a little amused snort at that. "I rather thought you might," she said.

Though the cold was biting, Sampson lingered a moment longer.

"Thank you," he said, staring at her. "For tonight. For…. Oh, love, you know I'm mad for you, don't you?"

"I know," she said, though he thought the words sounded sad, resigned rather than elated, and he hated that, hated that she was waiting for it all to go to hell.

There must be a way, if she would only trust him….

He must be patient, that was all. One day, she'd tell him the truth, and then… well, at least he'd know just how bad it was.

Chapter 13

"Wherein Gwenn accepts her fate."

Sampson escorted Gwenn back to her room and bade her goodnight with all the romantic reluctance she could have wished for in a lover. She'd barely a moment to close the door and try to soothe her scrambled wits, to make sense of what had happened, when a soft knock sounded. Wondering if Sampson had decided he couldn't wait to see her again she hurried to open it, only to find a teary Susan awaiting her.

"Don't feel well, miss," she croaked.

"Oh, you poor thing," Gwenn said, snatching up her dressing gown again. "Come, you ought not be wandering about in this chilly corridor. Back to bed with you. I'll make some willow bark tea."

She guided the girl back to her bedroom, to discover Selina huddled in a ball and shivering.

Gwenn clucked and fussed over them, fetching extra blankets and fluffing pillows, building up the fire in the hearth until it was crackling merrily.

"Now, you rest, and I'll make tea and then I'll read you a story. By the time I'm done, you'll feel much better."

Once all this had been accomplished, and the girls were dozing, Gwenn was exhausted. She got to her feet she began to creep furtively towards the door, only to be stopped by a pitiful whisper.

"Don't go, miss…."

Gwenn sighed and returned to her bedside vigil.

***

Sampson pushed his breakfast plate away and drew out his pocket watch, frowning at it. He'd been counting the minutes until he could see Gwenn again, and her failure to appear was making him nervous. Was she avoiding him? Was she angry or embarrassed? Did she regret what had happened between them after all?

He got to his feet just as the innkeeper's wife bustled into the room.

"Good morning, my lord. I trust ye slept well, and all is to your satisfaction?"

"I did, thank you," Sampson said, moving to the door.

"I took the liberty of sending for Mr Davies to see to your lordship's clothes. He's nae the kind of valet ye'll be used to, but he's the best ye'll find in these parts, if that suits ye?"

"That's perfect, Mrs Galbraithe. I shall be pleased to see him. And a lady's maid?"

"Oh, well I offered your Miss Wynter our Sally, but she said as how she was happy to see to your sisters, and that it was nae worth the bother."

Sampson frowned, unhappy with Gwenn acting the part of a servant, even though it touched him that she was willing to care for Susan and Selina. She was in no way proud and seemed perfectly content to do menial tasks. The previous governesses all had been very much on their dignity and would never deign to touch what they'd seen to be a lower servant's job. Not that he judged them for it; the hierarchy of the servants was a careful balance that you meddled with at your peril.

"I would like you to send Sally to her nonetheless," he said, and Mrs Galbraithe nodded.

"Right away, my lord. No doubt she'll be more willing after last night."

Sampson stilled, even though he knew the woman couldn't possibly be referring to *last night.*

"I beg your pardon?" he said, aware he sounded a little stiff.

"Ah, well the poor lassie was up all night with your sisters. Full of cold they are, the poor wee mites. Your Miss Wynter ordered some chicken broth early this morning and a weary sight she was too. Still, I'll send up the broth as soon as it's ready and that ought to do them all wonders." She gave him a reassuring smile. "I have a cough remedy also that should ease those sore throats and help them rest. I'll send it up as well."

"That's very good of you, Mrs Galbraithe," Sampson said, and hurried away to check on the invalids.

His first knock on the door was greeted with silence. Not wanting to disturb the girls if they were sleeping, he opened it a crack and peered through. The room was dimly lit, the curtains still drawn, though daylight crept about the corners. The subdued glow of the fire and a single candle guttering in its holder illuminated the room, and Sampson's throat grew tight as he took in the scene.

Gwenn was asleep in the middle of the bed, the book of Shakespeare's tales in her lap and a twin tucked under each arm.

Who was this woman, who could be the ideal governess, drive him wild with her passion and her touch, and who would care for his sisters as though they were her own children? His chest ached, his heart giving an uneven thud as he considered Gwenn as a mother. God, but she'd be perfect. Any child of hers would be so loved and cared for, so....

He stopped himself as he realised he wasn't imagining Gwenn's children, he was imagining *their* children.

Any possibility that he wasn't in grave danger of falling head over heels in love was swiftly set aside. That it was already far too late was something he could hardly ignore, either. Leaving Gwenn, or watching her leave him, was an idea he did not want to consider. Oh, bloody hell, he was an idiot and Samuel was a bastard. Perhaps if his brother hadn't intervened, he could have kept away, stopped this from happening. Yet, despite the dilemma that faced him now, he couldn't find it in his heart to regret it. He'd have time enough for that if he couldn't find a way for them to be together.

He stared at the charming tableau before him and knew he must find a way. Gwenn's golden hair was loose and tumbled beside the twins' pale blonde curls, and the way she had them hugged against her, despite their red noses and the likelihood that she too would fall ill, spoke volumes of the kindness of her heart. She made the girls as happy as she made him. He couldn't bear to consider how upset they would be if she left as she planned to. He had to make her want to stay.

Sampson moved silently to the bed and reached for the blanket, tugging it up a little higher to ensure they didn't get cold. Susan stirred and blinked up at him.

"Sunny?"

"It's all right, love, go back to sleep."

She sighed and did at once, her eyelids flickering as she turned to snuggle closer to Gwenn. His throat grew tight. The girl's mother was a sweet woman, but emotionally she was barely more than a girl herself. She'd been cosseted as a child and then thrown to the wolf that had been his father. She was a bundle of nerves and needed as much looking after as the girls did. Though she loved the twins, she was more like a doting sister than a mother, and didn't really know what to do with them. When the news and the manner of his father's death had reached her, she'd suffered a nervous collapse and gone back to live with her parents. Sampson had felt ill-equipped to be both father and mother to the girls, but he'd sworn to do his best—and made a hash of it.

Everything that had seemed so bloody impossible had been so easy once Gwenn had arrived, though. She made loving them and making them happy seem the easiest thing in the world. As easy as falling in love with her.

Sampson turned and snuffed out the candle before taking a moment to build the fire up again and, with one last glance at the bed, he crept out of the room.

***

Gwenn woke with difficulty. Her eyelids were heavy, her eyes gritty, and she felt weary and not the least bit refreshed.

"Sorry, miss. We didnae mean to disturb ye."

Propping herself up on her elbows, Gwenn squinted until she focused on a cheerful looking young woman who was braiding Selina's unruly locks into something tidy and pretty. Susan, sitting by the fire with her nose in a book, was already neatly braided. Dressed for the day—courtesy of this unknown maid, she guessed—though a little pale, they both looked far better than they had last night.

"I'm Sally," the woman clarified with a smile. "And the missus thought ye seemed worn to a thread. She told his lordship, and he said to send me to help with the girls. I'd go back to sleep, miss. Ye look done in."

"Thank you," she said, thinking that sounded like a fine idea. "How are you feeling, girls?"

"My nose won't stop running, but I feel fine," Susan replied, sniffing to illustrate the problem. "Selina has lost her voice, though," she added with a wicked grin. "So we'll all have some peace today."

Selina scowled and croaked something that sounded uncomplimentary.

"Oh, poor Selina," Gwenn soothed, smothering a laugh as the girl stuck her tongue out at Susan. "You must eat the soup Mrs

Galbraithe is having prepared for you. It will make your throat feel much better."

"Aye, I'm taking them downstairs for it now," Sally said, putting the finishing touches to Susan's hair. "Oh, and the missus sent that cough mixture up, too. She reckons it'll soothe that sore throat in no time."

Gwenn looked at the large, brown bottle on the bedside table. She reached for it, unstoppered the cork, and frowned as she gave a dubious sniff. "What's in it?"

"Oh, missus makes it herself. Swears by it, she does. It's liquorice, vinegar, salad oil, treacle, and tincture of opium."

Gwenn blanched. One of the men who could not afford her mother's attentions but was nonetheless infatuated and had followed her like a puppy, had been a poet—and an opium addict. He'd been kind to Gwenn and had been a sweet-natured, handsome man, until opium had destroyed him. The filthy stuff was going nowhere near her girls.

Her girls.

Gwenn swallowed as she realised what a foolish thought that was, and what a terrible mess she'd landed herself in. Forcing the fear rising in her chest aside, she held the bottle out to Sally who took it, setting it on the mantle shelf whilst she collected the dirty linens.

"Please thank Mrs Galbraithe kindly, but I do not approve of the girls taking opium for nothing graver than a sore throat."

"Very good, miss," the girl said, gathering yesterday's pinafores.

Gwenn nodded and turned back to the girls. "I shall make you some more willow bark tea but, for now, you must eat the soup that has been prepared for you."

"Yes, Miss Wynter," they chorused and followed Sally out of the room.

Gwenn fell back against the pillows. *Don't think about it,* she advised herself.

Don't think about how fond you are of those two funny little girls, don't think about how upset they will be when you tell them you are leaving them, don't think about him—don't think.

It was impossible, of course.

She thought about all of it.

She thought about the way she had behaved last night, and how very badly she wanted to do it again. The memory of having her hands on Sampson, of the power she'd felt when he had moaned and shattered sent heat radiating straight to her core. An insistent throb began between her thighs and she cursed, blinking back tears and burying her face in the pillow. Aunt Letty had been right, though the realisation was a bitter pill. The De Wynns had lustful natures; they were born sluts, and there was no escaping it. She ought never have tried. It would have been better if she'd simply trusted her mother's judgement. That way she could have avoided the inevitable heartache that awaited her now. For there was no fairy-tale ending to this story, and all her plans were at an end.

There would be no marriage to a decent man and a family of her own, not when the only man she could consider such a happy ever after with could never marry her. She could only bring him and his sisters shame and scandal, and she'd rather die than hurt those girls.

Not *her* girls. Never her girls.

So, there was nothing else to do. After Christmas she would leave, just as she'd said she would, but not to search out some new, hopeful future. She must go back to Marie—with her tail between her legs—and admit she'd been right about all of it. It would have to be a clandestine escape, too, with no fond farewells, for Sampson was too decent to let her go without trying to make things right for her and she couldn't endure that.

So, she would return—damaged goods—and Marie would be so angry at her stupidity. She wouldn't even have any bloody rubies to soften her ire.

That she would still have her virginity intact never even occurred to her. There was no way she could spend the coming days with Sampson and not give herself to him. She'd have that much of him, at least, a memory to warm her when she was living a different life, a life Sampson would abhor and have no part of.

Gwenn allowed herself the indulgence of a good cry, sobbing into the pillow until she fell asleep again. When she woke it was midday, and she was a deal calmer, resigned to her fate. There were the remaining days until Christmas and Christmas itself to enjoy, and she intended to do so. She would fill the coming days with all that she could not have in those that followed the holiday. The new year loomed, bleak and lonely, but she pushed it aside with impatience. She'd not think on it. There would be time enough for regrets. Why waste a moment on them now when she could be with Sampson and the girls?

Sliding out from under the covers, Gwenn hurried to wash, moving to the washstand to pour water from the waiting jug, when she heard giggling from outside the window. Curious, she set down the jug and drew the curtain back a little. The scene below made her heart leap to her throat and a smile curve over her mouth, even as her eyes prickled with tears.

Sampson was helping the girls make a snowman, the jolly, rotund figure smiling a broad coal-studded smile beneath a carrot nose as the girls each stuck in a twig for arms. Their big brother laughed as they launched themselves at him, grabbing for his hat. Sampson pretended to put up a fight until he allowed them to knock him down into the snow. Susan snatched up the hat with a cry of triumph and ran back to the snowman, setting it on his head at a jaunty angle.

Gwenn watched, finding it hard to breathe as Sampson got to his feet again, brushing snow from his clothes. He paused, as if aware someone was observing him, and looked up at her window. The smile that dawned on his face as he saw her robbed her of any remaining air in her lungs, and a lump settled in her throat. She laughed anyway, tears pricking at her eyes as he raised a hand and waved to her. Gwenn lifted her hand and waved back.

Sampson glanced about, checking no one was watching before blowing her a kiss. Gwenn touched her fingers to her mouth, believing she could feel the warmth of his lips on hers, which was utterly foolish, but she was foolish. For the coming days, she would give herself over to foolishness, to the inevitability that she would fall irrevocably in love with this man and that leaving him would break her in ways that could never be mended.

Foolish indeed.

Chapter 14

"Wherein the perfect day and the night..."

"Can we go outside now, please, *pleeease*, Sunny?" Susan begged, tugging at Sampson's arm.

They'd just finished a very fine repast which had finally warmed Sampson to his toes and he was not enamoured of going back out in the snow.

"Oh, yes, I must see this snowman," Gwenn said, mischief glinting in her eyes. "He looked a handsome fellow."

"Oh, he is," Selina said, her voice still faint but stronger than it had been this morning. "Please, Sampson."

How could he resist such pleas? Though teasing them a little was too much fun. "Oh, but Miss Wynter saw it from the window. No, no. It's too cold and it will be dark soon."

"It won't be dark for hours yet!" Susan exclaimed. "It's only two o'clock!"

"Oh, yes, but you two are not well, and you kept poor Miss Wynter awake all night... no, no, she must be worn out."

"I'm not the least bit worn out," Gwenn retorted, a glint in her eyes that made him aware of the blood surging through his veins, desire glittering like champagne beneath his skin. "I slept all the morning away. I expect I shall not sleep a wink tonight, unless I get some vigorous exercise."

"Is that so?" he said, a helpless smile tugging at the corners of his mouth as he considered just how vigorous he could be if she let him. "Well, in that case, I suppose we'd best visit the snowman."

The girls gave a pleased exclamation and shoved their chairs back, running to fetch hats, scarves, and pelisses. Sampson turned to Gwenn and reached across the table to her. He'd not been alone with her since last night and being in her company without being able to touch her made his skin ache with longing.

She took his hand, her slender fingers curving with his.

"I missed you," he said, knowing he sounded like a silly boy when they'd been together this past hour or more. He didn't care. "I want to kiss you so badly. I can't think of anything else."

Gwenn smiled at him, a sweet smile that seemed to settle in his heart, warming him from the inside out. "I know," she said, her gaze falling to his mouth and then to their hands, linked on the table. "I feel the same."

She slid her hand from his though, and he hated the loss of her touch. A moment later the twins burst back in, bundled up in their winter clothes.

"Come on!" they urged. Susan tugged at his arm whilst Selina tackled Gwenn. Laughing and exclaiming merrily, the girls hustled them from the room and into coats and out of the door.

Weak sunlight glimmered on the snow, the low hills around them sparkling white and pristine as though the world had been wiped clean of sin and could start afresh. Though it was beyond foolish in the circumstances, Sampson's heart was light too and full of hope. He could not remember a time when he'd known what it was to be so happy. Not like this.

Gwenn was laughing with his sisters, the three of them holding hands, shrieking as Selina slipped and fell on her behind with a thud. She stared up at Gwenn, her expression indignant for a moment, and then burst out laughing. Gwenn reached for her, helping her up and brushing her down before giving her a brief hug and taking her hand again. How easy it was to love her... for all of them.

Susan began singing a Christmas carol, her voice ringing out over the quiet, snow-hushed landscape. Selina joined in as best she could, a little raspy still, and then Gwenn's voice joined them together, pure and sweet and sending shivers down his spine as he realised that this… this was what he had wanted for the girls for Christmas, and for himself. He'd wanted them happy and carefree, and to know what it was to be loved. It had never occurred to him that a stranger could bring such things into their lives.

Sampson turned away, the scene filling his chest and his heart, and upturning everything he'd expected to have in his future. Everything that had seemed so important was shifting and muddling in his head. He thought about Samuel, and tried to remember the advice his brother had given him when they'd argued about the future, about the girls and Miss Wynter.

And then a snowball smacked him in the head.

He jolted back, his thoughts spinning away. Trickles of ice slid past his cravat as the snow melted on his skin and he spun around to find Gwenn laughing, delight in her eyes as she scooped up another handful of snow and sent it hurtling in his direction. It hit him square in the chest and Sampson looked down at the snowy patch on his coat, somewhere near his heart, which seemed apt. It wasn't the first time she'd hit him there, after all.

The girls cheered and chortled, gathering their own snowballs and lobbing them at him as he ducked out of the way.

"Right," he said with a deep growl, pretending to glare at them. "This means war!"

The three of them shrieked and ran for cover as he tore after them, his boots slipping in the snow as he threw snowballs at their retreating backs. He hit Gwenn in the back of the head, setting her bonnet all askew as she yelped in surprise.

"Oh!" she exclaimed, the light of challenge in her eyes. "You wretch, you'll pay for that!"

The next twenty minutes was filled with laughter and screams, so much so that some of the staff came out to see what was happening, and soon—with a little encouragement—everyone had joined in. Snowballs flew back and forth until the combatants were all rosy cheeked, red-nosed, and frozen to the marrow.

Mrs Galbraithe called a halt by announcing that there was hot chocolate for the children and mulled wine for the adults, and a plate of shortbread, still warm from the oven. Everyone bundled back inside in high spirits, chattering and filled with all the joys of the season despite their frozen fingers and toes.

They spent the rest of the afternoon sitting in the cosy private parlour beside a roaring fire, playing games with the girls. Though he was impatient to be alone with Gwenn, to hold her and kiss her, Sampson did not begrudge the time in the least. He simply enjoyed it, basking in the happiness shining from Susan and Selina's faces, the two of them delighted to have both their big brother's and Miss Wynter's attention at once.

They needed cajoling to go up to bed after supper, and though his blood simmered with anticipation, Sampson found he was sorry the day was over for them too. He promised them, and himself, that tomorrow would be just as much fun. He began to feel very fond of the snow heaped outside the door, and hoped it would linger.

"Goodnight, my lord," Gwenn said, her voice low as she moved to follow the girls out.

Sampson grabbed hold of her hand once the girls were out the door, stilling her.

"Gwenn?"

"Yes," she said softly. "Come to me."

His breath caught. It was hard to let her fingers slide from his grasp, but he did, watching her until she closed the door behind her.

***

Gwenn settled the girls to bed and read them a story, content that they should sleep well after the excitement of their day. They were fast asleep and snoring gently before she was halfway through the tale, and she set it aside with a smile. She took a moment to tuck them in, snuff the candles, and bank the fire before returning to her own room.

The air in her bedchamber was damp with steam and Gwenn was pleased to see the bath she'd ordered was ready for her. She went to her valise, taking out a small bottle of scented oil and added a few drops to the bath before undressing as fast as she could. The look in Sampson's eyes had suggested he'd not wait long to join her.

The water was good and hot, and she sighed with pleasure as she sank into it. She reached for the soap, lathering it between her hands. Her body was already alive with anticipation, knowing that he would soon be here, that his hands would be on her, and his mouth. She closed her eyes, remembering last night and imagining how good it would be to feel his skin, his body, pressed against hers. Her palms slid over her slick flesh, enjoying her own touch as she soaped her breasts, imagining it was Sampson who touched her.

There was a soft knock and a brief pause and suddenly he was standing there, as though she'd conjured him with the force of her desire.

He froze, staring down at her, his eyes so dark she'd never have guessed they were blue if she hadn't already known. Gwenn smiled and continued to caress herself, rolling her nipples between her fingers until they were taut. Sampson's breath hitched, and the sound sent a jolt of pleasure between her thighs.

Gwenn licked her lips and allowed her hands to slide over her torso, below the waterline, to touch herself and ease the ache that throbbed and demanded her attention. She wanted him to touch her, wanted his hands upon her, but the look in his eyes was such that she knew he wanted to watch her—and she wanted him to watch. She sighed as her fingers sought the little nub of flesh that clamoured for him and Sampson groaned and went to his knees, his eyes never leaving hers.

"Tell me what you are thinking," he said, and the words were ragged, rough with desire.

"I couldn't do that," she said, smiling a little as she teased him. "It's far too wicked."

"Oh, God, please."

She tilted her head to one side, considering him. "You're wearing too many clothes."

He moved at once, shedding his coat and waistcoat, throwing them to the floor in a careless heap before tugging his shirt over his head and casting it aside.

"Tell me," he demanded.

Gwenn closed her eyes and let out a soft moan, arching a little as her hand moved beneath the water. She cupped her breast with her free hand and squeezed, sighing again before regarding him through heavy-lidded eyes, allowing her gaze to roam over him with slow appreciation.

"Undo the buttons," she commanded, smiling as he leapt to do her bidding.

His hands didn't seem entirely steady as he unfastened the fall and shoved his trousers and small clothes down his hips. His cock sprang free, and Gwenn drank in the sight of him with greedy eyes.

"How lovely," she murmured, her body heated and eager for him but enjoying his desperation too much to stop yet. "Is that for me?"

"God, yes. Yes, you know it is. All of me. I'm yours."

For a moment those words struck her heart, a sharp pain that she pushed aside and refused to allow to wound her. She knew what he meant, and he didn't mean that he belonged to her. He was hers for now, for this night and those that followed, until Christmas and the end of the holiday, and her dreams.

"Tell me, Gwenn," he said breathlessly. "Tell me what you are thinking of, what is making you sigh with pleasure?"

"Your mouth," she said on a sigh, holding his gaze. "I'm thinking of your mouth."

She watched, riveted to the sight of his large hand curling around his cock and stroking.

"Where?" he asked. "Where is my mouth?"

Gwenn swallowed, the torment far from one sided now as her heart thundered in her chest. She didn't answer him but stood up, the water cascading down her body as Sampson stared up at her, wide-eyed.

"Gwenn," he said, her name spoken with such reverence she knew she'd never forget how it sounded on his lips, as if it was precious, as if it was his alone to speak that way. "I've seen nothing so beautiful as you in my life."

She felt beautiful then, and not merely for the quirk of nature that had given her a face and figure that made men lust for her. She felt beautiful because she was happy, because this man made her happy and she was the person she wanted to be when she was with him.

Gwenn reached for the towel and covered herself, stepping from the tub and watching him in silence.

"Let me see," he begged. "I want to see."

She moved closer to him, taking her time, and allowing the towel to fall a little farther with each step until she was right in front of him and it tumbled to the floor.

"Tell me," he said, staring up at her, stroking himself as his eyes roved over her body. "Tell me where my mouth was."

Gwenn gave a soft laugh and trailed her right hand between her breasts, her fingers drawing a sinuous path down across her belly until she reached the little thatch of curls between her thighs.

"Oh, yes," he breathed rather than spoke the words. "Please say it."

"Here," she said.

He reached for her, his hands grasping her hips as he leaned in and pressed his mouth against the curls. His tongue traced the seam of her sex and Gwenn gasped, trembling at the sensation of his sleek tongue touching her so intimately. She reached out, grasping his hair, as much to keep herself upright as to keep him from moving, watching the thick red strands cover her fingers and glint like garnets in the candlelight.

Sampson moaned against her skin, parting the soft curls and sucking gently on her private flesh until she cried out and her knees buckled. He steadied her, looking up with laughter glinting in his eyes.

"I have you, love," he said, and the truth of that was undeniable. He had her, body, heart, and soul, with no escape.

"I can't... can't stand any longer," she said, dazed now and grasping the bedframe to keep herself upright.

She heard a low chuckle and then watched with amusement as he shed his boots and the rest of his clothes with frantic impatience. He got to his feet then and swung her up into his arms as she gasped and clung to his neck.

"I hope you don't think you're finished," she said, the words tart, though she was struggling not to laugh.

"Indeed not," he replied, with the utmost gravity. "As if I would leave a job half done?"

"That's all right, then." She sighed as he placed her on the bed.

For a moment he just stood, staring down at her, and Gwenn let her thighs part in open invitation. He grinned, a look of such wicked delight her heart skipped with happiness, desire, and all the wonderful things she could not think about losing, not now, for it would destroy her.

He climbed onto the bed, moving over her and leaning down to nuzzle the tender skin below her ear, kissing a path down her neck to her breasts, where he lingered.

"So lovely," he murmured against her skin, trailing a damp path around one nipple with his tongue before taking it in his mouth and suckling. Gwenn cried out as the sensation tugged elsewhere and the insistent throbbing began again, so demanding it was impossible to think past her need.

"Please," she whimpered. "Please...."

He took pity on her and continued his exploration, while his hands cupped and squeezed and stroked and she thought she would lose her mind if he didn't return his mouth to where she needed him. Finally he did, the heat of his tongue gliding over her, having worked her to such a pitch by now she shattered at the first touch upon her sex, crying out and clutching at his hair as pleasure rippled through her, so intense she was still dazed by it long after the climax had subsided.

Gwenn fought to draw a shaky breath, a little stunned. It was hardly her first orgasm. Her body would be her fortune and knowing how to please herself every bit as important as how to please a man. The difference between finding one's own pleasure however and... and *this*.... Good heavens! There was no comparison.

She forced her eyes open, blinking as his intense blue gaze fell upon her, looking impossibly smug. Gwenn gave a rather unladylike snort of laughter, but then she wasn't a lady, as she'd just proved by dallying with a man who was not and would never be her husband.

Don't think of it, she told herself. *Not now.*

"My, don't you look pleased with yourself," she said, reaching for him.

Sampson settled beside her, pulling her into his arms. "I should say I do. I'm the cat that got the canary, and the cream, and it was sweet indeed."

He buried his face in her neck and nibbled at her ear and Gwenn giggled and squirmed. She sighed as he raised his head again, staring down at her, emotions alight in his eyes that she didn't dare guess at, for fear she would read too much into them.

"You're wonderful," he said, sounding as though—in this moment, at least—he truly meant it.

"As are you, my lord," she said, striving to keep things light, afraid of betraying what this meant to her.

He frowned, his eyes troubled.

"Sampson," he corrected and kissed her, slowly and with such tenderness that she wanted to believe this wasn't just a dalliance, that perhaps the memory of her would linger in his mind once she was gone.

Her memories would be filled with him, she knew that much and refused to regret it. Marie had survived betrayal, she'd had her heart shattered by the man she loved, a man she'd born a child for... a child he'd never seen, never acknowledged. How that must have hurt Mama, and yet how strong she was. Gwenn would be strong, too; they were made of the same stuff, after all. Perhaps she had inherited a wanton nature, but she'd inherited that resolve, the determination to not only survive but to live, and live to the full.

For the first time, Gwenn thought she understood her mother's extravagance and her lust for money and power. Never again would a man have a hold on her. Her body and her fortune were her own, and no one would ever touch her heart again. Gwenn had tried to escape her fate, wanting something more than such a life could give her, but perhaps it was the only way for an unmarried woman to survive and keep herself intact.

Yet even as she understood she could feel nothing but sorrow, because Marie might have jewels finer than any royal princess, but Gwenn suspected her heart still belonged to the man who had broken it all those years ago.

So this was her destiny too, to follow in her mother's footsteps, but without avoiding the dangers of which Marie had tried to warn her daughter.

Sampson's hands were warm, his touch at once soothing and inflaming as he caressed her, drawing her closer. The heat of his body blazed against her, the combination of silky skin and hard muscle intriguing and wonderful. The coarse hair on his chest grazed her sensitive nipples, and she shivered with pleasure.

"Gwenn...." He sighed her name, pulling her hips close against him and tilting his hips so his arousal slid over her sex, making her cry out—

"Miss Wynter?"

The both froze, horrified at the muffled voice on the other side of the door.

"Christ!" Sampson muttered, surging to his feet. "I didn't lock it."

Panicked, Gwenn scrambled off the bed.

"J-Just a moment, darling," she called as Sampson lunged to gather his clothes and Gwenn pulled on her dressing gown.

Her hands were shaking, and it took her several tries to do up the ties. She gestured for Sampson to move back into the far corner of the room, out of sight of the door before hurrying to open it, stepping outside and closing it behind her.

"Selina?" she said, finding a sleepy looking twin awaiting her.

"Susan," the girl amended, rubbing her eyes and yawning. "Selina can't stop coughing and she's keeping me awake," she grumbled. "I was going to give her some of that cough mixture to shut her up, but I thought perhaps I ought to ask you if that was all right."

"Oh, my goodness. No!" Gwenn cried, appalled at what might have happened if Selina had not gotten an answer at the door or, worse, if she'd tried the handle and come in. She went hot and cold, assailed with guilt at the idea of the girl finding her in such a way with her brother. "I told Sally to take the wretched stuff away with her."

"I think she forgot, miss."

"Oh, Susan." She pulled the girl into her arms, blinking back tears. "You did very well to come and ask me first and I... I'm... so sorry."

Susan frowned up at her, a little bewildered. "S'all right," she said, obviously perplexed. "It's only shouting at her won't make her stop, so I wondered if you might be able to."

Gwenn gave an uneven laugh that threatened to turn into a sob and hustled Susan along the corridor. "Come along, then. Let me see what I can do."

By the time Gwenn had temporarily soothed Selina with a honey and lemon sweet whilst she made her some willow bark tea and then rubbed the girl's chest with camphor oil, Susan was fast asleep. Selina put her empty teacup aside and settled back on the pillows with a sigh.

"Do you think you can sleep now, love?" Gwenn asked.

"Yes, miss. Thank you. I'm sorry we woke you up again."

Gwenn reached out and smoothed the girl's hair from her head as self-loathing rose in her chest. "That's all right, dear. That's what I'm here for. Sweet dreams."

She left the room, closing the door quietly behind her and stood for a long moment in the dark. The girls were so sweet and innocent. It had been a very long time since she'd known what that meant. Had she *ever* been that innocent, that pure? If she'd taken that away from them, sullied them by opening their eyes to the kind of woman she was… oh, God. What kind of wicked, sluttish creature was she to seduce their brother as she had? He was a good man, a loving brother trying to do his best for his family, and she….

Gwenn closed her eyes, overcome with remorse. It was a few minutes before she could find the will to return to her own room. To her relief, Sampson was gone. She couldn't have faced him then, couldn't have borne the shame of it. As it was, she fell into bed and prayed for sleep, though she doubted it would come any time soon. Worse, as she turned her head into the pillow, she could still smell him upon the sheets, the faint aroma of bergamot, soap, and the musky spice of a male body that filled her with longing.

"Oh, Marie," she sobbed, covering her face with her hands. "Oh, what have I done?"

Chapter 15

"Wherein the snow melts but ice forms."

"It'll please yer lordship to know the snow's melted."

Sampson blinked awake to regard Mr Davies, his temporary valet. The man placed a cup of coffee on the nightstand before holding out Sampson's dressing gown to him.

"Sun's out, too, and it looks like it'll be a fine day."

Supressing a curse with difficulty, Sampson shoved his feet into his slippers and allowed Davies to help him into his dressing gown before stalking to the window. He flung back the curtains, wincing in the glare of sunlight, and saw that Davies was correct. Much of the road was already clear, and the sun was melting that which remained at quite a pace. They could go on their way.

No, damn it.

He didn't want to leave. Not yet, certainly not while everything was so up in the air after last night. *Bloody hell.* There was no reason to keep them here now, though, and he didn't doubt the staff were already preparing their departure. Yesterday had been so idyllic he'd been looking forward to another day just like it. Yet last night, when that little voice had called for Miss Wynter, he'd seen the horror in Gwenn's eyes, and had felt it himself at the thought one of the girls walking in on them.

They must be more careful in the future.

That there would be a future was not in doubt. Not in his mind. He still did not understand what that future held. He couldn't, until he knew what it was Gwenn was running from. All he knew was that he couldn't turn away from her, couldn't turn his back on her, or on the feeling in his chest which seemed to grow exponentially with each day he spent in her company. It was too late to run from it, impossible to deny it. All he could do now was accept it, and pray she would trust him enough to give him a chance to help her, to make things right and find some kind of future for them.

Perhaps he'd not be able to marry her, not without hurting the girls, but that didn't mean he would give her up. It simply meant he couldn't marry her *yet*. Not until the girls were settled, at least. Would she endure that, he wondered? Was he enough to wait for when it would likely deny her the chance of having a family of her own? It would be ten years at the very least before the girls were settled, possibly even twenty. Could she bear to be his mistress for that long?

Well, that was a question he needed to ask, but not yet. This was all too new, too fragile, and he must speak to her before they had to spend an entire day together with the girls.

"I must dress at once," he instructed Davies, and hurried about his ablutions with speed.

***

He was too late.

Gwenn was already at breakfast with the girls when he came down.

"Good morning," he said, smiling at them and trying to gauge Gwenn's mood.

Perhaps he could have a few moments alone with her after breakfast.

"Morning, Sunny," the girls chorused, though his heart clenched as he noticed Gwenn did not meet his eyes.

"Good morning, my lord," she said, the words stiff and formal.

Hell.

"Sampson, the snow is melting, and our snowman's nose fell off," Susan said, taking his hand and pouting at him.

"He's going to disappear," Selina added with a heavy sigh. "It's so sad."

"Never mind, girls," Gwenn said, her voice soft. "All good things must come to an end."

"Nonsense," Sampson replied sharply, his chest tight with anxiety, the words too obviously prophetic for him to ignore. "I expect it will snow again when we get to Tor Castle and, even if it doesn't, there is plenty to look forward to. You'll meet your new brother and his wife, and there's Christmas and a castle to explore, and no doubt you'll be spoiled beyond bearing. Indeed, there is nothing to be the least bit sad about, as *nothing* is ending today."

The girls grinned at him, this rather emphatic statement cheering them up at least, but Gwenn still didn't look at him.

"Eat your breakfast please, girls," she said, keeping her own eyes on her plate. "We have packing to finish, and we must not keep the horses waiting for us. There's still a long way to go."

"I'm so excited to see the castle," Susan said, her blue eyes alight with excitement. "Do you think there will be ghosts, Miss Wynter?"

"There's no such thing as ghosts, Selina," Gwenn said, the statement a tad sharp.

"I'm Susan."

Gwenn stilled and then looked up and smiled at Susan. Sampson saw that the expression didn't meet her eyes, which were heavy, as though she'd slept ill. "I do beg your pardon, Susan, but you must not worry about ghosts."

"Oh, I wasn't worried," Susan carried on, spearing another sausage with her fork. "I think it would be marvellous to see one."

"So do I," Selina chimed in.

"Don't speak with your mouth full, Selina," Gwenn said, though Sampson could hear a weary note to her voice that made his chest ache.

"How is your cough this morning, Selina?" he asked, desperate for Gwenn to look at him, to acknowledge him in some small way as anything other than her employer.

Gwenn's fork clattered against her plate as she dropped it. She glared at him, such fury in her eyes his breath caught.

"How did you know I had a cough, Sunny?" Selina asked.

Sampson's heart skipped for a moment and he covered the taut silence emanating from Gwenn by reaching for a bread roll. He could hardly tell her he'd heard her from the wrong side of Gwenn's bedroom door.

"Oh, I think Davies mentioned it this morning," he said, striving for an easy tone. "Valets know everything, you see."

"They're omnificent," Susan said, nodding sagely.

Despite the tightness in his chest, Sampson smiled. "I think you mean omniscient," he corrected. "But I'm not sure even the finest valet could claim that."

"Omniscient means they know everything," Susan told her sister, looking smug.

"Well, you're not omniscient, 'cause you got it wrong," Selina said, smirking.

Susan huffed.

"Have you ever been to Scotland before, Miss Wynter?" Sampson asked, fishing desperately for a way to get Gwenn to speak to him, to thaw the ice that she'd encased herself in to keep him at a distance. "I don't think I've ever asked you."

"No, my lord," she said, never taking her eyes from her breakfast.

Sampson busied himself with filling his plate, though he'd no appetite and his throat felt too tight to swallow. What if she shut him out for good? What if she'd not see him? Panic flapped in his chest like the wings of some giant bird desperate for freedom.

"Tor Castle is quite a sight," he pressed on, aware he was babbling but needing to fill the space her withdrawal made in their previously happy party. "It's not pretty, rather grim on the outside really, but the views are spectacular. It's in the shadow of Ben Nevis, you see, so snow is very likely. Ross, my brother, he's been renovating the place. It will be interesting to see what he's accomplished since we were last there."

His voice seemed too loud, too forcibly cheerful, and he longed to reach out and take her hand, to beg her not to do this to him.

"Ross is actually our *half*-brother," Susan added, for Gwenn's benefit. "He's a bastard."

"Susan!" Gwenn said, sounding more startled than shocked. "That is not a word that a young lady uses."

"But he is," Selina objected, cutting in. "Our father put a baby in his mama's belly even though she didn't want it, and he was already married so he couldn't marry her. She killed herself once he was born. So, Captain Ross is an orphan *and* a bastard."

Gwenn gasped and Sampson closed his eyes. Could this morning get any worse? He'd thought they'd not heard that story, and he felt a wash of shame for having not shielding them better. Their minds and hearts ought not be sullied by such vile stories, true or not. Gwenn had clearly not come across that particular tale of his father's life, judging by her obvious shock. Though there were plenty more where that came from.

There was a tense silence. Susan and Selina glanced at each other, and then back and forth between Gwenn and Sampson.

"Where did you hear that, girls?" Sampson asked, struggling to keep his tone calm, because he would thrash the life from whatever wretch had told them.

The twins shrugged, retreating into silence.

Sampson let out an unsteady breath. "Well," he said. "I'd like to know where you heard it, as it is not something I wanted you to know, however…." He smiled at them, willing his face to relax enough to put them at ease. "You already know our father was not a very nice person. I'm afraid that everything you said was true, but still, I'd like you not to say that word again. It may be true, but it is a word people use in an insulting manner. Ross is our brother, and we are glad to have him, aren't we?"

"Oh, yes," the girls said at once.

"He wears a skirt," Susan said with a grin.

Sampson held his tongue and didn't correct her. With a bit of luck, she'd say that in front of Ross. He glanced at Gwenn, hoping to share the joke, but she wouldn't look at him.

The great flapping bird in his chest made another bid for freedom.

"Susan, Selina, listen to me," he said, looking at each of them and praying they would trust in him, even if Gwenn wouldn't. "If ever you hear anything else about our father, or about any of our family, even me, I want you to come and talk to me about it. Especially if it troubles you," he added, his voice firm.

"But won't you be cross?" Selina asked, glancing at him and back at her plate.

"Not with you," he said at once. "Never with you. I don't like gossip, but our father created a great deal of it and… and I'm afraid your brothers, myself included, have only added to it. What you must never do is think it in any way makes you a part of it. None of us are perfect. Far from it," he added with a wry smile. "We all do reckless or foolish things, things that other people might look down on us for, but that doesn't make us bad people, or mean we ought to be punished. Life is complicated, and... well, we must muddle through as best we can."

"Yes, Sampson," Susan said, reaching out and slipping her hand in his.

Sampson clung to it, ridiculously glad of the gesture, as he felt as if his life was being upended on all sides.

"We will, Sampson," Selina echoed, and then, as she couldn't reach him across the table, she got to her feet and ran around to give him a hug.

Sampson hugged the girl's slight frame to him, overwhelmed by how much these little girls meant to him, and how badly he wanted Gwenn to continue being a part of all their lives. He let out a breath.

"I needed that, thank you," he said, tweaking her nose as she released him.

Daring to hope, he turned back to Gwenn, but she had turned away from him and was staring out of the window.

Sampson lingered over his breakfast, hoping he'd have an opportunity to speak to Gwenn alone. Once the girls had finished, she rose to shepherd them out of the room and he tried to stop her.

"Miss Wynter, might I have a word?" he asked as she reached the door.

She didn't turn around. "Certainly, my lord. There's plenty of time once we are settled in the carriage. I must finish my packing now, or we shall be late."

"Gwenn," he said, lowering his voice. "I don't give a damn for the packing or being late. I must speak with you."

For a moment, she hesitated, and then she turned and faced him. "There's nothing to say, Lord Cheam," she said, with such

165

cool precision he felt the chill of the words in his heart, and then she left the room.

***

Gwenn tried to do better for the rest of the morning. She hoped the girls had been unaware of the strange atmosphere between her and Sampson after the fun of the previous day, but that would not continue. They were bright children and it would soon become apparent that something was amiss. Besides which, she could not allow the girls to suffer for her own selfish actions. Whilst she knew that she was not entirely to blame, and that Sampson had pursued her, she could not help but believe her own nature had led them to this pass.

She knew what people said of her family, particularly of the De Wynn women, and the truth of those comments made her cheeks heat. The De Wynn family was littered with fallen women, mistresses and courtesans, scandalous women who had taken their pleasures where they liked, how they liked, and to the devil with the consequences. Families had been ruined, duels fought, and hearts broken over her kin, and now she saw how it happened. It was in her nature, in her blood. Perhaps there was something inherent in her that she couldn't even see, that called to men and tempted them to act in a self-destructive manner? Could that be possible?

She forced her mind from such thoughts and back to the children. Though the effort at appearing happy and vivacious was exhausting, she'd been trying her best and doing a fair job of keeping them entertained she hoped. With Sampson—no, *Lord Cheam*—it was far harder. Trying to keep her manner cool and professional and yet not unfriendly, for the girls' sake, was wearing on her nerves. That his gaze constantly returned to hers, full of warmth and an almost puppyish desire for forgiveness, was enough to make her head pound. She wanted to throw herself into his arms and cry and have him soothe her and tell her everything would be all right, but she wasn't a child and, whilst she wanted to hear the lie, she knew it would only unravel when faced with reality.

Better to face it now, head on. She'd been a fool to think even these coming days were hers to have, not when it risked his relationship with his sisters. Over and over again, her mind returned to the image of the two of them intimately entwined in her bed, of exactly what they'd been doing... and then the little voice beyond the door, asking for her. She closed her eyes and shuddered. No. She'd not risk the girls finding them in such a way. She might be wanton and no better than she ought to be, but she'd not ruin a family like this to satisfy her own lust. Even she wasn't that depraved.

With luck, they would catch up with his brother and his aunt tonight, and she could keep her distance without being obvious about it. She knew it would be best if she left now, before Sampson could try to persuade her back into his arms. He *would* try, that much was obvious, but the twins were so excited for her to see the castle and share Christmas with them all.

How could she disappoint them both?

That she was not ready to leave Sampson yet was also true, if an exercise in self-flagellation, but that she must endure the coming days without touching him seemed to be a fitting punishment for her foolishness. *Let it be a lesson to you, Guinevere de Wynn*, she told herself, staring out over a landscape that was harsh and untamed and stunningly beautiful, *that kind of life is not for the likes of you.*

***

On the western shore of Loch Lomond, stood a charming little village built of local sandstone to house the workers from the nearby slate quarries. Not that there was a great deal to see at this late hour past shadowy shapes, the edges highlighted with what remained of the snow, as the carriage finally rumbled ponderously through the main street and halted outside The Drovers Inn.

Sampson had long since subsided into gloomy melancholy. Though he'd put on a cheerful front to keep the girls happy—as Gwenn had obviously done—they were all dozing now. He suspected she was only pretending, but he knew it was hopeless when the girls were with them. His heart was leaden. He was afraid she'd never allow him the chance to speak with her, to make her understand what he felt. It appeared she had decided things were at an end between them, and there was nothing he could say to change her mind.

Well, damn that.

He wasn't letting her go without a fight.

When he saw Samuel waiting for them on the front step of the inn, he didn't know what to feel, whether to punch him in the bloody nose or embrace him in thanks.

"Well met, Sunny," Samuel said with a grin after hugging each of the twins. Aunt May came out to join them, her keen gaze scrutinising both him and Gwenn in a manner that gave him pause.

"Come along, girls," Miss Wynter said, chivvying her charges out of the cold and into the warmth of the inn.

Aunt May followed them, leaving Samuel and Sampson alone. Sampson watched Gwenn go and knew she'd not reappear tonight. She'd plead a headache and eat in her room, and he'd have no opportunity to see her. The Drovers was a busy place and he could not risk a furtive excursion to her bedroom, even if he thought there were the slightest chance she'd let him in.

Samuel took one look at his expression and hurried him off to a private parlour where they could have a drink.

"I half expected you to break my nose," Samuel said with a grin as he poured a generous measure from a decanter into a glass and handed it to him.

Sampson didn't even know what it was, but knocked it back without bothering to ask. He didn't much care. Whisky, he realised, relishing the harsh burn as it lit a fire down his throat.

Sam stared at him and Sampson gave the glass back.

"Ah," he said, frowning at Sampson and refilling the glass before returning it. "Want to talk about it?"

"Not much," Sampson growled, downing the next glass in two large swallows and handing the glass back again.

"I take it the objective is getting drunk?" Samuel said, taking the glass and regarding him with concern.

"Correct."

Sam reached for his own glass, emptied it down his throat, grimaced and then filled it again along with Sampson's before pulling a chair up and sitting down.

"We'll regret this in the morning," Samuel said with a lopsided grin, putting the glass back in his brother's hand.

Sampson snorted and took a large mouthful.

"Oh, come on, Sunny, spit it out," Sam coaxed him. "I take it all is not sunshine and roses with Miss Wynter?"

"I ought to kill you," Sampson said, rubbing a hand over his face. "But—"

"*But?*" Sam repeated in surprise. "There's not usually a but after that statement. It's normally unequivocal."

"Yes, well," Sampson grumbled. "Depending on what happens over the next few days I may retract the *but*."

"All right," Samuel said, wary now. "So shall we play twenty questions, or are you going to tell me?"

Sampson glowered and took another large swallow from his glass, though his empty belly protested.

"Right you are, then." Samuel shuffled his chair closer. "Have you kissed her?"

Feeling his brother's intent gaze on him, Sampson frowned. He wasn't certain he wanted to discuss this with anyone, but... oh, hell, he'd go mad if he didn't, and Sam *was* his brother.

"Yes."

His idiot brother grinned at him. "Well done, Sunny," he said, reaching forward to clap him on the shoulder.

Sampson smacked his hand away. "Don't you dare speak of her like some common strumpet," he snapped, fury rising in his chest. "She's a lady, a fine one at that, and I happen to... to...."

Samuel sat back and stared at him. He was the only one of them who had inherited their father's glass green eyes, and they missed nothing. Sampson looked away from him.

"Forgive me," Samuel said, the regret in his voice sincere. "I meant no disrespect, in any case, but I'm sorry if I offended you."

Sampson downed the rest of his drink and shoved the glass towards his brother.

Samuel took it but looked uneasy. "You're in love with her."

"For what it's worth," he agreed, at least, he assumed that's what the stabbing pain in his chest was.

Gwenn had said it was an infatuation, that he was besotted. Was that all it was? Could something as simple as that make him feel as if he was losing his mind, as if his life would never be the same without her?

"And does she love you?"

He drew in a deep breath. "Currently, she can't stand to look at me."

"Ah. And... before?"

Sampson allowed his mind to drift back to the perfection of yesterday, to snowball fights and laughter and singing, and of the most erotic experience of his entire life, when he had watched Gwenn pleasuring herself in her bath.

"I don't know," he admitted. "I… I'd thought perhaps…." He sat forward and ran a hand through his hair. "Christ, I don't know. Give me another bloody drink."

Samuel downed his own glass and poured another measure into both his and Sampson's but hesitated before he handed it over. "Shouldn't you try and sort it out rather than… well, this?"

He gestured with the glass and Sampson reached out and took it from him.

"I would, but she's avoiding me, and there's nowhere I can be private with her. It will have to wait until we get to Tor Castle, though I don't know how I can endure waiting. Then, brother dear, you will help me to be alone with her, seeing as you're so bloody adept at it."

Samuel had the grace to look a little sheepish and raised his glass to chink against Sampson's. "Then let us drink and be merry, for we may not die tomorrow, but after a couple of hours on the road, we're going to bloody well wish we were dead."

Chapter 16

"Wherein a drunken Romeo gets his just desserts."

Gwenn jolted awake from an uneasy sleep, certain she'd heard a noise but unsure of what it had been or where it had come from. She lay still, blinking into the darkness and waiting for it to come again, and nearly leapt out of her skin as something tapped on her bedroom window.

Scolding herself for even contemplating ghosts, she got out of bed and hurried to the window, and almost screamed as she pulled back the curtains.

Sampson was outside and, considering the bone-breaking drop beneath him, she could only conclude that he'd run mad or was thoroughly foxed.

"Are you insane?" she demanded, thrusting the window up as he swayed precariously on the thickly tangled ivy stems that covered the back of the inn. The answer was obvious enough when he spoke.

"Had to speak to you, Gwennie," he slurred, and she exclaimed with fury as she realised he was more than foxed, he was thoroughly soused. "B'fore I go mad."

"Get in here, you blithering idiot," she cursed, hauling him inside before someone saw him or he broke his stupid neck. He landed with a heavy thud on her bedroom floor and groaned, clutching his head as he sat upright.

"What the devil are you playing at?" she demanded, trying to scold him furiously without ever raising her voice, which was frustrating to say the least. "Do you have no thought for your sisters? I believed you were a good man, doing your best to keep scandal from dirtying your name any further, but this...."

She gestured at the state of him and he shook his head.

"Don't scold me, love," he said, the words slurring a little and sounding so pitiful she didn't know whether to throw something at him or hug him. "I know. I know I'm an idiot, I know I don't deserve you or the girls, but you wouldn't see me, wouldn't talk to me, and I can't bear it. 'Sides," he added, his forehead furrowing, "it was Sam's idea. He told me I ought not let you have time to think about leaving me, because the more time you had the better the idea would seem."

"Oh, Sampson!" she exclaimed, shaking her head just as a soft knock sounded at the door.

They both froze as the handle turned, and Aunt May crept into the room.

"Ah," she said, spotting Sampson and closing the door behind her. "I thought as much when I heard the thud."

She smiled at Gwenn's horrified expression. "Don't worry, dear. My room is next to yours and I had an ear out for something of the sort. Once those two start drinking, trouble isn't far behind. They're not called The Scandalous Brothers for no reason. Impulsive devils when the drink takes them, and it was easy enough to guess why this one wanted to drown his sorrows."

She folded her arms and stared down at her nephew with a combination of dismay and amusement, while Gwenn found a searing blush scalding her cheeks. Sampson leant his head back against the wall and closed his eyes with a groan.

"Mrs B-Bainbridge," Gwenn stammered, horrified to imagine what the woman must be thinking, and feeling far worse as she realised it was all true.

"Oh, hush, child," she said, with a tut. "For starters, it's Aunt May, and there's no need to be so missish about having a man in your room. I was young once, you know, so don't look so appalled. The question is, what do we do with him now?"

Gwenn blinked in astonishment, gaping at her. Sampson began to snore.

Aunt May rolled her eyes. "Oh, how I long for the good old days. We were far wilder and freer than your generation, you know. Now it's all appearances and morals. Nothing's changed in the least, it's just people pretend they don't get up to all the naughty things we did with glee and no shame at all."

She laughed as Gwenn continued to regard her with wonder.

"I had a great many beaus, I'll have you know," she said, smiling. "Until Father forced me to marry Arthur Bainbridge." She grimaced and shook her head. "He was disgustingly rich and very respectable, and not a bad man when all's said and done, but how I wished I'd taken my chance to run off with his younger brother when he asked me. Not a shilling to his name but, oh… oh, what a man, and so handsome too. I think we'd have been happy. Such a long time I've regretted it."

Gwen stared as Aunt May's eyes grew misty and she put a hand to her heart. When she spoke again her voice was faint, the sorrow audible.

"He died a couple of years later, in a duel. I always wondered if…." She watched with her heart aching as the woman pressed her lips together, fighting for composure. "But never mind that," she said briskly, though her voice trembled a little. Suddenly she shook her head as if casting the memories aside and gave Gwenn a dazzling smile. "What to do with Sunny, then? Silly boy. He's fallen head over ears for you, of course, I could tell the moment you arrived this evening. It was written all over his face."

She gave Gwenn a shrewd look. "You should marry him."

The words were such a shock that Gwenn had to sit down on the bed, as though the force of them had knocked her backwards.

"Don't tell me the thought hasn't occurred to you?"

Gwenn fought for breath, for an answer, but none came. Nothing sensible, anyway. "I-I'm a governess," she stammered.

Aunt May snorted and folded her arms. "And I'm the Queen of Sheba." The woman didn't look away, just held Gwenn's gaze, the light of challenge in her eyes.

"He can't marry me," Gwenn said at length. "I'm... not respectable." The words were stiff, and she almost laughed at the magnitude of the understatement.

"No, I didn't think you were," Aunt May said with a sigh. "Must be why we all like you so much."

Despite herself Gwenn smiled. "I like all of you too," she said. "Very much."

"And Sampson?"

Gwenn's eyes were drawn to the slumbering figure beneath her window, and she sighed. "I like him best of all," she admitted. "So much that I won't cause the most shocking scandal this family has ever seen."

To her surprise, Aunt May snorted and moved to sit on the bed beside her. "Good luck with that, young lady. You've a way to go, believe me." She reached out and took Gwenn's hand, squeezing her fingers.

"Oh, I can do it," Gwenn said, with a wry huff of laughter. She met the older woman's eyes. "He won't want me when he knows."

"Perhaps," Aunt May allowed, with a prosaic shrug. "But that's his decision. You should at least allow him to make it."

Gwenn swallowed around the knot in her throat and clung to Aunt May's hand.

"He'll be fine," she said unsteadily. "And the girls won't have to face any more scandal. Sampson will marry a nice, respectable girl, and—"

"And spend the rest of his life wishing he'd run away with you," Aunt May finished for her. "Look at him," she instructed, pointing at the figure slumped on the floor. "He's not drunk like that in seven years or more, and he only drank then to escape his wretched father."

"Don't," Gwenn said, tears stinging her eyes as she held back a sob. "Please... don't make it harder."

Aunt May sighed and put her arms about her. "You're just what this family needs, Miss Wynter, or whatever your real name is. Damn scandal, damn the *ton*, damn what anyone else thinks. Love, that's what's important. Those girls need it. Their mother is a silly bit of nonsense who'll never be a role model for them, but you... you could show them what it means to be a woman with spirit and a brain in her head and, as for Sampson...." She sighed and shook her head. "Well, I've said my piece. I'll not say it again. Only, it breaks my heart to see young people making mistakes out of some misguided sense of obligation or twisted morality."

Gwenn wiped her eyes, beyond touched by her words, but still steadfast in her belief that even a broad-minded woman like Aunt May would balk at her nephew marrying a woman the world knew had been raised by a courtesan to be a courtesan.

"Promise me you'll think on what I've said, child."

"I will," Gwenn said, knowing she'd think of nothing else over the days to come.

"Well, then." Aunt May got to her feet. "I shall track down his partner in crime and see if he's in any state to handle moving his brother."

Gwenn watched as the woman got up and left, her eyes inexorably returning to the gently snoring figure beneath the window. Knowing she was a fool, but quite unable to stop herself, she moved to him, kneeling by his side. Tenderness welled in her heart for him, for his reckless and foolish behaviour, which she knew well would be a source of mortification for him in the morning.

"Poor darling," she said, brushing his thick hair from his forehead.

His eyes flickered open and settled on her as a hazy smile curved over his mouth.

"Gwenn," he said, reaching for her.

Gwenn took his hand before he could pull her into his arms, aware that Aunt May and Mr Pelham might be back at any moment. Yet she couldn't resist lifting his hand to her mouth and kissing his fingers. In all likelihood he'd not remember this in the morning, in any case.

He sighed.

"I missed you," he said, the words so stark and honest they tore a ragged hole in her heart. "You were right there in front of me, and I missed you so badly. Don't cut me out, Gwenn. I can't bear it."

Gwenn closed her own eyes, unable to stop the tears that slid down her cheeks.

Sampson reached out with his free hand and wiped them away. "Let me love you," he whispered, his eyelids heavy with fatigue and drink as he gazed at her.

The door opened and Gwenn let go of his hand and moved back, taking a breath and trying to compose herself before she turned and rose to her feet.

"His idiot brother is just as drunk as he is," Aunt May said in disgust. "I tried to rouse him, and he almost pulled me into his lap. He called me *his little darling*. I may never recover," she said with a shudder. "My only consolation is the look on his face tomorrow when I tell him," she added, with a wicked glint in her eyes.

Gwenn laughed a little, though it was the hardest thing not to weep.

"We'd best let Sampson sleep it off here. There's no way we will move him without causing a stir," Aunt May said, frowning at Sampson, who appeared to be asleep again. "For propriety's sake, you may share my room tonight. Not that I care, but just in case anyone sees him here. We'll make something up about a mix up with room keys if necessary."

"Thank you," Gwenn said, too tired and emotional to argue or think of any better solution.

"Oh, it's not a problem. I sleep very little these days, so we shall be up in plenty of time to rouse him before everyone wakes tomorrow."

Aunt May took her arm and gave her a warm smile. "There, there, child. Things won't look so bleak in the morning after a good night's rest. Come along, now."

***

Sampson could feel his Aunt's gaze boring a hole in his head, but he kept his eyes tightly shut. His brain felt like it had been sliced in two by the bloody great sword Ross had carried when in full Highland regalia, and he didn't need anyone to tell him what a prize ass he'd been last night. When he thought of it, a prickle of horror ran down his spine. Good God, what if someone had seen him? He could have ruined Gwenn and caused exactly the kind of scandal he'd been determined to keep their family away from.

This was what came of drinking to excess, and he ought to have known better. He *did* know better, only he'd been heartsick and frightened that Gwenn was slipping from his grasp, and he'd wanted a few hours of oblivion to settle the emotions battering him on all sides. Besides which, it was all Sam's bloody fault. It had been his stupid plan, and Sampson had been too foxed to see it as anything but a marvellous idea. That alone should have rung every alarm bell at full pitch. From the moment his youngest brother had come of age, most every scrape Sampson had ever gotten into had Sam at the bottom of it somewhere.

The carriage hit a rut in the road and Samuel groaned beside him. *Good,* Sampson thought with grim satisfaction, as he gritted his own teeth.

"Idiots, the pair of you," Aunt May said, shaking her head as Sampson dared a glimpse at her through slitted eyelids.

Though Sampson had protested—as loudly as his sore head would allow—Aunt May had insisted that Gwenn have the girls and a carriage to herself. According to her, the young woman had put up with quite enough extraordinary behaviour for one day and needed some time away from them. What was more, Aunt May was going to thoroughly enjoy watching her nephews suffer, and give them a stern talking to along the way.

Sampson and Samuel had exchanged looks of pained resignation and had submitted to the inevitable, albeit it rather gracelessly.

"Well then, Sampson?" she said, quirking one eyebrow at him just a little, but managing to convey a world of disdain in the slight movement. "What are your plans?"

"Plans?" he rasped as his stomach roiled. "You mean other than dying in a ditch?"

"Yes, dear, other than that. It's entirely your own fault, so please don't expect any sympathy. I mean I have no argument with climbing in through the girl's bedroom window, assuming she is happy to let you in, but you might have thought to make it a romantic gesture," she said with a tut.

Sampson stared at her, too scandalised to speak. He knew Aunt May had a colourful past, but she'd been the paragon of respectability for most of his life, and it was hard to credit.

"For example," she continued, "being sober enough not to fall on your head and land her in the devil of a scene would have been a start. Bearing flowers or poetry, perhaps?"

"It's the middle of December," Sampson objected, torn between indignation and embarrassment at the scolding. "And it's snowing. Where in God's name could I find flowers?"

Aunt May waved this away as if it was a minor detail. Samuel sniggered.

"And you can shut up," she said, turning her steely gaze in his direction. "Sampson already told me whose bright idea it was. Not that I hadn't already guessed."

"Tattle-tale," Samuel muttered, folding his arms.

Sampson shot him a dark look and said nothing.

Aunt May snapped her fingers at Sampson, making him wince. "Pay attention," she commanded. "You need a plan, and it had better be a good one. What are your intentions towards Miss Wynter?"

Sampson opened his mouth, about to retort that they were honourable, but he realised with a wash of shame that he could make no such claim. Not until he knew what Gwenn was hiding from him. If it was merely a minor scandal, then their marriage would be enough to silence the gossip mongers. Perhaps not completely, but enough that he could be happy that, by the time the girls were of age, such a story would be long forgotten.

If not, though....

He was responsible for those girls. When they'd been born, he'd made a promise to them—and to himself—that he'd look after them, that he'd try to be someone they could depend on. It hadn't happened overnight by any means, but Sampson had curtailed his drinking and carousing, and had tried to be the man their father ought to have been. Little by little, he'd done what he could to grow into the role of their guardian, with mixed success perhaps, but he had tried his best. He couldn't forget that now, and he could not let them down.

"I don't know," he said, hating the words, and himself.

Gwenn deserved the best of everything. She deserved a man who would give up everything to be with her. Sampson wanted to be that man, would have been no matter the nature of the scandal, if not for two little girls who needed him even more than he needed Gwenn. He was a man, after all, an adult who knew how to look the world in the eye when everyone was sneering and gossiping about his family. Losing Gwenn might feel like having his heart cut out with a spoon, but he'd live, after a fashion. He couldn't subject the girls to such treatment.

"How can I know until she tells me who she really is, and what she's running from?" he demanded, feeling the need to defend himself. "She won't trust me enough to tell me, and I can't make any decisions until I know. The girls...."

His aunt's face softened.

"You've been a wonderful brother to them, Sampson," she said, soothing now after her rather abrasive scolding. "No one could have asked more of you, and no one should," she added, surprising him. "What those girls need is a loving home, an example of what that home looks like. That's what is most important to them now."

Sampson felt his throat tighten with emotion, so taken aback by his aunt's words that he was unequal to the task of finding a reply, and then the carriage lurched and swayed, and it transformed into an urgent desire to cast up his accounts.

"Stop the coach," he rasped, and flung himself out the door.

***

Their midday stop was a brief affair. The brothers looked like they'd been recently dug up by resurrectionists and Gwenn was too emotional to swallow. Only Aunt May and the twins enjoyed their repast, but the girls were so excited to reach Tor Castle and meet their new brother that they inhaled their food, barely chewing a bite, and Gwenn was too distracted to scold them for it.

As Sampson had predicted, and much to the twins' delight, the snow began falling mid-afternoon and slowed their progress, but the girls were all merriment now and nothing could dampen their spirits. They sang carols and spent a deal of time wondering about what Christmas presents they'd get. By the time the glowering castle was silhouetted on the horizon against what remained of the daylight, they were beside themselves.

"Girls," Gwenn said, smiling despite her own low spirits, "please remember that you are young ladies. Your excitement is understandable, and I have no desire to quash it, only do try to remember your manners, please, or it will reflect badly on your poor governess."

"Yes, Miss Wynter," they chorused, returning impish smiles and bouncing in their seats.

Gwenn laughed. Their company had done her good. They were so cheerful and good-natured that it was impossible not to be buoyed by them. The realisation that she would miss them dreadfully sent her spirits tumbling back into an abyss, however, and she had to work to rearrange her face into something approaching pleasure in their arrival.

She had Christmas to look forward to, she reminded herself. She had always longed to experience a family Christmas. Marie was always morose during the holiday, as it was the one time a husband really could not escape being with his wife and children. They would have a fine meal and lavish presents, naturally, but it was just Marie and Gwenn, and Gwenn spent her time trying to coax Marie out of her sulk. Oh, Marie would arrange parties, naturally, but not the kind of wholesome gatherings that families enjoyed, nor the kind that Gwenn was allowed to attend. There were no innocently silly games, raucous laughter, or noisy children. This year would be different. Likely it was the only time she would ever get to experience such a thing, as her future would no doubt follow the same pattern as Marie's had, so she ought to attempt to enjoy it.

That was the most depressing thought of all, and she fought back a surge of melancholy as she climbed down from the coach with no little trepidation.

Chapter 17

"Wherein a warm welcome on a cold winter's night."

In the gloom of the winter's evening and with snow falling in a gentle hush around them, the girls came face to face with their new brother for the first time.

Although bursting with anticipation, they became suddenly shy when presented with the magnificence that was Captain Ross Moncreiffe.

Gwenn could not help but smile at the thought that Marie would have been salivating, had she been here. Sampson and Samuel were not small men. Tall, lean, and broad-shouldered, they were impressive specimens of masculinity, but Moncreiffe was built on rather larger proportions. He was as solid as the mountain that stood at his back, every inch an Englishwoman's romantic ideal of what a Scottish warrior should be. Dressed as he was in full Highland regalia, he was a sight to behold.

To Gwenn's amusement, he blushed a little under her and Aunt May's open-mouthed appraisal as the twins hid behind them and peeked around with wide blue eyes.

"Ach, pay all this nae mind," he said, his broad accent warm and rough as he gestured to his kilt and sporran and all his finery. He sent a frustrated glare towards the small dark-haired woman at his side. "'Twas Freddie's daft notion, though I told her it made me look like a prize ar—"

"Ross!" the woman cried in alarm as the big man glowered and snapped his mouth shut. "Ladies and children present, remember, and it was not daft. I bet the girls have been longing to see a real Highland warrior." She smiled at the twins and held out her hands. "Now remind me, which of you is Susan, and which is Selina? I never could get it right."

"I'm Susan," said a small voice as the girl stepped forward.

"Susan, and so you are Selina. Oh, it's so lovely to see you both again." Freddie held out her arms to the girls. "I've missed you very much, and now I'm your brother's wife, which makes us sisters. Isn't that wonderful?"

Selina crept closer too, both sisters moving to hug Freddie and stare up at the mountainous Scot beside her.

"Ah, and what do you think of your brother?" Freddie said, lips quirking a little. "I know he looks very fearsome, but he's really not."

"Good evening, ladies," Ross said, executing a formal bow to the twins that made them giggle. "And welcome to Tor Castle. I am *verrry* pleased to meet ye." He accentuated his accent, rolling the r's and winking at them as they grinned in delight.

"Why do Scottish men wear skirts?" Susan asked, gazing up at him in wonder.

There was a snort of laughter from Samuel, and Ross narrowed his eyes, pointing a finger at him.

"Ye put the lassie up to that," he said with indignation as Sam dissolved.

"I didn't, I swear," Sam said, shaking his head. "Which makes it even more priceless."

Ross harrumphed and turned back to the girls. "It's a kilt, lass, nae a skirt, and only a *real* man can wear it," he added, glowering at Samuel, who just went off again.

They were hustled into the castle and out of the cold and the rest of the introductions made.

"Good to see you, Ross," Sampson said, greeting his brother warmly. "This is your Aunt May."

"We apologise in advance," Samuel added with a smirk.

Aunt May glowered at Samuel before turning to Ross. "Oughtn't you be wearing a sword with that get-up?" she demanded.

Ross, who looked a little taken aback by both Samuel's introduction and Aunt May's brisk tone, nodded.

"Aye, but Freddie didnae want to frighten the girls."

"A pity," Aunt May said, sending a meaningful look towards her nephew.

"Ye may borrow it with my good blessings, though," Ross added with a grin.

Aunt May stared up at Ross with approval. "I like you." Ross gave a low chuckle. "Aye, and I like ye fine too. Yer very welcome here."

Aunt May beamed at him and turned back to her nephews. "What lovely manners your brother has. Perhaps you could learn a thing or two whilst you're here."

Before either Samuel or Sampson could protest, she brought Gwenn forward.

"Ross, Freddie... may I call you Freddie, dear?" she asked the big man's wife.

The young woman laughed and nodded. "I shall be most offended if you don't, Aunt May."

"Thank you, then may I present our dear friend Miss Wynter to you."

Gwenn froze, astonished by the introduction. Rather than have Gwenn presented as the governess, a servant of sorts, she had given her the status of a guest. For a moment Gwenn thought she might cry, her throat was so tight, but then she realised she could not allow them to believe she was something she was not, no matter how much she wanted to. She was hiding enough of herself without making things worse. A respectable family would never invite her into their homes, not if they knew who—and what—she was.

"That is very kind, Mrs Bainbridge," she said, forcing her voice to remain steady. "But not entirely accurate. Good evening, Captain Moncreiffe, Mrs Moncreiffe, I am so pleased to meet you. I am in fact employed by Lord Cheam as governess to Susan and Selina."

The captain and his wife greeted her with warmth whilst casting curious glances between their guests, aware that there was something amiss but too polite to ask.

"Digby," Ross called to the butler, a tall, thin fellow with an immaculate appearance. "Did Mrs Murray say something about shortbread?"

The man turned and smiled, a surprisingly warm expression from a fellow who had up till now been the discreet and starchy epitome of a top-notch butler. "Indeed, she did, Captain. In fact, I should say she's bursting with impatience to meet the young ladies."

Gwenn's surprise deepened as she recognised a decidedly English accent. She wondered how a man like the captain had acquired such a butler in the wilds of Scotland. On first sight, he'd seemed top lofty enough to serve a duke, but the way he treated his master was far more familiar than was usually approved of.

"Are ye ready to meet my housekeeper, ladies?" Ross asked of Susan and Selina. "She is a very fine cook and will stuff ye like a pair of plump partridges before the end of your stay, so I give ye fair warning. Her shortbread is a thing of beauty. Would ye be interested in tasting some?"

The girls chorused an enthusiastic reply, and Freddie laughed and took their hands.

"Come along then, to the kitchens with you."

"Should ye prefer to go to yer room now, Auntie?" Ross asked Aunt May who gave an emphatic shake of her head.

"With shortbread on offer? I think not."

"Excellent," Ross replied. "We'll all go to the kitchens for tea and shortbread. Mrs Murray will be in raptures, but I'm afraid ye will find us very informal here."

"Refreshingly so, I believe," Aunt May said, before adding with a rather imperious air. "You may give me your arm."

"It would be an honour, Auntie," Ross replied with exaggerated politeness.

Samuel made a gagging sound and received a clip round the ear from Aunt May on her way past, which made Ross snort with laughter.

"Ach, yer just jealous that she likes me better than ye," he said to Samuel, who rolled his eyes as Ross glanced at his wife and added with a wink. "Most people do."

Gwenn hesitated, longing to follow them but unsure if she ought to until Sampson caught her eye. He moved towards her and held out his arm.

"Come along," he said, smiling at her with such tenderness her chest ached. There were too many emotions battering her on all sides and she felt raw and exposed, too open and vulnerable to withstand that smile. The warmth of their greeting from everyone at the castle and the easy banter between them only brought to life all her hopes and dreams and proved they existed… for some. This was what she'd run away for, hoping to find some small taste of a life like this. Now she could see the reality of it before her, but she was like a child with her nose pressed against a sweet shop window and no money to go inside. Perhaps a thief would be a better analogy, she thought bitterly as the sweet, vanilla scent of shortbread enveloped them, for she could surely contaminate all of this with the taint of scandal, if she didn't leave them be.

***

Mrs Murray was a small woman with luxuriant white hair and dark eyes, bright with intelligence and good humour, and Sampson was gratified to receive a warm welcome from her. She'd treated him with a distinct lack of respect and great suspicion at their first meeting, though in the circumstances Sampson could hardly blame her. He'd brought her beloved Captain Moncreiffe home bleeding and nearly out of his mind with fever, after their father had shot him when his back was turned. It was only her considerable skill as a healer that had saved him. That she'd believed Sampson every bit as vile and wicked as his father had been obvious, and she'd taken a while to come around.

It seemed he'd passed some test, however, and she was all smiles and showed every sign of being genuinely pleased to greet him, especially as he'd brought his little sisters to stay.

"What bonnie lasses," she said, beaming, her rosy cheeks flushed with the heat of the kitchen, which was the cosiest place Sampson had ever known. "Have another shortbread," she whispered, loud enough for everyone to hear as she snuck another biscuit into their eager hands and then smacked Ross's away when he reached for one himself.

"Ye've already had one," she said, wagging a finger at him. "Ye'll spoil yer dinner."

"Ye gave the girls three," Ross retorted, indignant as she snatched the plate of biscuits away.

"Ach, take the food from the mouths of bairns, would ye?" she demanded as Ross huffed and folded his massive arms, looking as sulky as a three-year-old denied a treat.

Sampson laughed despite the heaviness in his heart. How good it was to be here. The girls had already lost any shyness in the presence of their half-brother and had taken to Freddie at once too. They would have a wonderful Christmas and be spoiled rotten, and that was everything he'd hoped to give them.

Unbidden, his gaze drifted to Gwenn. She was watching everything with rapt attention, an uneaten shortbread held in her elegant fingers. Her eyes were a little too bright as she stared at the girls. They were talking with Freddie and laughing as Ross looked down at the three of them with amusement. He stroked his wife's hair, an openly tender caress, and she looked up at him, such adoration in her gaze that Sampson smiled and turned back to catch Gwenn's eye to share in the warmth of the scene. As he looked up, he saw her turn abruptly away. She stood before the fire, staring down at the flames, and Sampson watched as she raised a hand to face and wiped her cheek. His heart clenched with misery. The longing for her, the longing to go to her and promise that they could have that too, was so overpowering it took everything he had to hold himself still.

A prickling sensation up the back of his neck told him he was being watched, and he looked around to find Mrs Murray studying him. Slowly, her gaze travelled from him to Gwenn and back again.

Sampson turned away, unable to look her in the eyes, unable to meet her piercing gaze when it asked the unspoken question, *what the devil are you playing at?*

He didn't have an answer.

***

Gwenn slept badly despite the embrace of a soft mattress and soft, thick blankets and quilts. She got up earlier than usual, unwilling to linger and allow her mind to travel back down the same paths it had trodden in circles all night, and hurried to pull on her dressing gown. A maid had coaxed her fire to life recently, but the flames had yet to take the chill from the room.

From behind the curtains, a bright slant of daylight hinted at a sunny winter day, just perfect for Christmas Eve, and Gwenn tugged them open and froze, captured by the beauty of the scene before her. The rugged landscape of valleys and massive hills sparkled beneath a carpet of snow and, towering over it all, Ben Nevis dominated the vista, as white as a freshly iced bride cake.

Although Marie could never have been accused of being a godly or pious woman, she believed in God and had instilled the same belief in her daughter. Marie swept aside any suggestion that her lifestyle was a sin and that she was destined for hell with the rejoinder that Mary Magdalene had been a fallen woman and Jesus had liked her well enough. Gwenn always forbore to point out that Mary had repented of her lifestyle; it really wasn't worth incurring Marie's wrath. In this moment, though, Gwenn thought that any god who had a hand in creating something as beautiful and awe inspiring as this scene would have love and understanding enough to forgive a flawed creature like Marie… or her.

At least, she hoped so.

I'm nothing compared to that, she thought, staring at the immutable mountain. It had been there thousands of years before Gwenn had been born and would still be there when she had long been consigned to dust. Strangely, it was comforting to be such a tiny part of a history which would swallow her up and never give her a second thought. She was an imperfect creature, but her mistakes would not bring the world to an end any more than her good deeds would change its course. The realisation gave her a measure of peace and, though heavy eyed and weary, she went down to breakfast with more equilibrium than she'd been able to find last night.

Though the household was not yet awake, the servants were already up and doing. Gwenn dithered in the entrance hall, uncertain of where to go as Digby was still preparing the breakfast room and she did not wish to disturb him. The delicious scent emanating from the kitchen made her mind up for her and she followed her nose, pushing open the heavy door.

Mrs Murray looked up as she hesitated in the doorway and her friendly face split in a wide smile.

"Come in, Miss Wynter, and bide awhile. I've fresh bannocks and there's tea in the pot."

"I don't want to get in your way," Gwenn said, as Mrs Murray waved this notion away with a snort. "Ach, if I can work around Captain Moncreiffe, a wee slip of a thing like yerself is nae gonna bother me none."

Before she could say another word, Gwenn found herself hustled to a spot at the huge, scrubbed oak table and sat down with a plate of bannocks, a dish of creamy golden butter and a large jar of jam. Mrs Murray hefted an enormous brown teapot, which seemed the size of Gwenn's head and poured out a strong cup of tea, before pushing a jug of milk and a bowl with sugar lumps at her.

"Tuck in."

"Thank you," Gwenn said, reaching for a bannock and slathering the warm, crumbly surface with fresh butter and a healthy dollop of jam. She almost moaned as she took a bite. The buttery, oaty bannock against the sweet, tart bite of the jam was heavenly. "That," she said, staring at her plate. "Is the most delicious thing I ever tasted."

Mrs Murray beamed at her, clearly delighted. "Hawthorn jam," she said and then gave Gwenn a wink. "Good for the heart, it is."

Gwenn paused, the bannock suspended an inch from her mouth. Somehow, she knew Mrs Murray was not speaking of her health.

"I'm sorry?" she said, aware she sounded a little stiff as her mind whirled, wondering if she'd somehow given herself away last night.

"Forgive me," Mrs Murray said as a frown gathered between her eyes, she hesitated, wiping her hands on her apron. "'Tis none of my affair, I know, only I had come to like Lord Cheam but... if he's forcing his attention where it is not wanted, mayhap he's more like his father than I imagined."

"He's nothing like his father!" Gwenn burst out before she could think to hold her tongue.

It was too late now, though, and Mrs Murray stilled, watching her.

"He's a good man," Gwenn said, her throat growing tight. "It's me... me that...." To her shame the little aura of calm she'd discovered evaporated in an instant and all the emotions she'd been struggling to keep in check burst free as she dissolved into an ugly bout of tears.

"Ach, lassie!" Mrs Murray cried, bustling over and pulling her into a fierce embrace.

Gwenn allowed it, comforted by the homely scents of baking as the small woman crooned and rocked her like a child. "I'm sorry. I never meant to upset ye so. I ought never to have opened my mouth. Blathering on and interfering is my besetting sin, as anyone will tell ye."

"It's all right," Gwenn managed between sobs. "B-But how—"

"I saw him looking at ye last night," Mrs Murray said, her voice gentle as she stroked Gwenn's hair. "Pure longing in his eyes. A man in love if ever I saw one."

"L-Love?" Gwenn said, her heart bursting despite everything.

Except then she realised that it changed nothing. It only meant Sampson would be just as wretched as she was when this came to its inevitable end. She cried harder.

"Aye, lass," Mrs Murray said. "And I could see plain that ye were burdened down with a heavy weight. I wondered if perhaps ye did not enjoy his attentions and feared for ye, but I see that's not the case."

"It's not." Gwenn shook her head and accepted the handkerchief that Mrs Murray pressed into her hand. It smelled of lavender and she inhaled, trying to calm herself and failing. "I l-love h-him, but it's... it's impossible," she said, and dissolved into another round of sobbing.

The sound of a door opening reached their ears and Gwenn stiffened, glancing to where Captain Moncreiffe had just come in.

"What is it?" he demanded, staring at Mrs Murray who was clutching Gwenn to her bosom. No doubt she looked a fine sight, red-eyed and dishevelled after her outburst.

"Out!" Mrs Murray commanded, and with such force Gwenn jumped.

She watched the captain with trepidation, waiting for the moment when he shouted at his housekeeper to mind her tongue and remember to whom she was speaking. Instead, he stared, open-mouthed, and then turned smartly on his heel, and went out as instructed.

Gwenn glanced back at Mrs Murray, a little astonished.

The old woman shrugged, a glint in her dark eyes. "I was the nearest thing to a mother he ever had. I patched that boy up when he was a wee bairn, and tanned his hide a time or two an' all. For all he's a big braw captain now, he'll nae forget it. Besides which, the bravest fellow will take to his heels at the sight of a woman's tears."

Gwenn laughed a little, and Mrs Murray patted her cheek. "I have just the thing," she said with a wink and hurried off, returning with a bottle of whisky. She laced Gwenn's tea with a generous measure before putting it in her hand. "Drink that and finish those bannocks, and the world won't seem so cold, lassie. Then we'll talk... if ye wish it."

She moved away without another word, busying herself with preparing the breakfast as Gwenn sat and ate and sipped at her tea, and discovered that Mrs Murray was quite correct. The old woman's presence soothed her as did the scent of fresh bread. The tea, or rather the whisky in it, eased a little of the tension and chased away the desperation she'd felt, for now at least.

Gwenn picked up the bannock she'd set down before her outburst and decided, for the moment, to concentrate on simple pleasures.

Chapter 18

"Wherein Gwenn decides her fate."

"Morning, Ross," Sampson said as he came down the stairs. He'd slept badly, too consumed with how to get Gwenn to tell him the truth of her past so that he might find a way for them to have a future. Ross was standing in the middle of the vast hallway, rubbing the back of his neck, his thick eyebrows drawn together. "What is it? Forgotten to put your trousers on?"

Ross looked up and rolled his eyes. "Ye are just jealous ye have nae the legs to wear a kilt, ye damned Sassenach."

Sampson snorted and smacked Ross on the shoulder. "Yes, that must be it," he said, his tone grave.

They walked to the breakfast parlour and sat down whilst Digby served coffee and ensured their plates were loaded with bacon, sausages and eggs before leaving them alone.

"Tell me about Miss Wynter."

The coffee went down the wrong way, such was Sampson's surprise at the question and Ross thumped him on the back so hard he was almost winded. Once he'd gotten his breath back, Ross regarded him curiously.

"Well, that was nae the reaction I expected."

"Wasn't it?" Sampson retorted tersely as he met Ross' suspicious gaze.

"Dallying with the governess was nae what I expected of ye, nae."

Ross' expression had hardened and, for a moment, Sampson felt a burst of fury. It dissipated as he realised he had no right to the moral high ground: he *had* been trying to seduce the governess, to make her his mistress if he couldn't have her for a wife. With the circumstances of his own conception, Sampson could hardly blame Ross for viewing the affair in a less than romantic light.

"It's not what you think," Sampson said, and then gave a huff of laughter as he realised how pathetic that sounded. He groaned and rubbed a hand over his face. "I'm not like him, Ross. I don't want to be dishonourable—"

"Then don't be," Ross replied, his voice hard as he speared a sausage with a rather too violent stab of his fork.

"Now look here," Sampson said, growing a little irritated now. "You don't know the circumstances, so don't go giving me the protective laird defending the innocent girl treatment. I want to marry her, I… I just might not be able to."

"Then ye ought not to hae put yer hands on her," Ross growled, setting down his knife and fork and glaring at Sampson.

"I haven't!" Sampson retorted, though perhaps not with as much conviction as he might have bearing in mind that *a,* it wasn't entirely true and *b*, it wasn't for lack of trying.

"Oh, aye?" Ross said, scathing now as he folded his arms. "And why is she in the kitchen sobbing her heart out with Mrs Murray if she has nae yer bairn in her belly, or the likelihood of it?"

Sampson felt the colour leave his face. It was the strangest sensation. His guts twisted into a knot as his chest grew tight and a cold wave rolled over him. Not his child of course, but… but could it be someone else's? He forced himself to sit and think before jumping to conclusions. Nothing about Gwenn made any sense. The sensuous woman who knew how to please a man, who knew just what to do and say to drive him wild, was at odds with the girl who had seemed hesitant when he kissed her, as if uncertain, as if she'd never done it before.

He put his head in his hands, trying to think but coming up empty. All he knew was that Gwenn was in the kitchens, crying, and likely it was his fault.

Sampson pushed his chair back and stood but Ross grasped his wrist, his hand like an iron manacle. "Where are ye going?" he demanded.

"Where do you think?" Sampson tried to snatch his arm free, but Ross held it firm.

"I'll not hae ye chasing an unwed lass under my roof if yer intentions are not honourable."

"They are honourable, damn you," Sampson snapped, before sighing and adding. "Mostly."

"That's nae good enough."

"I know that!" Sampson said, frustrated now. "Don't you think I know that? This is not all my fault, Ross. I know it looks bad, but... can you not trust me? I'm your brother. I thought that meant something." He stared into Ross's eyes: green like Sam's, like their father's. "I'm not like him, Ross, I swear it. I would never abandon her. I *want* to marry her, but it's just not that simple."

Ross searched his gaze, and whatever it was he was looking for he seemed to find as he let go of Sampson's wrist. "Aye, well. I suppose I'd better give ye the benefit of the doubt." He picked up his knife and fork again, pointing the knife at Sampson. "But if I find ye have played me or the girl false... I'll make ye sorry."

"Fair enough," Sampson said with a tight smile, before stalking from the room.

Aunt May, Samuel, and the twins were just making their way down the stairs as Sampson crossed the hallway. He greeted them, dithering to speak to Samuel.

"What's wrong?" Sam said, ever alert to his moods.

"I don't know, but Ross said Gwenn... Miss Wynter is in the kitchens, crying."

"Ah," Sam said, and Sampson felt a rush of affection for him at not needing to say another word.

"We're supposed to be going out to pick greenery to decorate with," Sam said, grimacing a little. "I'll make your and Miss Wynter's excuses and keep the girls away. You should be safe until lunchtime."

Sampson let out a breath and grasped his brother's arm. "Thank you," he said, with real gratitude.

Sam shrugged. "That's what brothers are for," he said, adopting a pious tone, before adding. "Besides which, now you owe me."

"I do," Sampson said with a snort. "Though if you could also try to get Ross to understand I'm not some vile debaucher of innocents, I'd be much obliged, and you may add it to the tally."

"Oh?"

"I'll explain later," Sampson said, shaking his head. "I need to find Gwenn."

With no little trepidation, Sampson made his way to the kitchen. On sticking his head round the door, he discovered Mrs Murray, but no Gwenn.

"She's nae here," the woman said, giving him a shrewd look.

Realising there was no escaping, and that he was likely in for another dressing down, Sampson took a breath and walked into the room, closing the door behind him.

"Get it over with then," he said, just wanting to be free to find Gwenn and find out what was wrong.

He steeled himself as Mrs Murray folded her arms, her dark eyes glinting. It had hurt that Ross had been so ready to condemn him, but somehow this would be worse. He'd enjoyed the warmth of the old woman's regard last night, as he felt he'd earned her respect, but he hadn't the time or the inclination to explain himself to her or Ross, especially as that would mean exposing Gwenn as being less than respectable, whatever that really meant.

"I admit, I was ready to blame ye when the poor lassie began weeping her heart out," Mrs Murray said, and then, to his surprise, her gaze softened. "I saw the look ye gave her last night, and though my first instinct was that ye loved her something fierce, I feared ye had gone the way of yer father. I was wrong, though, and I'm sorry for it. Ye have my apology."

Sampson raised his eyebrows, a little taken aback. For a moment he said nothing, not sure what to say.

"I love her," was all he could manage. "But it's not that simple. I have the girls to think of."

Mrs Murray nodded. "Aye, she said as much."

"Did she... did she say anything else?"

"Nae." Mrs Murray smiled at him, her expression full of understanding. "I'm sorry, my lord. I only know that she believes ye have nae future together, and the knowledge is tearing at her heart."

Sampson nodded, feeling the same sensation in his own chest at her words. "Mine too," he said softly.

Mrs Murray nodded. "I thought as much, and I'm sorry for it."

"Do you know where she is?"

"In the captain's study. She said she might read a bit to settle herself down, and no one will disturb her in there today. Ross is going to take ye all out on a walk down to the river, aye?"

Sampson nodded. "Thank you, Mrs Murray."

"Ye are welcome, laddie," she said, and Sampson smiled, touched rather than irritated by her not using his title.

It had been a sign of affection and sympathy, and he took it as such.

***

Sampson hurried to the library, determined to have the truth from Gwenn and face it, whatever it might be.

Gwenn sat in a large armchair by the fire, a book in her lap. With her head resting on one hand, her legs curled beneath her, she looked ridiculously young and terribly vulnerable. She glanced up as he walked in, and his heart reacted at the emotion in her expression on seeing him. God, she was beautiful. Even though he could see she'd been crying, and her eyes were heavy with tiredness, she was perfection. A wave of longing swept over him. Desire caught him up, not only the desire to take her to his bed, but to keep her with him, to protect her and ensure her happiness, always.

He moved towards her and she smiled up at him. There was something in her gaze that he didn't recognise, something both sorrowful and determined. He didn't like it.

"Gwenn?" he said, as she set aside her book and held out her hand to him. He sat beside her, perched on the edge of the armchair.

"Did Captain Moncreiffe send you?" she asked.

Sampson snorted. "Not exactly. I was threatened with pistols at dawn if I didn't treat you with respect."

She laughed at that, a low, throaty sound that made him feel a little dazed. "I knew I liked him."

He huffed, at a loss for anything else to say, and Gwenn raised his hand to her mouth and kissed it.

"I like you too," she said, amusement in her lovely eyes. "I like you best of all."

"Gwenn," he said, helpless to say more, yet it had all been in her name, the anguish and the yearning quite audible.

She looked away from him and stared at the fire.

"Why were you crying?"

He saw a slight movement of her shoulders as she shrugged. "Because I want what I cannot have," she said simply. "It was ever thus," she added, flashing him a twisted grin.

"Don't," he said, finding it unbearable suddenly. "Don't make light of it. Not when I feel like my heart is being ripped from my chest."

Her eyes filled with tears and she stared up at him.

"Truly?"

Sampson got to his knees before her and took both of her hands, kissing first one, then the other as he tried to find the words. There were none, he realised. Perhaps if he'd been a poet or a more imaginative man, but he didn't know how to put it into words. "Truly," he repeated, hoping the sincerity of his reply would say what he could not.

He heard her let out a heavy breath before giving him a tremulous smile.

"Tell me," he said, squeezing her hands and willing her to trust him. "Tell me who you are, Gwenn. Tell me what it is you are running from."

She stared at him for a long moment.

"Is everyone going out?" she asked, as he frowned at the change of subject.

"Yes. Samuel has promised to keep the girls entertained until lunchtime at the earliest. We won't be disturbed. We have a whole morning together," he added with a smile, though his heart wanted him to tell her they had a lifetime together.

The knowledge that he could make no such claim made him feel raw, angry, and a little wild.

"Good," she said, and he thought he heard resolution in the word.

He moved back as she stood and did the same, daring to put his hands to her waist. "Gwenn, don't try to divert me. I want to know. I want to know everything. I won't let you down. Can't you trust me?"

"Yes," she said, smiling at him.

She leaned in and kissed his mouth, a tender brush of her lips over his. The sensation was like putting a match to dry tinder. He would have caught her to him, pulling her into his arms to take more, but she backed off.

Sampson stared at her, aware that she must see the hunger in his eyes.

"Not here," she said, and moved to the door.

"Wait," he said, moving after her. "Where are you going? You must tell me, Gwenn."

"I will," she said, not looking at him. "But not now. I don't want to talk now."

She turned and met his eyes, and his breath caught in his throat at what he saw in her gaze, at the reflection of his own need.

He watched as she slipped through the door and went after her, following at her heels like a puppy. Christ, in this moment he felt he'd follow her anywhere if she asked him to. The closed door muted the sounds of laughter and the chink of crockery from the breakfast parlour and no one saw them go back up the stairs. No one saw Miss Wynter open her bedroom door and go in.

No one saw him follow her.

Chapter 19

"Wherein an inescapable fate approaches."

This morning, in the aftermath of a good cry, Gwenn had made her decision. She had promised herself that she would have this much of him, as long as she was sure there was no risk of the girls finding out. She could not hurt them or Sampson in such a way, but with Samuel's promise she could feel certain they were safe for a few hours, and she would take those hours as her own. They were all she would have.

She locked the door and then turned to look at Sampson. Her emotional outburst and Mrs Murray's calm good sense had cleared her head, and she knew there was no point in dragging things out. It would only hurt them both. She would have this time with him, and she would stay for Christmas Day, to make the girls happy. Then, early the next morning, she would leave.

Mrs Murray understood and had promised to help her go with no one the wiser until she was well on her way. The woman did not know all the details, but from what Gwenn had told her she saw a hopeless love affair as clearly as anyone else could. If Gwenn stayed, she would only bring shame to herself, and to Sampson and his family, and that would do no one any good.

She'd been a fool to think she could outrun fate, but she could not regret having tried. To be loved by such a man was perhaps worth a lifetime of regret, for she could see the truth of it in his eyes. She would not have rubies but, unlike Marie, she would know that it had been real for them both.

"Ross was ready to kill me," Sampson said, breaking into her thoughts, his voice sounding loud in the quiet of her bedroom though he'd spoken softly. "He thought... he thought you carried my child."

"I'm sorry," she said, feeling her guilt weigh heavier as she saw she was already damaging him, besmirching his reputation when he wanted so badly to show the world he was not that man. "I hope you told him otherwise."

He nodded, though there was a question in his eyes and Gwenn smiled, unable to condemn him for thinking it.

"Nor anyone else's either," she said.

He let out a shaky breath.

"There's been no one," she added, needing him to know that she did not give herself lightly, without love. Not yet, at least. Perhaps not ever, though that would make her future career somewhat challenging. She must learn to separate her body from her heart, she supposed, but for now—for him—they were inextricably linked. "I've never...."

Sampson moved closer and reached out, tracing the line of her jaw with his fingertips. Gwenn closed her eyes, revelling in his touch, in the way he made her feel precious, beloved.

"I can't pretend I'm not glad," he said, his voice low. "But it wouldn't have changed anything."

She smiled up at him, knowing it was true even as she knew that it would not be for most men. In doing this, she was ruining all of Marie's carefully wrought plans, but she didn't care. This was for her. She would choose who would be her first lover, not by deciding which man had made the most generous offer, but by following her foolish heart. There would be no debt for taking her innocence—such as it was—she would give herself freely with no thought of recompense or anything beyond the fact she loved him.

After that....

Well, she would not think of what came after that.

"Gwenn, we must talk," he said, his expression grave. "About the future. I can't just… I'm not an utter bastard, darling, no matter evidence to the contrary." He took her face between his hands. "I want to be with you. I *need* to be with you. I want to know how we can make that happen. I'll do anything I can—"

Gwenn kissed him.

She couldn't listen to anymore, couldn't hear the sincerity in his voice without hoping, and there was no hope. There hadn't been from the start, and she'd known it then as she knew it now. There was so little time left, she would not waste it.

This time she employed all the seductive arts she knew. Perhaps her first kiss with him had been tentative, but that hesitation was gone now, and she intended to make this memorable. She slid her hands into his hair, pulling his head down, insisting he deepen the kiss as she pressed her body against his.

Sampson groaned, his hands falling to cup her behind, lifting her against him. She moulded herself to him, one hand moving to trail a teasing finger along his clean-shaven jaw. Drawing back, she nipped at his mouth before setting her own to the strong contour her finger had just traced. She pressed a line of delicate kisses against his skin until she reached the tender spot below his ear and kissed him there, touching him with her tongue and breathing in the heady scent of him. He filled her mind, and she catalogued every detail, needing to remember it all for the endless future when she would have only memories. He smelled clean and fresh, starched linen and soap with a hint of bergamot, and the warm musky scent of a man with a willing woman in his arms.

"Gwenn," he said, her name unsteady as she reached for his cravat and untied it with deft fingers.

She'd tie it just as precisely, too, when it was time. Another thing at which a first-class whore must be adept.

"Shh." She soothed him and kissed the corner of his mouth, dropping the cravat to the floor before pushing his coat from his broad shoulders.

"You're sure?" he asked, helping her strip the coat from him and making her smile by casting it aside without a backwards glance.

"I've always been sure," she said, reaching for his waistcoat buttons. "I just didn't want…." She hesitated, not sure of how to word it. "The girls."

He nodded, understanding her without the need to say any more.

The waistcoat went the way of his coat and she tugged his shirt free of his waistband, sliding her hands beneath and luxuriating in the warmth of his body, the undulation of powerful muscle under smooth flesh. She moved higher and found the silky skin of his nipples and toyed with finger and thumb until the tiny nubs were hard from her touch.

"Take it off," she instructed, her voice sultry as he shed the shirt with obvious enthusiasm, dragging it over his head and throwing it to the floor. Gwenn smiled and leaned in, flicking her tongue over the taut flesh she'd teased to a sensitive peak.

Sampson gave an uneven huff of laughter, and she bit down on him, not hard enough for pain, but enough to make him gasp. She looked up to find him watching her, a wary mixture of amusement and surprise in his gaze.

Gwen chuckled and reached for the buttons on his trousers as he reached for the fastening on her gown. She pushed his hands away, flashing him a wicked smile.

"Ah-ah," she taunted, shaking her head. "Ladies first."

Sampson opened his mouth to protest, but she'd found her goal and curved her hand around his erection as whatever he'd been about to say died in his throat. She watched, captivated as his eyes closed and his breathing quickened. He was hot beneath her touch, and so aroused that her hand grew slick with his desire.

He murmured a low curse and then his eyes opened, the pupils wide and dark, but the iris such a startling shade of blue in this moment, she was caught in his gaze, trapped and unable to look away.

"How you make me feel...." he rasped, capturing her face between his hands. "Oh, God, Gwenn."

He kissed her, ravenous and demanding, and she melted into it, pouring all the longing and need she felt into the touch of her mouth on his, in the hopes he would understand what she offered: not eternity, but all of now, everything she had to give condensed into this one shining moment.

Sampson reached for the fastening of her gown again and she wriggled free of him, shaking her head.

"Lay on the bed," she said, wondering if he would obey her.

She doubted he was used to being ordered about in the bedroom and suspected he wanted to balk and take control. There was curiosity in his eyes, though.

"You're very dictatorial," he said, not moving, one corner of his mouth tugging up a little.

"I am," she agreed, keeping her voice low and soft. Gwenn tilted her head to one side, staring unabashed at his almost naked body. She allowed her gaze to linger on that very male part of him for a long moment before looking him in the eyes again. "But don't worry, I can be very biddable, too... later."

There was a promise in the words, and his eyes darkened further.

"As you wish, then," he said.

Gwenn could not hide her smile of triumph, and feeling magnanimous, bent to help him remove his boots. She remained on her knees, enjoying the view as he swept his trousers and small clothes past his narrow hips and kicked his feet free of them.

He stood still, allowing her to watch him, though she was viscerally aware of the tension in him. It was like being in the presence of something wild that might pounce at any moment. Slowly, she leaned in, not looking away from him. He stared down at her, and she suspected he was holding his breath as she touched her tongue to his erection. It was barely a caress, but his cock jerked, and he gasped.

She chuckled and moved back, daring him to complain. Sampson's eyes narrowed, but he said nothing, stalking to the bed and laying down as she'd instructed.

"Such a good boy," she murmured, eliciting a snort of amusement.

"Biding my time," he said darkly, though there was laughter glittering in his eyes.

She smiled at him, a purely joyful smile at his acquiescence, at allowing her to tease him and have her own way, when it would have been easy for him to play the dominant part here.

Gwenn faced him, her heated gaze roaming his naked body. Not taking her eyes from his, she reached for the fabric of her skirts, raising the hem a little at a time, watching him track the movement. His eyes followed as she revealed her ankles, her stockinged legs, and the frivolous satin pink of her lacy garters. She paused for a moment, aware of the sharpening of his interest as she raised the hem a tiny bit farther, to reveal a glimpse of the dark gold curls at the apex of her thighs.

"More," he said, the word demanding and somewhat urgent.

Gwenn tsked. "Say please."

"Please," he said at once.

She pursed her lips, considering as she looked at him. "Touch yourself first."

His eyes widened with surprise as she quirked an eyebrow at him.

Gwenn's breath hitched as he took himself in hand, and she obligingly lifted her skirts higher, watching as he stroked himself. Gathering the voluminous skirts in one hand, she touched herself with the other and gave a soft moan of pleasure.

"Christ, Gwenn, please," he said, sounding as if he was choking the words out.

"No," she said, pure devilry thrumming through her. "Tormenting you is too much fun."

She let her skirts drop with a wicked chuckle as he gave a groan of protest. He stilled as her hands went to the fastenings of her gown, and she silently thanked providence that she'd put a front fastening dress on today.

Gwenn stripped for him slowly, drawing it out as her dress slid to the floor with a sensuous rustle of material. She continued disrobing in a leisurely yet deliberate way that she knew he was finding maddening. Finally, down to stockings and chemise, she moved closer, though not close enough for him to touch her, and cupped her own breasts, pinching her nipples until they were aching, taut and visible beneath the sheer fabric.

"Have pity, love," he said, reproach in his eyes.

Gwenn bit her lip and shrugged and, in one swift movement, tugged the chemise over her head and threw it at him. He snatched at it, never taking his eyes off her. and lifted it to his face, inhaling her scent.

"You are going to pay for this...." he growled.

"I certainly hope so," she said, batting her eyelashes at him.

He laughed, and the sound of it settled in her heart. Everything was so right with him, so easy. She moved then, knowing he was at the limit of what he would endure, and raised her leg so her foot was on the end of the mattress. Reaching for her garter, she made a show of untying it and rolling the stocking down before throwing it aside. She shifted, raised her right leg, and deliberately widened her stance, ensuring to give him a glimpse of the hidden place between her thighs.

His breathing was ragged now, and she felt the pulse of her own desire, pounding in her head and throbbing in her heated centre. In the moment between her dropping the next stocking and it hitting the floor, he lunged for her.

Gwenn shrieked as he swept her up and threw her onto the bed, holding her arms captive above her, staring down at her.

"A taste of revenge is due, you little devil," he murmured, excitement glittering in his eyes.

His sex was a burning, heavy weight between her thighs and she arched against him, sliding her own slick flesh against his. The groan that movement forced from him made her shiver with anticipation but, before she could do it again, he'd bent his head and taken one nipple into his mouth and suckled hard.

Gwenn's breath caught as the sensation tugged deep inside her, adding fuel to the heat of the insistent throb that was demanding *more* and *now*. He repeated the action upon her other breast until she was squirming beneath him.

He looked up, wickedness glinting in his eyes.

"Retribution is sweet indeed," he murmured.

"Go ahead," she sighed, arching voluptuously under his weight. "Do your worst."

A low chuckle rumbled through his chest, a smug quirk pulling at his lips.

"Oh, I will."

He did. Moving down the bed and pushing her thighs wide, he settled to the task of tormenting her aching flesh. His tongue was wicked and drove her to the brink, inching so close to a tumble into a glittering release before retreating again, leaving her clutching at the bed sheets with unfulfilled need and frustration simmering through her.

Sampson knelt back, regarding her through heavy-lidded eyes and with a deal of satisfaction.

"Oh, I feel better now," he said, amused by her glare of indignation.

She laughed then, knowing she'd earned her torment and not regretting a moment of it.

"Sampson," she said, all the teasing gone from her voice. She reached for him and he went to her at once, gathering her in his arms and kissing her. Such a kiss it was, too, an endless tangle of tongues as their bodies entwined and Sampson rocked against her until she was trembling with need.

"Please...." she begged him, arching her hips towards his.

"Gwenn," he said, his forehead against hers as the blunt head of his sex pressed against her, between her thighs and her body clamoured for him.

"Yes," she said, urging him forward and gasping with surprise as he surged into her, filling her in one smooth movement that stole her breath.

"Love?"

She let out a little huff of laughter and looked up at him, rendered speechless by sensation. It hadn't hurt, though it felt strange and not terribly comfortable. He kissed her, slowly, tenderly, and her body relaxed around his, accepting the intimate invasion without further protest.

When he moved again, her breath hitched once more, though not from discomfort. He stared down at her, such emotion in his eyes that she wished this moment might endure, captured in amber like a dragonfly to preserve it for always. Foolish of her, when she knew such pleasures were fleeting, but that look of adoration would live in her memory for as long as she lived, and would warm her heart when everything else left it cold and untouched.

She drank him in, all of it: the weight of his body, the slide of his passion-damp flesh under her palms, the sounds of pleasure torn from him, and the gentle murmur of sweet words that she wanted written on her skin so she might have them with her always.

"Gwenn," he said, her name a helpless sound of devotion as the pinnacle beckoned them on, urging them to the end of this transitory burst of happiness. "I love you."

The words sank into her, into her bones, her heart, and her soul, and she laughed, though she was breaking into pieces and would never be whole again.

"Yes," she said, needing him to hear it too. "I love you, Sampson. I do."

He held her as the climax shook her body and sent her spiralling into ecstasy and then withdrew with a tortured groan, turning his head into his arm to muffle his cries as he spent, his seed splashing hotly upon her skin.

Gwenn tried to catch her breath, to gain a hold on her emotions, but they were hurtling out of control. He'd done it to save her, fearing an unwanted child, she knew that, knew that he was taking care of her, that he always would take care of her, if she let him. Yet it broke her heart, this evidence that they had no future together.

Sampson kissed her and held her, and she clung to him, turning her head into his neck and breathing in deeply, the combined scents of heated male flesh and their lovemaking sharp and intimate. They stayed that way, clinging together, and then Sampson got up and poured water from the jug into the bowl and wet a cloth, returning to clean and dry her with such careful attention that her resolution to be brave faltered.

You're being ridiculous, she told herself, and knew it was true. Hadn't she already resigned herself to there being only this… this one time together?

As he removed the cloth she saw that there was only the faintest trace of blood, barely discernible, and wondered at the fact such a high price was put on it, that without that tiny hint of innocence the world would consider a woman ruined and worthless.

Not *her*, mind.

Yes, she had devalued herself, Marie would tell her so in no uncertain terms, but she'd been ruined at birth, the illegitimate daughter of a courtesan.

Her future was written in stone, or it may as well be.

Despite her best intentions, she burst into tears.

Chapter 20

*"Wherein a seasonal celebration marks the closing of the year…
and of a love affair."*

Sampson smiled, watching his sisters' enthusiasm as they decorated the castle. Everywhere the clean scent of pine and rosemary permeated the air, along with the spicy perfumes of Christmas treats that emanated from the kitchen. They'd returned to the house at midday, rosy-cheeked and happy, sitting on a cart loaded with huge pine boughs, holly, ivy, and laurel.

Aunt May, Freddie, and Gwenn had set to, ordering everyone about and making garlands to decorates mantles, windows, and every available surface. They decorated them with apples, clove-studded oranges, red ribbons, pinecones, and Christmas roses, and made a kissing bough, too, with evergreen and mistletoe. Ross had been quick to steal a kiss from his wife and Sampson had fought a burst of jealousy. It was so easy for them to be together, especially here in the wilds of the Scottish Highlands. Why could he and Gwenn not love each other so openly and with no shame? Bitterness rose inside of him and he forced it down, determined not to spoil the pleasure of watching his family enjoying themselves.

He looked at Gwenn, who had thrown herself into the celebrations with enthusiasm. A little too much enthusiasm perhaps, he thought, an uneasy feeling in his heart. There was a touch of desperation to her happiness, a sense of someone grasping for every drop of joy that could be wrung from the day.

Sampson remembered that morning and his chest ached with longing for her, to have that with her again. Making love to her had changed something in him. He couldn't say exactly what, only that

215

he felt he'd gained some deeper understanding of what it meant to love someone. He knew now, and with clarity, the difference between lust and infatuation, and the kind of love that endured for a lifetime.

He remembered too, the devastation of her tears, the way she'd clung to him. She'd lied to him then. At first, he'd feared she regretted giving herself to him, but it wasn't that. She'd told him she was emotional because she was so happy to be with him, and that wasn't a lie, but it wasn't the only reason for her tears. Sampson wasn't a fool. He knew she feared the future as he did, but she knew the reasons that would keep them apart, he did not. Was it so bad? What kind of scandal was she embroiled in that she was so scared of it touching him and his family?

Although he'd not wanted to, she'd made him promise not to speak of the future until after Christmas. She didn't wish to think of it now, or for the troubles that awaited them to take the joy from this happy time. Though he was frustrated to keep living in ignorance when he wanted to face their problems head on, he'd not had the heart to insist. Gwenn had promised he would know everything as soon as Christmas Day was over. She would reveal the whole story to him. So, it was only one more day. He could give her that time and, if he could not be open in his feelings for her, at least he could enjoy having her near. He could share his family's happiness with her at their first proper Christmas together, out from under the shadow of their father, at last.

***

Christmas Day was a raucous affair and Gwenn was glad of it. The girls were thoroughly over excited and the castle rang with the sound of laughter and chatter as presents were opened and silly games played. By the time dinner was served, everyone was starving and ready to be impressed by everything Mrs Murray had achieved. Ross had employed some girls from the village to help her as it was to be such a lavish dinner, and she'd made full use of them. The table groaned under the weight of food and everyone exclaimed with delight as they saw the treat set before them.

A roasted boar's head with an apple in its mouth was the centre piece of the magnificent spread. Gwenn declined that particular delicacy, but there was also a roast goose, roast beef, a huge brawn, and a raised pie so heavy Digby looked strained as he carried it to the table. It was stuffed with every variety of fowl and game you could think to name, and obviously a source of great pride to Mrs Murray. There were also dozens of side dishes, roast potatoes and vegetables and mince pies, and Mrs Murray insisted that everyone try everything on offer.

Gwenn sat down with relief after participating in a particularly energetic game of blind man's buff. The mulled wine had gone to her head somewhat, and she felt rather giddy, so she followed the example everyone else set and filled her belly until she felt she would burst. Sampson sat on her right and, though she did her best not to let it show, she was terribly aware of him. He would touch her whenever he could, just a brush of his fingers against hers as he passed her a plate but enough to send awareness and longing thrumming beneath her skin.

It was lovely, if surprising, to find Mrs Murray and Digby eating with them at the table, with Digby's wife, Maggie, also in attendance. As Ross had told them on arriving at the castle, they were very informal, and Gwenn smiled at the affectionate banter between him and Mrs Murray. She was clearly a motherly figure and, despite the way she teased him, she also saw that Ross got the best of everything and stuffed him as if he was being fattened for next Christmas.

"Ach, no more," he protested as she tried to persuade him to a third helping of Christmas pudding. "I'll burst, and that'll nae be pretty."

Everyone laughed, and he got to his feet and raised his glass. "I propose a toast to Mrs Murray, the finest cook to be found anywhere in Scotland. Despite fearing the sharp side of her tongue, she's the heart of this castle, and we'd all go to the devil without her. God bless ye and keep ye, Mrs Murray, for all our sakes."

Everyone cheered and raised their glasses as Mrs Murray blushed and dabbed at her eyes and scolded everyone for being so daft, though her pleasure in his words was obvious enough.

Once everyone had settled again, they looked back to Ross who had clearly not finished. "I'll not keep blethering on long," he promised, ignoring Samuel's heckling from the far end of the table with dignity. "But... I would like to say how glad I am to see you all here. Some of us are blood kin, and some of us are not, but we are all family."

Gwenn felt her eyes prickle with tears, touched by his words, knowing he knew well of her affair with Sampson, but knowing too that this family would never be hers.

"People say ye cannae choose yer kin, but I disagree. Perhaps there are those we'd rather not have a tie to, but there are also those we can bring into our lives and keep close. So, to all my kin, blood or nae, I wish ye all a very merry Christmas, and that the coming year brings ye happiness, health and all the blessings ye deserve. *Slàinte mhath!*"

Beneath the table Sampson sought her hand and held it in his grasp, firm and reassuring, a promise to her that he would make things right. It took everything she had not to cry then, but to smile and release Sampson's hand to raise a glass and toast the good fortunes of the family's future. That, at least, she could do. She wished them joy and prosperity, good health and good fortune, and everything they deserved. There was a part of her that knew she should wish that Sampson could fall in love with a respectable woman, that he could marry and have a family... but she wasn't strong or selfless enough for that.

Perhaps one day, but not yet.

"Merry Christmas."

Gwenn turned to see Sampson smiling at her, too much emotion in his expression. She looked away from him before glancing about the table to see if anyone else had noticed, but everyone seemed to be chattering and occupied.

"Merry Christmas to you," she replied softly, not looking at him.

"Gwenn."

She turned then and found herself caught in eyes as blue as a summer sky. *I love you*, they said, without him ever speaking a word. Gwenn stared back, hoping he could read the truth of her heart in her own expression, knowing this day was their last. He didn't know they'd shared their last kiss, did not know that when she bade the family goodnight, it would be the last time he saw her. It was best he did not know, for she did, and her heart was breaking.

***

It was late before they could persuade Susan and Selina that the day was truly over, though they were both dropping with exhaustion, their eyes open only through sheer determination. Gwenn went into their room to wish them a good night and sat on the edge of the bed they shared.

"What a marvellous day," she said, smiling at the two sleepy faces looking owlishly back at her.

"Oh, it was," Susan said, nodding.

"Marvellous," Selina agreed.

They looked at each other and grinned. "The best Christmas ever," they said in unison.

Gwenn laughed as Susan reached out and took her hand. "But every Christmas will be like this now, for we shall all come back every year. How lovely it is to have Ross and Freddie and Mrs Murray and Digby, and especially you, Miss Wynter."

"Oh." Gwenn gave a hiccoughing laugh, struggling not to weep as she realised how upset they would be tomorrow when they discovered she was gone.

"Well, I'm sure it will be just as wonderful whether or not I am here," she said, striving for levity, but the girls both sat up and stared at her, shaking their heads.

"Oh, no," Selina said, her expression grave. "That's not true. Everything is better since you came. Even Sampson is happier, and he's always so worried about everything."

"About us," Susan said, nodding.

Abruptly and before she could lose what remained of her composure, Gwenn leaned toward them and pulled them both into a hug.

"You are, without a doubt, the most wonderful, beautiful, clever girls that ever lived," she said, her voice increasingly thick. "And don't you ever believe otherwise. I… I am… most terribly fond of you." She kissed each golden head in turn before giving them a dazzling smile as she fought to keep her tears at bay. "Now, go to sleep, for I expect the captain has more to entertain you with tomorrow, so you mustn't sleep the day away."

This idea seemed to win them over, and they settled down as Gwenn tucked them in.

"Goodnight," she said, taking one last look at them. "God bless."

Somehow, she made it out of the room without dissolving into tears. Though she knew she ought to return downstairs, she couldn't face it. Longing to see Sampson again was a grave temptation, but she was too raw, too close to tears, and he would notice and demand she explain. No, she must end this little idyll, and do it now, before she discovered she was too weak willed to make the break.

Digby nodded a greeting as he passed her in the corridor on his way downstairs and she waylaid him.

"Please send my apologies, but I won't go back down. All this enjoying myself has worn me out."

"Of course, Miss Wynter," he said, his smile warm. "I'll make sure they know you have retired for the evening. Good night, miss."

"Goodnight, Mr Digby."

She watched him go before going to her own room and shutting the door behind her. Gwenn leaned against it and closed her eyes. Well, that was that, then. Sampson would not seek her out. He had been as shaken by their near discovery as she had been and, though he'd said he'd get Samuel to give them some more time together, he would not risk coming to her room. She would not see him again this night, or any other night.

She wept as she gathered her things and packed them away. The girls had made her a present each for Christmas, sweet little paintings of her and the two of them together with Sampson. Beside them stood a huge snowman with a beaming coal black smile. Gwenn packed the paintings with care, careful not to crease the paper, not allowing herself a moment to study the charming scene and everything it implied, lest her resolve falter.

Sleep didn't come, not that she'd expected it to, and it was still dark when Mrs Murray gave a light tap on the door.

Together they carried her luggage down to the front door, to where a burly Scot with a thick beard and an impenetrable accent awaited her with a pony and cart.

"This is Angus," Mrs Murray said. "He'll take good care of ye and see ye to the mail coach. Ye can trust him, lass, he'll see ye safe away."

"Thank you, Angus," Gwenn said, trying to find a smile for him.

The man nodded and snatched his cap from his head, muttering something Gwenn didn't understand.

"His niece is at Fort William," Mrs Murray said, translating for her. "She'll attend ye on the journey as far as Carlisle, where she'll visit her auntie. Ye will swear to me ye'll find another to travel in her place, Miss Wynter, or I'll raise every soul in this castle afore I let ye go."

Gwenn smiled, touched by the woman's concern.

"I promise I shall, and I shall take care of myself. I'm not a green girl, you know."

She smiled, but was unable to keep the sadness from her voice at the truth of that statement. If only she had been, how different her life might be.

Mrs Murray gave a taut nod. "This is for the journey," she said, thrusting a heavy basket at her which Angus took and put in the cart. "There's some of my pie, and bread and cheese, and... and some things to keep the cold out."

Mrs Murray's voice quavered, and Gwenn burst into tears, throwing herself into the woman's embrace.

"Oh, lassie, I'm so sorry."

"Me too," Gwenn said, wiping her face to no avail as the tears came thick and fast. "But I won't bring shame on them. I couldn't bear it, and... and there's no other way."

"Are ye quite sure...." Mrs Murray began. "Is it really so bad?"

"Yes," Gwenn said simply. "It really is. Take care, Mrs Murray and please, would you see that everyone gets these?" She handed the little bundle of letters into the woman's keeping, letters she'd written in the lonely hours of the night whilst everyone slept.

"I will lass. Will ye write me an' assure me ye are safe an' well when ye get home?"

Gwenn nodded, too overcome to speak, and gave the woman one final embrace before climbing into the cart.

"Thank you, for everything," she managed, her voice thick with tears.

Mrs Murray raised a hand as the pony began to move. "*Gabh mo leisgeul,* Miss Wynter."

Turning in her seat, Gwenn returned the gesture, staring back at the shrinking figure and the vast castle at her back, until they turned a corner and Mrs Murray was no longer visible.

Chapter 21

"Wherein… the truth."

Sampson pushed his empty plate away, surprised at how much he'd eaten. After last night's feast he'd been certain he'd not face another bite for days, but he'd woken ravenously hungry. Everyone was up late this morning, however, and only the twins had kept him company whilst he ate. They'd gone off to find Freddie, who'd promised them a game of cards, and Sampson had the breakfast parlour to himself. He'd called in on Samuel before he came down, who'd cursed him roundly and told him to go to the devil. Before he'd left his brother in peace, Sampson had extracted a promise that he'd entertain the twins this afternoon for a couple of hours, and he was eager to tell Gwenn. It was snowing again and being outside was not as appealing as it had been on Christmas Eve, so Sam would keep the girls occupied indoors and give him and Gwenn some private time together.

Today, he would discover what it was she was hiding from him and, as much as he dreaded it, he wanted to learn the truth. Once Sampson knew what he was fighting, he could think of possible ways to get around or lessen any scandal. He was a wealthy man, after all, and money was a powerful motivator. Surely there would be something he could do.

He wondered if Gwenn was up yet. Mrs Murray had said she had woken with a headache and was having a lie in, but that had been ages ago. Sampson hoped she wasn't sickening for something. Though he'd told her she didn't have to act the part every moment of the day, she was scrupulous in her work as governess and never left the girls to another's care unless Sampson insisted. It was unlike her to leave them for others to attend to. He decided to ask Mrs Murray to take her up a cup of tea and see how she was faring.

As he passed Ross's library on the way to the kitchen, he heard an almighty row coming from inside. From the sounds of things, Mrs Murray and Ross were at odds, and Sampson jumped in surprise as the door flew open and Ross stalked out with a face like thunder.

"Interfering old buzzard...." he muttered under his breath until he saw Sampson and stopped in his tracks. "Sampson."

"Ross," Sampson replied, amused. "Good morning."

There was something in his brother's eyes, something that made foreboding prickle down his spine. "I'm afraid it is nae that, *mo bhràthair*," he said, his expression sombre. "I was just coming to find ye. Ye had best come in. Mrs Murray has something to say."

Ross's words and the bleak expression he wore set Sampson's heart to pounding in his chest, and he was breathless by the time he faced Mrs Murray and saw the stark white of her complexion.

"What is it?" he asked. "My God, is it Gwenn? Is she ill?"

The woman twisted her apron between her hands and shook her head, but her eyes were filled with tears. "Nae, my lord. 'Tis nothing like that. The lass is well."

"Then what?" he demanded, looking between her and Ross.

His brother looked away from him and went the decanter on his desk, busying himself with pouring out two glasses.

"What?" Sampson said again, wanting to shake the woman.

"Miss Wynter... she asked me to give ye these," she said, reaching into the apron pocket and handing him a small bundle of letters. "There's one for yerself, and another for the girls, and one for their auntie."

Sampson stared down at the letters in confusion. Why was Gwenn writing him letters when she could speak to him?

"I don't understand," he said, hearing the panic rising in his voice as a terrible suspicion grew in his mind.

"She's gone, laddie," Mrs Murray's voice trembled, and a tear rolled down her cheek. She swiped it away and stood a little taller, raising her chin. "She told me that... that she had to go, that if she stayed she would hurt ye and yer kin, and bring shame upon yer family and herself, and that she could nae bear to do."

Sampson couldn't move, couldn't speak. He stared stupidly down at the letters, his heart thudding too hard and too fast, his brain so stupefied he couldn't think.

"When?" was all he managed.

"Hours ago," Ross said, holding out a glass to him. "And the snow's coming down thick and fast. I'll willingly take ye to Fort William, but I fear ye'll nae get much further."

"Perhaps she's stuck too?" he said, hope rising in his chest at the idea.

"It's possible," his brother said, nodding.

"I need to leave. Now."

Ross downed his drink with a grimace. "I'll ready the horses." He moved to the door but paused, putting a heavy hand on Sampson's shoulder and squeezing. "I'll help ye however I may, brother. I know what it is to see the one ye love slip from yer grasp."

Sampson nodded, praying that he could catch up with Gwenn as Ross had caught up with Freddie.

"Perhaps ye had best read the letter first, my lord."

Sampson turned to stare at Mrs Murray, wanting to hate her for helping Gwenn run from him, but he saw the misery in her eyes and knew she'd done what she'd thought best. Yet why hadn't they trusted him?

"Why?" he said, his voice rough. "Why did you—?"

"Because she needed a friend, and she needed to return to her kin," Mrs Murray said, the words sure, though her eyes were full of tears. "I could nae tell her not to go. She told me plain that to marry her would be to ruin those sisters of yours, and she'd not live with that on her conscience, and she knew ye could nae either. She wanted to save ye the heartbreak of telling her so." Mrs Murray nodded at the letters. "She said it was all in there, and that you would understand, once ye had read it."

Sampson stared at the letters, his hands trembling.

He looked up as Mrs Murray reached up and touched her weathered fingers to his cheek.

"It fair breaks my heart to hurt ye so with this news, but I could nae refuse her. Forgive me."

She went out, closing the door behind her. Sampson set aside the letters for his sisters and his aunt, unable to even consider how he would tell the girls that Gwenn had gone.

He broke the seal and took a breath before unfolding the paper. The writing was smudged in places and his throat closed as he imagined her distress when she'd written it.

My darling,

Please forgive me for leaving you in such a cowardly manner, but I could not bear to look you in the eye and see your opinion of me change when I told you my story. I could not take the risk, either, that your heart is even greater than I supposed, and that you would forgive me, for I might never then find the strength to leave you. You will see now, though, how impossible it is.

My name is not Gwendoline Wynter but Guinevere de Wynn. My mother is Marie de Wynn. Yes, the very same, the most scandalous and infamous of courtesans. I am the illegitimate daughter of the Marquess of Davenport. No doubt you have heard the tale of the Davenport rubies. My mother wears them with pride.

I think perhaps you have also heard of her daughter, Guinevere, who is destined to be the greatest whore who ever lived. She is soon to make her come out, and the richest and most powerful men of the ton have been invited to bid for her. I have often wondered if you received such an invitation, for I do not remember your name on that list. I suspect that you declined, and that alone tells me I am right to do as I have.

Marie has raised me to excel at my occupation. Any innocence has long since vanquished from my mind, even as my body remained untouched lest I devalued myself. When I foisted myself upon you under the guise of governess it was with the intention of running away, of finding another life, another way of living, and instead... I found you.

I regret nothing that has passed between us. No matter what you may think of me now, please know that my heart was honest and loved you in its entirety.

I shall <u>always</u> love you, Sampson.

I love you and your beautiful sisters too well to hurt you any more than I must. I hope they can forgive me for deserting them but tell them what you must. I beg that you will find a governess who will be kind to them and remind them every day how special they are. You will never know how much I long for it to be me, but I discover that I cannot outrun fate. I care little for the future in this moment, nor for what happens to me now. I only know that I understand what it is to love and be loved, and that there will never be another.

Goodbye my darling. Please find it in your heart to forgive me and know that you will always be in mine.

Yours,

Gwenn.

Chapter 22

"Wherein life goes on."

London. 3rd April 1821.

Sampson looked up from his desk as his butler, Brent knocked and came in.

"Captain Moncreiffe to see you, my lord."

"Ross!" he exclaimed, moving to greet his brother. "This is a surprise."

The two men embraced as Brent withdrew and closed the door behind him.

Ross studied him, holding him at arm's length, his scrutiny unnerving. Sampson moved away, avoiding his gaze, knowing what he would see only too well. He'd faced it in the mirror every morning for more than three months.

"Ye look bloody awful," Ross said, earning himself a huff of laughter.

"Thank you," Sampson said, moving to pour them a drink. "I must ask you to drop in more often lest my ego run away with me."

"It's nae funny," Ross growled, scowling at the drinks Sampson carried as he handed one to him. "Is that yer first of the day, for I doubt it. Ye've lost weight," he added, his tone accusing.

"For God's sake, Ross, you're not my bloody mother," Sampson snapped, though he knew it was all true enough. He drank too much and slept too little. Not that he cared. The only thing that kept him from falling utterly to pieces was his sisters.

They'd already endured a vile father; he'd not be the brother that let them down. Well, not yet, at any rate.

"Nae, but someone needs to take ye in hand, and it may as well be me. I'm yer big brother, remember."

Sampson stared at him, as an uncomfortable suspicion formed in his mind. "Why are you here?"

"I just told ye," Ross growled. "Yer brothers and yer aunt and even those wee girls have written to me more than once over these past months, worrit to death about ye, but the last letter was more than I could bear from a distance. So, now ye are bloody stuck with me."

He stared at Ross, torn between surprise at how much the gesture touched him—that Ross would come all this way on his account—and intense irritation that his family had been bothering the man behind his back.

"Ye have heard the news, then?"

Sampson gave him a dark look. "Of course I've heard the bloody news."

"Aye," Ross replied, unsurprised. "Then what are ye goin' to do about it?"

Well, wasn't that the question.

"None of your business."

"Ach, but I intend to make it my business. It may have escaped yer notice, but ye are the head of this family now, and ye had best make a better job of it than yer father did, or ye will have me to answer to."

"He was your father too," Sampson shot back, downing his drink and slamming the empty glass down. He glowered at Ross and reached for his glass, filling it again.

"So, I'll ask again. What are ye going to do?"

Sampson stared at the huge Scot, who seemed to take up more than his fair share of the study. His face was hard and implacable, his stance one of a determined mountain range, but there was warmth and a depth of sympathy in his eyes that made Sampson's throat tight. He shook his head and sat down by the fire, staring into the flames.

His mind wandered back to that morning so many months ago, the morning Gwenn had run from him. Ross had been as good as his word and they'd made it to Fort William despite the dreadful conditions. It had been a damned hard journey and all for nothing. By the time he'd gotten there, Gwenn was long gone, having escaped before the weather closed in and the roads became impassable. Sampson had followed her as soon as he could, but he'd never caught up with her.

By the time he reached London and discovered where the infamous Marie de Wynn lived, it was only to be told that the family had left England. He'd tried bribery and intimidation, but no one would tell him where the lovely de Wynns had gone. Now, though, everyone knew that they were returning. The scandal sheets were full of the news, and extraordinary bets filled the book at White's where the favourite for winning the prize was the Duke of Sherringham. For Guinevere de Wynn was returning to London from wherever she had hidden herself and would finally make her long awaited debut.

Over his dead body.

"Ye intend to run with her, don't ye?"

Sampson's head snapped up in shock, to see Ross's shrewd green eyes studying him. His heart thudded in his chest and he knew Ross had figured it out. How, he didn't know, but though they'd known each other such a short time, his brother seemed to always know what was in his mind.

"I cannae take all the credit," Ross said, his expression wry. "It was Samuel who first suspected. He was curious as to why ye were spending so much time on getting the family's affairs in order this past month when ye had neglected everything for weeks after she ran from ye. It seemed obvious enough to me what ye had planned."

"If we leave, if we disappear, the scandal will die down, and by the time the girls come out we'll have been forgotten."

There was a snort of derision. "I doubt that, and in the meantime those girls will break their hearts over the loss of ye."

Sampson put his head in his hands. He was being torn in two and the pain was unbearable, but he could not see Gwenn forced into a life that would destroy her, and it *would* destroy her. He knew her, knew her heart and all that it longed for. Such a life would break her spirit in no time at all. Even if he could find a way to live without her—which after the past months seemed doubtful—he could not live with that.

"What would you do?" Sampson asked, his voice bleak. "What would you do if it were Freddie?"

Ross nodded. "I ken well that I'd kill any man whose name was on that godforsaken list, but I would nae abandon my family."

"Christ!" Sampson exploded, surging to his feet. "You think I do this without a second thought? You think it isn't tearing me apart to even consider leaving...."

His voice broke as he remembered Susan and Selina's devastation in the days after Gwenn had left and the uncannily silent journey back to London. They'd clung to him, unwilling to let him out of their sight, as if they'd known his heart was more damaged than their own, and feared to leave him alone.

Sampson walked to his desk and leaned upon it, struggling to keep his composure when he wanted to scream and rage and weep and destroy everything he could lay his hands on. For a short time he'd seen the world in the brightest colours, he'd seen the possibility of everything life could be with the woman he loved beside him, and now all he could see was an endless swathe of grey.

"Nae," Ross said, getting to his feet. "I dinnae think that nor anything of the sort." He laid a heavy hand on the back of Sampson's neck. "But I think ye are too broken to see what is before ye, and I intend to set ye straight, for ye cannae leave those girls, Sampson. They've lost one father and, whether ye like it or nae, ye have taken his place. If ye leave, I fear what it'll do to them."

"They'll have Sam, and Sherbourne and Solomon, it's not as if they'll be alone," he said, though his heart was filled with guilt, shame, and sorrow, and he couldn't bear the idea of not being here with them, to see them grow and keep them from harm himself.

"It's yerself they look to, Sampson, and I ken how it feels to be abandoned. I'll nae let ye do it, *mo bhràthair*."

Sampson spun around, knocking Ross's hand away. "Then what?" he raged. "What would you have me do, for I cannot... I cannot...." To his horror, his throat closed, and tears spilled from his eyes and he turned away and put his head in his hands.

"Ye have forgotten something important, brother," Ross said, his voice low and sure. "Ye have a family around ye. I dinnae ken what that meant for a long time, but I now I do, and I mean to teach ye for ye have forgot. Ye also have friends. I saw that myself the night I came here to face the evil bastard that sired us, may he rot in hell."

Sampson rubbed a hand over his face and steadied himself, turning to face Ross. "And so...?" he demanded, hoping to God Ross had something worthwhile to say, for if he was getting his hopes up for nothing, he'd bloody kill him.

Before he could answer, the door burst open and Susan and Selina came through at a run, launching themselves at Ross.

"Ross!" they cried in unison as the big man scooped them up, one in each massive arm, beaming at them and kissing their cheeks as they threw their skinny little arms about his neck and hugged him.

"Ach, well I never did see such bonnie wee lasses in my life," he said, hugging them until they squealed. "What a grand welcome, and worth every minute of the wretched journey just for that."

"Have you come to make Sampson happy again?" Susan asked, such hope in her eyes that Sampson wanted to bawl.

"Will you help him get Miss Wynter back?" Susan added breathlessly.

Sampson's heart twisted in his chest. Though he'd tried his best, he knew the house had been smothered in gloom since they returned, as if Gwenn's absence had stolen some vital part of the world and the sun no longer deigned to shine upon them. That the girls had felt it so keenly though, that tore at his soul... and that they knew the reason for his misery was even worse.

"I have," Ross said, his tone decisive. "And I will."

"Ross!" Sampson snapped, too shocked and furious to hide his anger. "You have no right to say such things, to make promises that you can't possibly keep."

"Oh, ye think I cannae?" Ross said, something steely in his eyes. "Ye forget who ye talk to, does he nae, my beauties?" he said to the girls.

"He thinks people won't speak to us if he marries Miss Wynter," Susan said, shocking Sampson to his bones as she summed up the situation to a nicety.

Where in God's name had she heard that?

"But that's stupid," Selina chimed in. "Because we don't want to speak to the people who wouldn't like us if he married her."

"Aye," Ross said, nodding at them as though that was the wisest thing anyone had ever said. "Quite right, too."

"Susan, Selina." Sampson took a deep breath, trying to explain without making them too unhappy, but he must not allow them to hope. "You are too young to understand, and Ross too pig-headed to accept it, but one day you will want to marry, and if such a scandal is attached to our name——"

"It will scare off all the stupid men we wouldn't like to marry anyway," Susan said, looking at him as if he was daft. She clung tighter to Ross, her blue eyes glittering and angry now. "Anyone who can't see that Miss Wynter is the most perfect lady is utterly stupid."

"Yes," Susan said, in perfect accord with her twin. "Guts for brains, leather-headed lobcocks, cod's heads——"

"Susan!" Sampson exclaimed, shocked and startled by both her outburst and her vocabulary.

"That was very good," Ross said, looking impressed. "Will ye teach me some more later? I liked 'leather-headed lobcock,' very descriptive."

The girl giggled and nodded, and Sampson threw up his hands. "Madness," he muttered, moving to fix himself another drink.

"Leave that glass be," Ross growled, a threatening note to his voice. "The girls have given ye some very sound advice, and I am about to give ye a deal more, and then, we are going to go and call on some friends."

Unwilling to cause a scene before the girls, Sampson put the glass down—for now—and contented himself with glowering at his brother. "What friends?" he demanded, wondering what the hell Ross had in mind, and not allowing himself to dare hope it had a chance in hell of succeeding.

Ross kissed each of the girls on the forehead and set them down, telling them to run along and leave everything to him. They did, having implicit belief in Ross's ability to make everything all right. Sampson stared at his brother, some childish corner of his heart wanting to believe the same thing.

"What friends?" he said again, once the door had closed and the girls were out of earshot.

Ross grinned at him and winked. "Dangerous ones, aye?"

Chapter 23

"Wherein dangerous friends make useful allies."

Alexander Sinclair, the Earl of Falmouth, regarded them from behind his massive desk, his face impassive. Sampson fought the urge to fidget. He felt like he used to when hauled before the masters at school, usually in the moments before being sent down.

Alex steepled his fingers, considering, and Sampson wondered at his cool demeanour. If anyone had just made such an outrageous suggestion to him, he'd be throwing a fit.

"Just so we are clear," Alex said, his grey eyes moving between Sampson and Ross, the two of them sitting side by side as they awaited his reply. "You wish to know if either myself or my son-in-law have any hold over the Marquess of Davenport?"

"Aye," Ross said, leaning forward in his seat.

Sampson was glad Ross answered as his own tongue was tied in a knot, too terrified to form words. Whether that was because he feared Alex was about to throw them out of the house or agree to a plan which could probably see them all hauled up before a judge with God knew what charges against them, he wasn't sure.

"And if we do, you wish for us to use whatever influence we may have on him to—"

"Aye," Ross said again, clearly impatient as he waved a hand at Alex. "Ye have understood just fine, my lord. The question is, have ye, and will ye?"

Sampson glared at his brother for treating Alex in such a cavalier fashion. It was true that Alex had been a good friend to Sampson in the past. It was also true that his reputation was the kind that suggested it was a bad idea to upset him. A *very* bad idea.

Sampson noted the first threads of grey in the thick black of the earl's hair, though there was no question that the fellow was still in the prime of life. Those wicked grey eyes glinted, a slight curve twitching the corner of a mouth that appeared cruel and implacable.

"We have," Alex said, satisfaction in the words. "And yes, I rather think we will."

Sampson let out a breath he'd not realised he'd been holding.

"Did you doubt me?" Alex regarded him, a mild look of reproach settling upon Sampson. "You know well enough that I have promised to support you and your family in the past."

"Yes," Sampson agreed, knowing it was true, but acknowledging a friendship instead of cutting someone in the street was not the same as this... this *outrageous* plan, if one could even call it that? Treasonous, perhaps? Insane, certainly. "But... but this—"

"This is exactly the kind of scheme that will make my wife think me a heroic figure who will do anything in his power to ensure love triumphs over all obstacles," Alex said with a wry smile. "Believe me when I tell you my motives are entirely selfish."

Sampson laughed, knowing—as all the *ton* knew—that the terrifying Earl of Falmouth was besotted, enamoured with, and utterly devoted to his wife, a beautiful French *émigrée* many years his junior.

"And Black Rule?" Ross asked. "What of him?"

Sampson waited Alex's answer with interest. Luther Blackehart, or Black Rule, had been crowned Lord of London's underworld years ago. There were rumours that he'd become respectable in the time since he'd married Alex's daughter, but no one would say that to his face. The man was universally believed to be ruthless, dangerous, and best avoided.

Alex chuckled. "Believe it or not, my son-in-law is a pussy cat. He'll agree. For one thing, neither of us are much enamoured of the marquess. Davenport is a weak man who treats those he ought to care for with contempt. He never makes provision for his illegitimate children, the callous bastard." The earl's face darkened. "His wife was a good woman, a kind soul who died too young. She deserved a great deal better than he ever gave her, as do his children, *all* his children. I think I shall very much enjoy calling in his debts."

He sat back in his chair and met Sampson's eye. "So, Guinevere de Wynn. Is she as beautiful and mysterious as the rumours suggest?"

"More beautiful," Sampson said softly. "But not the least bit mysterious. Not to me, at least. Her heart is an open book. She wants security and love and a family around her, not...."

He waved his hand, unwilling to put the life Gwenn was resigning herself to into words.

Alex nodded, his smile warm. "Well, then. We had best call on Luther. There are plans to be made."

***

Gwenn stared at herself in the looking glass as Marie fussed around her, tweaking a lock of hair here, tugging at her neckline to expose a little more of her décolletage. She said nothing, allowing Marie to do as she would. She didn't much care. When she had returned to London—once the flames of Marie's fury had died away—her mother had been swift to act. She had packed up her household with the efficiency of a wartime general and taken her daughter to Italy. There she had hidden Gwenn from the world and allowed her the time to grieve for her broken heart.

This much, at least, her mother had understood, and she would not let her daughter ruin her chances by exposing her to scrutiny before she was ready.

It was impossible to hide from her fate forever, though. During those days, hidden away in a tiny village in a beautiful valley, she had stared at the lovely scenery and wept until she had no tears left, and little by little she had ceased to be herself. As she mourned the loss of everything she'd never really had, she set her heart to one side and learned to wear the mask of the perfect courtesan, just as her mother had taught her. She had become a commodity, something to be bought and sold.

Marie stood back, regarding her daughter with a critical air. "I almost hate to admit it, but I think you are more beautiful than I ever was."

"Surely not, Mama," Gwenn said, smiling a little. "I find that hard to believe."

Marie gave a low laugh and moved to her daughter, taking hold of her hands. "It's true." She stared at Gwenn, warmth and sympathy in her eyes. "Strangely enough, I think it is the sorrow in your eyes that adds to your allure. There is an air of fragility, of something that needs protecting that the men will find irresistible. I was so angry with you when you returned. Such a foolish, foolish thing to have done, but now... I cannot help believe that this doomed love affair will not affect your price at all."

"I'm so relieved you are not disappointed," Gwenn said, the words brittle.

Marie gave a bitter laugh, shaking her head. "I know you think me a cold bitch, Gwennie," she said, her voice low and sad. "But I would have saved you this heartache. I did try," she added. "The world is far crueller and colder than I, my girl, and we must all do what we can to survive. Women have little power, and that which we do have must be stolen and snatched at. That pretty face will only endure so long, my love, as I can attest to." Marie sighed with regret and Gwenn knew it was her moment to ensure Marie that her looks were not fading, but she could not find it in her heart to soothe her mother's ego tonight.

Marie laughed again, amused now, no doubt aware of the petty turn of her thoughts.

"Come, my beautiful daughter. The wealthiest and most powerful men of the *ton* await you, and you may take your pick from them. I think you'd do well to choose Sherringham. He's known for being a generous lover and he's a good man at heart, not one you need fear would ever abuse you, but it will be your decision. I will not interfere in this. Only, think carefully before you decide."

Gwenn nodded, too numb to speak. She felt sick. The urge to run, to flee, was rising in her chest. It had all seemed so inevitable when she'd left Sampson. The life she'd been bred for was all she knew, and if she could not have him... well, what did it matter? Yet, it did matter. It mattered a great deal. How could she give herself to another man, a man she didn't even know yet, let alone care for—after everything she had shared with Sampson?

A sob rose in her throat and she forced it down. It was too late. There was no escape.

"There will be an hour for the men to put in their offers," Marie continued, unaware of the turmoil in her daughter's breast. "That will give them a chance to view you and realise just what a prize there is to win, as well as note their competitors. Then I will select the best ten for you to make your choice from. You will announce your choice at midnight."

Gwenn nodded again. Her chest was tight, and she could not breathe. What would Sampson think of her, if he could see her now?

Don't think of it, she told herself, fighting for calm. *He's lost to you, they are all lost to you. What other talents do you possess, who would employ you? Who would you lie to next? You cannot starve on the streets, nor become a burden to Marie.*

You must do this.

"Are you ready?" Marie asked her.

You have no choice.

Where will you run to?

Who would you go to?

Who else would you taint with the burden of your name?

"Yes, Mama," she said, turning away from the mirror, from the image of the greatest whore that the great city would ever see. "I'm ready."

***

Sampson glanced at the unhappy figure beside him. Luther Blackehart was the only man he'd ever met who could match Ross for breadth and height. A veritable mountain of a man, he possessed an innate quality of power that sent other men scattering before him. Although—like Sampson and every other man here— he was in impeccable evening dress, he was not a gentleman, and no one would ever mistake him for one. The ragged scar that marred the right side of his face suggested this was not a man who was a stranger to violence. It would be correct. He was a survivor of the worst that London and poverty could throw at a man.

He was also in a bad mood.

"Thank you for this," Sampson said, aware of the fellow's unease at being here.

Blackehart grunted.

"I am in your debt."

He turned then, black eyes glinting against a dark complexion that attested to his gypsy heritage.

"You are," the man agreed. "My wife was not pleased that my name was on that bloody list."

Sampson cleared his throat. "I doubt they wanted to risk offending one of the most powerful men in London," he said, trying not to dwell on his own fears for the evening and concentrate on his companion's troubles. It might settle his nerves and take his mind of what he was about to do. Unlikely, but it was worth a try.

"I know *why* my name was on the bloody list," Blackehart growled.

"Right," Sampson nodded and decided he may as well shut up.

His guts were roiling now as he imagined everything that he was about to expose himself to. If this went wrong, he'd be a laughingstock and everything he'd tried to save the girls from would be nothing compared to the scandal he'd create.

What if she'd changed her mind? They'd known each other such a short time, what if it had been an infatuation? What if….

"It will be all right."

Sampson looked around, startled to discover Blackehart had addressed him, and more so by the sympathy in his eyes.

"Will it?" he asked, unnerved to find his voice rather less forceful than it ought to be. Sampson cleared his throat and looked away. A heavy hand rested on his shoulder for a moment.

"You love her," he said, as if that made everything clear. "You will make it all right, for her."

Sampson met the man's dark gaze again, read the understanding in his eyes. "Yes," he said, his voice sure now, certain. Gwenn loved him, and he loved her. He would make it all right. With a little help from some dangerous friends. A smile curved over his mouth. "Thank you," he said, meaning it.

"You're welcome," Blackehart said. "But you still owe me."

Sampson laughed, but the sound died in his throat as a hush settled over the assembled company. Marie de Wynn's lavish home was filled with men, and a glamorous selection of less than respectable women, but now every one of them turned their heads to look up at the grand staircase that descended in an elegant sweep to the magnificent entrance hall they'd been waiting in.

Marie de Wynn made her entrance then, clad in red satin, the infamous Davenport rubies sparkling at her ears, throat, and wrist. Unlike Gwenn, her mother was dark, luxurious thick mahogany curls tumbling carelessly to her shoulders, pinned here and there with ruby combs. Nonetheless, Sampson could see the likeness in the elegant line of her jaw, in her lush curves, and something in the way she carried herself... like a queen.

The woman did not prevaricate; she knew well how to command attention.

"Ladies and gentleman," she said, her voice rich and earthy, the sensual tones of a woman at ease in her own body, with her own power. "I present my daughter, Guinevere de Wynn."

Sampson's heart leapt to his throat as a slender figure moved forward. Her golden hair glimmered in the warm glow of hundreds of candles and she was dressed in a simple if provocatively low-cut ivory satin gown. A single row of pearls encircled her elegant neck. She was indeed lovely, but her astonishing beauty was marred for him as he saw that the light of laughter and love—and the vivacity of her spirit, for which he'd fallen so hard—had dimmed. He watched, transfixed, as she paused at the top of the stairs, and at once he recognised the haunted quality of her gaze, the terror. Every protective instinct rushed to the fore as her chest rose and fell too fast, staring about the room, eyes wide like some wild creature backed into a corner with nowhere to run.

"Beautiful," said a masculine voice, full of admiration from somewhere to Sampson's left.

"Stunning."

"Magnificent."

"Incomparable."

The murmurs of interest and approval rang through the gathering and Sampson wanted to kill every one of them for daring to think what they were undoubtedly thinking.

He couldn't breathe, his gaze fixed on the woman he loved, and he wondered if he alone saw the little shove her mother gave her, to force her down the steps.

Damn Marie de Wynn.

This had to end. *Now.*

He moved forward, shoving men aside left, right, and centre as he elbowed and pushed his way through, oblivious to the curses and indignant shouts as he made his way to Gwenn.

She was almost at the bottom of the stairs when she saw him, the look of dazed terror morphing to one of mingled delight and horror.

"No," she said, her voice faint. "Oh, no."

For a moment, he thought she would faint, but she held tight to the rail of the bannister, frozen with shock.

"Lord Cheam," Marie said, moving to stand beside her daughter. She did not look pleased. "I did not expect to see you here."

"No doubt," Sampson said, not looking at Marie, never taking his eyes from the woman who held his future in her hands. "But here I am, and here I will stay, with Gwenn."

"No, Sampson," Gwenn said, her eyes filling with tears. "No, you must not. Think of the girls! You cannot do this to them."

"I cannot condemn the girls to live a life with a brother who is dead inside. I cannot give them such a poor example to follow, either. A man must fight for what he loves, he must do everything in his power to protect those he cares for—all of them. I should not want them to choose a man who would do any less for them than I would do for you."

"Very pretty, my lord," Marie snapped, taking hold of Gwenn's arm, her intention clear as the murmurs of interest rose about them. "But that is all it is, pretty words. A woman cannot live on them."

"Marry me, Gwenn."

Everyone stilled, falling silent as Sampson's voice rang out across the room, strong and sure of itself.

"W-What?" Gwenn was staring at him, looking at him as if he'd run mad, when in truth it was the first time he'd felt sane since the moment he'd heard the news that she'd run from him.

"Marry me, Guinevere de Wynn," he said, his voice softer now. "I love you, and I cannot go on without you beside me. Besides which, the girls miss you desperately. They begged me to make sure I brought you home. I promised them I would. Don't make me break that promise."

"O-Oh, Sampson," she said, shaking her head, tears sliding down her cheeks now. "T-That's n-not fair."

"I know," he said, grinning at her. "I'm not intending to play fair. In fact, I'm prepared to play very dirty indeed, as your father has recently discovered."

Both Marie and Gwenn were staring at him now.

"M-My father?" Gwenn stammered.

"Everything will be all right, darling." He stared at her and held out his hand. "I won't let anyone or anything ever hurt you, or Susan and Selina. This is the right thing to do. I will make it all right—with a little help. Trust me, love, *please.* Let me prove it to you."

Gwenn stared at his hand and Sampson held his breath.

Marie tugged at her daughter's arm. "He'll break your heart," she said urgently, her eyes glittering with tears as she encouraged her daughter to turn away from him.

Sampson watched as Gwenn looked up at her mother and touched a hand to her cheek.

"No," she said gently. "He won't."

Marie stared at her daughter and made a sound of distress and then pulled her into her arms, giving her a fierce hug. "Go, then," she said, her words a mixture of anger and hope. "Go and find what I could not." With that, she turned away from Gwenn and faced the crowd. "A little change of plans, gentleman." Clapping her hands, she gestured for a pair of liveried footmen to open the grand doors to the ballroom. "Let us see what other entertainments can be found this evening."

Like an empress, Marie swept through the crowd as they followed in her wake, eyes turning back as they left, lingering to stare at Gwenn, many of them clearly angry and muttering unhappily.

Sampson paused as the Duke of Sherringham caught his eye. The man lifted a glass of champagne in a silent salutation, a wry smile at his lips, before following Marie to the ballroom.

He turned back to find Gwenn staring at him and, once again, held out his hand to her.

"Come home, love, it's been so bloody awful without you."

Gwenn did not take his hand. Instead, she threw herself into his arms, and Sampson spun her around, laughing even though his throat was closing, and his vision seemed strangely blurry. He held her to him, tight enough that she would know he would never let her go.

"Are you sure, Sampson?" she said, looking up at him, her beautiful eyes still full of concern, concern for him and the girls. "I couldn't bear it if—"

"If you don't marry me now, I shall look a fool," Sampson pointed out. "There's no getting out of it, I made very certain of that."

"Yes, but how...?"

He stopped her question by the very effective method of pressing his mouth to hers. She melted into him, kissing him back with a passionate desperation that told him she'd been every bit as wretched as he since the moment they parted. At last he let her go, putting distance between them and clasping her hand firmly in his.

"Let's go home and see the girls. They'll be beside themselves if they wait much longer."

Gwenn nodded, staring at him with undisguised adoration. "Yes, please, Sampson... take me home."

Epilogue

"Wherein gossip runs amok."

19th May 1821. St George's, Hanover Square, London.

Sampson turned and looked down the aisle.

Gwenn was walking towards him, a smile on her face that made his heart sing and his breath catch in his throat. Behind her, Selina and Susan skipped along together, heads held high, beaming with pride and very grown up in the lovely gowns that Gwenn had chosen for them. Such pretty girls, with their blonde ringlets bouncing, and so happy.

Sampson blinked hard. He was, without a doubt, the luckiest man alive.

***

It was the wedding of the season.

Sampson knew it had astonished everyone when the Marquess of Davenport had officially recognised his illegitimate daughter. He had done so in the full view of the *ton*, escorting her to the theatre and musicales, and to several balls, before finally walking her down the aisle on the day she married Viscount Cheam.

Of course, no one else knew that the marquess was privately outraged, but too terrified to look anything but enchanted that his estranged daughter was reconciled to him. A late-night visit to the marquess from Black Rule and the Earl of Falmouth seemed to have concentrated the man's mind with quite startling effect. They had clarified that his daughter *would* be welcomed with open arms, or not only would the marquess's impressive debts be called in at

once, but that stories—and proof—of some of his more scandalous
peccadilloes would find their way to the biggest gossips in town,
not to mention the press. The underlying message that the two men
would also be *very* displeased if he did not comply may also have
contributed to his eagerness to help.

A dirty tactic, but an efficient one.

What had surprised even Sampson was the guest list to their
wedding. Something Falmouth had insisted on overseeing. It
seemed the earl had powerful friends, and at least half the *ton* were
in his debt or owed him favours. The Duke of Ware and his best
friend, the Duke of Sindalton, were both in attendance with their
families, as was the usually reclusive Marquess of Winterbourne.

To Sampson's astonishment Viscount DeMorte, a man he had
never met in his life, and with a reputation every bit as dark as
Sampson's father, had also attended. Alex had just smiled and
reassured him that DeMorte was as much a victim of gossip as
anyone, and not to judge a book by its cover.

Sampson had remained a little sceptical until he'd seen the
look of adoration the man had cast the delicate blonde on his arm.
It seemed Lady DeMorte was responsible for taming a man with
one of the worst reputations in the *ton*.

The illustrious names kept coming, and the *ton* were agog with
the romantic story of how Sampson had saved the lovely Miss de
Wynn from her fate. That the gossip was sympathetic rather than
judgmental was further proof of Blackehart's and Falmouth's
influence.

Of course, Alex had attended too, with his vivacious wife on
his arm, and his aunt, Lady Seymour Russell at his side. The old
woman shared Alex's sharp grey eyes and had a tongue that
matched. Few people ever dared contradict her. Blackehart had
refused the invitation, however, certain that his presence would do
no good whatsoever, and content to retreat to the wilds of
Dartmoor where he had made his home. He had, however, sent his

best wishes and a generous gift, along with an invitation for Sampson and his wife and sisters to visit them in the near future.

Sampson's family were there too, naturally, his brothers overflowing with good cheer and a great deal of aggravating taunting, which Sampson bore stoically enough, and his Aunt May, sobbing into a lace edged hanky and looking pleased as punch.

So, with the acceptance of some of the most powerful families of the *ton*, any scandal that might have rocked the establishment to its foundations was squashed to a mere whisper. Oh, people would still talk, but not openly, and no one dared to cut a woman whose husband had such formidable and daunting friends.

***

"My word, what a marvellous day!" Susan exclaimed, flopping down into a seat in a flurry of silken skirts.

"The best day *ever*," Selina confirmed, doing a little twirl in the middle of the room to send her own skirts fluttering about her legs.

Sampson put his arms about Gwenn and tugged her closer, nuzzling her neck. "Hmmm, not certain it's the best day ever… *yet*," he murmured, nipping at her ear as she squealed and laughed.

"Not in front of the girls," she scolded him, though happiness shone in her eyes.

Sampson made a show of huffing and moving away from her, though his arm stayed tight about her waist. He looked about his home, to the private parlour where the family had retreated now the wedding breakfast was over and only they remained. Solomon and Sherbourne had collapsed in a heap, too stuffed with food and wine to move. Aunt May was dozing, her soft snores barely audible over Susan and Selina's excited chatter. In the main reception rooms, servants bustled back and forth, tidying away evidence of the lavish meal they'd given, but here, peace reigned. Well, as much peace as Selina and Susan ever allowed, but he rather liked it that way.

Sampson cast Gwenn a look which must have spoken volumes, as she blushed and looked away. He was eager to have her to himself now, to escape up to their bedroom, and leave everyone else to their own amusements... but how to extricate himself without the twins asking where they were going?

Sampson sighed, considering how best to manage it as he caught Samuel watching him with glee. It was clear his brother well knew of his predicament. He watched as Sam elbowed Ross, who was standing beside him with Freddie on his arm. Sam then whispered something that made the big man give a wicked chuckle as he glanced at Sampson. Sampson watched, wondering how his brothers planned to torment him further with trepidation.

"Ach, 'tis a pitiful sight," Ross lamented, giving a mournful shake of his head as he regarded Sampson. "We'd best put the poor bas—" Ross choked as Freddie stamped on his toe.

"Children present," she muttered, glaring at him.

"We'd best put the poor fellow out of his misery," Ross amended, giving Freddie a rueful smile.

"Oh, not yet," Freddie said, tugging at his arm. "You must give them Mrs Murray's gift."

"Oh, aye," Ross said, smacking his head with his palm. "Thank God ye reminded me. I'd have been in a deal of trouble had I forgot. I think I'm too big to fear her tanning my hide these days, but I'd rather not risk it."

Freddie chuckled as Ross rushed out of the room and returned a few moments later with a small gift, wrapped up in soft paper with a pretty yellow ribbon.

"Here ye go," Ross said, putting it in Gwenn's hand. "Mrs Murray bade me tell ye how very happy she was, and to tell ye she'll be most offended if ye do not return for Christmas this year."

Sampson smiled as Gwenn's throat worked, aware she was holding back tears. "We wouldn't miss it for the world," she said, before reaching up on tiptoes and pressing a kiss to Ross's cheek. "Would you give that to her for me, please?"

"Aye, that I will," Ross said, looking pleased. "Now, open it up. We have to give her a detailed description of your expression when ye see it."

Gwenn laughed and tugged at the ribbon, and then made a soft sound of wonder as she saw the tiny knitted bonnet and booties. Sampson's own throat felt a little tight as he saw the longing in her eyes as she touched a finger to the delicate items.

"She seemed to think these would come in useful soon enough," Ross said, winking at his new sister-in-law as Freddie elbowed him.

"Ross!" she exclaimed, laughing. "You'll make the poor girl want to disown us."

"Ach," he said, smiling fondly at his wife. "There's no need to be jealous. Mrs Murray knitted ours ages ago."

A look passed between the two of them that Sampson suspected meant there would be news from that quarter soon. He smiled with a deep sense of contentment at knowing this family was not only going to survive, they would thrive now and grow stronger together.

"Mrs Murray also asked that ye forgive her," Ross said, looking to Sampson. "She's broken her heart these past months and I know the guilt weighs her down."

Sampson smiled and tugged his wife a little closer. "You may tell her there is nothing to forgive, and I shall look forward to seeing her at Christmas."

Ross nodded, pleased, and then he gave a soft laugh. "Ah, well, I suppose I'd best put ye out of ye misery, ye poor devil." He turned then and regarded the twins. "Right then, lasses. I'm growing bored here, have ye no games to entertain me with?"

The two girls stared at him in stunned amazement, being well aware that grown-ups seldom volunteered for such things after a busy day.

"Yes!" they shrieked in unison, before running off, likely to fetch every game they could lay their hands on.

"Away with ye, then," Ross said, winking at them. "Ye had best not disappoint Mrs Murray. She's expecting those wee knitted booties to be filled nine months from now."

"If not sooner," Samuel murmured under his breath so only Sampson could hear.

Sampson did not need asking twice. He tugged at Gwenn's hand, pulling her in his wake as he ran up the stairs. She laughed as she hurried after him, still clutching Mrs Murray's gift in one hand. Ushering her into the part of the house that held his private rooms, he closed the door and locked it behind him.

"There's no escape now, Lady Cheam," he said, grinning at her.

"Thank goodness," Gwenn said, staring at him with such happiness in her eyes he felt quite dazzled by it. "I never want to be parted from you again. Nor the girls," she added.

"I can't help but wonder if you didn't marry me for my sisters," he said with a rueful smile.

Gwenn smiled and moved closer to him. "I do adore those girls," she said, her voice soft. "But I have to admit that you have a certain appeal, too."

Sampson chuckled and took the tiny knitted garments from her hand, staring down at them and imagining her round with his child. The image pleased him more than he could credit. He wanted that. "A big family?" he asked her, knowing what the answer would be.

"Yes, please," she said, her voice a little breathless now. "A big noisy, chaotic family, full of love and laughter."

He set the items down on his dresser and turned around to smile at her. "Poor Mrs Wilson will have her hands full."

"I like Mrs Wilson," Gwenn said, sliding her arms about his neck.

Sampson nodded. "You can thank Mrs Murray for finding her."

In the days after Gwenn had left and Sampson had followed her back to London, Mrs Murray had sought out a governess. Mrs Wilson was a no-nonsense Scottish lady, a widow who had raised two sons and a daughter. She was also warm and kind and had been immediately taken with her two charges. Susan and Selina had resisted her at first, too distressed by Gwenn's departure to take to another governess, but now it was clear there was a strong bond between them, and the girls were happy.

The girls were happy.

The knowledge settled in Sampson's chest, and any last shred of anxiety he'd held onto these past weeks faded away. The girls would be fine, better than fine with Gwenn to guide them. They also had him and the rest of the family to protect them and keep them safe, not to mention some surprising friends. Blackehart, rather to Sampson's astonishment, had turned out to be a devoted family man, and had taken to the twins at once. Naturally, they adored him. Any young man with less than honourable intentions towards those girls in the future would think twice and run in the other direction. The idea made him smile.

"You're happy," Gwenn said, stroking his cheek.

Sampson nodded. "Happier than I ever dreamed, than I ever realised was even possible."

"I know," Gwenn said, laying her head on his chest. "I feel the same way."

"It was good of your mother to miss the wedding."

Gwenn's smile was rueful. "She said watching my triumph from afar was gift enough and that she'd never been prouder. I think that's the nicest thing she's ever said to me."

"We'll not cut her out of the family, Gwenn," Sampson said. "I won't stop you seeing her or visiting."

"Thank you." The smile she gave warmed him to his toes. "I would not like to lose her. She's not an easy woman, but... well, I love her all the same. Anyway, I believe Alvermarle has bought her diamonds to soften the blow of having a married daughter, so she's happy."

Sampson laughed. "And what should I buy my lovely wife to make her happy?"

Gwenn sighed and touched a finger to his lips. "The only thing I want right now is this wicked tongue."

She tugged at his neck and Sampson went willingly, desire rolling through him like a heated wave as their mouths met and her tongue sought his. He kissed her, slow and languid and deep, before drawing back.

"Where else do you want my tongue?" he asked, already breathless with wanting.

She let him go and turned away, sauntering to the bed, perching on the edge of the mattress. Sampson watched as she kicked off first one shoe, then the next.

"Hmmm," she said, a low sultry sound that made his cock twitch with anticipation. "You may kiss my foot."

Gwenn extended one dainty foot and beckoned him with a crooked finger. He went to her, of course, and got to his knees before her, sliding his hands over her silk clad leg before bending his head to press his mouth to her instep.

"And here?" he asked, kissing her ankle.

"No, not there," she said, so he moved his attention to the inside of her knee.

"Here?"

"No."

Sampson watched as she gathered her skirts and raised them higher, parting her legs. His mouth went dry. Slowly, he leaned in and kissed her inner thigh, the scent of her teasing his senses, lily of the valley and the feminine heat of her need for him.

"Here?" he asked, his voice rough.

"No," she said again, though she was breathless now.

Spreading her legs wide, he looked up at her before sliding his tongue through the soft curls at the apex of her thighs to touch tiny bud hidden beneath. He drew back.

"Here?"

"Yes. Oh, yes."

She lay back on the bed, holding her skirts out of his way, and Sampson gave a low chuckle of pleasure at her obvious desire.

"Your wish is my command, Lady Cheam," he murmured, more than happy to settle to his task. He teased and tormented her, bringing her to the edge of what she could bear, until she was clutching at the bedsheets, her body bowed before leaving her suspended at the moment before she climaxed.

"Sampson!" she exclaimed, her voice tight with frustration.

"Wait for me, love," he said, pressing a kiss to her thigh before standing and undressing himself. She sat up with a huff to watch him disrobe and he grinned at her, quite unrepentant. "You're wearing too many clothes," he observed, once he was naked.

A shiver ran over him as her heated gaze took him in, lingering on his cock, hard and aroused. She slid from the bed and turned so he could unhook her dress, and he worked as quickly as his eager fingers could manage, throwing the beautiful gown to one side and discarding stays and petticoats with speed until only her stockings remained.

He sighed as she leaned back against him, the lovely swell of her bottom cradling his sex as he reached around and cupped her breasts, squeezing and pinching her nipples until she moaned her pleasure.

"So beautiful," he murmured. "And all mine."

She laughed then, a breathless sound of pure happiness. "All yours. Always."

Sampson carried her to the bed and made love to her, taking his time to show her everything he felt, until his wife could be in no doubt that she was loved and adored, and would be cherished, always.

Much later, when the house was sleeping and skies beyond the windows dark and starlit, they lay together, sated and sleepy.

"Where did you go?" he asked her.

She understood at once, though they had never spoken of it before.

"Italy," she said, toying with the hair on his chest. "Tuscany. A tiny village in the hills. It was extraordinarily beautiful. Not that I could appreciate it. I was too unhappy."

Sampson turned on his side to look at her and took her fingers, kissing each one in turn. "We'll go back there, and you can show us all and make it a place of happier memories. I don't want you to think of such a lovely place with sorrow, Gwenn. You will never be unhappy again."

She smiled at that and touched her hand to his face. "I think life sends everyone challenges, and it is not within our power or our right to be happy all the time, but I do know I will never be alone again, and we will face any troubles that come our way together. I know, as the girls know, that you will always be with me, that you will always be there for me."

"That I *can* promise," he said, staring into her lovely turquoise eyes and seeing a beautiful future stretching out before them in the sparkle they contained.

"Then that is all I desire," she said with a soft sigh.

"*All* you desire?" he repeated, a devilish note lingering in the words.

"Oh, well...." A naughty smile curved over her lush mouth and she leaned in to nip his lower lip. "Perhaps not *quite* all."

Sampson gave a low chuckle of delight and turned her onto her back, eager to discover just what it was his delicious wife desired next.

Don't miss Samuel's story... coming soon!

Characters Referenced from Other Books

If you missed *The Earl of Falmouth*, *Black Rule* or *Ross Moncreiffe's* story, you'll find them in the **Rogues and Gentlemen Series**, details below…

Alex Sinclair, The Earl of Falmouth:
Book 2 – ***The Earl's Temptation.***

Luther Blackehart (Black Rule):
Book 14 – ***The Blackest of Hearts.***

Captain Ross Moncreiffe:
Book 16 – ***The Scent of Scandal.***

Turn the pages for links to these books and more!

Girls Who Dare– The exciting new series from Emma V Leech, the multi-award-winning, Amazon Top 10 romance writer behind the Rogues & Gentlemen series.

Inside every wallflower is the beating heart of a lioness, a passionate individual willing to risk all for their dream, if only they can find the courage to begin. When these overlooked girls make a pact to change their lives, anything can happen.

Ten girls – Ten dares in a hat. Who will dare to risk it all?

To Dare a Duke

Girls Who Dare Book 1

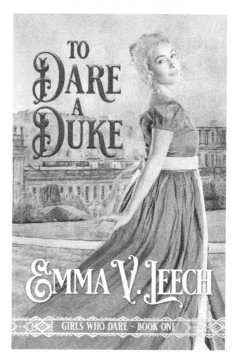

Dreams of true love and happy ever afters

Dreams of love are all well and good, but all Prunella Chuffington-Smythe wants is to publish her novel. Marriage at the price of her independence is something she will not consider. Having tasted success writing under a false name in The Lady's Weekly Review, her alter ego is attaining notoriety and fame and Prue rather likes it.

A Duty that must be endured

Robert Adolphus, The Duke of Bedwin, is in no hurry to marry, he's done it once and repeating that disaster is the last thing he desires. Yet, an heir is a necessary evil for a duke and one he cannot shirk. A dark reputation precedes him though, his first wife may have died young, but the scandals the beautiful, vivacious and spiteful creature supplied the ton have not. A wife must be found. A wife who is neither beautiful or vivacious but sweet and dull, and certain to stay out of trouble.

Dared to do something drastic

The sudden interest of a certain dastardly duke is as bewildering as it is unwelcome. She'll not throw her ambitions aside to marry a scoundrel just as her plans for self-sufficiency and freedom are coming to fruition. Surely showing the man she's not actually the meek little wallflower he is looking for should be enough to put paid to his intentions? When Prue is dared by her friends to do something drastic, it seems the perfect opportunity to kill two birds.

However, Prue cannot help being intrigued by the rogue who has inspired so many of her romances. Ordinarily, he plays the part of handsome rake, set on destroying her plucky heroine. But is he really the villain of the piece this time, or could he be the hero?

Finding out will be dangerous, but it just might inspire her greatest story yet.

For a sneak peek of Emma's exciting new series, turn the page!

Members of the Peculiar Ladies' Book Club

Prunella Chuffington-Smythe – first Peculiar Lady and secretly Miss Terry, author of The Dark History of a Damned Duke.

Alice Dowding - too shy to speak to anyone in public and often too small to be noticed.

Lucia de Feria - a beauty. A foreigner.

Ruth Stone - heiress and daughter of a wealthy merchant.

Matilda Hunt –blonde and lovely, and ruined in a scandal that was none of her making.

Bonnie Campbell - too outspoken and forever in a scrape.

Jemima Fernside - pretty and penniless.

Kitty Connolly - quiet and watchful, until she isn't.

Harriet Stanhope – serious, studious, intelligent. Prim. Wearer of spectacles.

Chapter 1

My dear Alice,

The fateful day of departure is approaching like a dark cloud on the horizon, blowing lace and frills and inanity in our direction. Are you as miserable as I at the prospect? Oh, Lord, how will I tolerate it? Thank heavens for you and the girls. We <u>will</u> endure and survive another season. The ton will not crush us. We will overcome! Together.

—Excerpt of a letter from Miss Prunella Chuffington-Smythe to Miss Alice Dowding.

***

1ˢᵗ April. Otford, Kent. 1814

The duke crossed the ballroom, tall and handsome, dark, wicked eyes flashing fury as everyone around held their breath...

Prue stared down at her inky fingers, her brow furrowing. There was something lacking, something.... She tapped the end of her quill against her chin, her lips pursed.

Ah, yes.

The duke ~~crossed~~ prowled the ballroom, tall and handsome, dark, wicked eyes flashing fury as everyone around held their breath...

She smiled, pleased by the addition. A depraved, cold-hearted man like her duke would certainly prowl. It recalled night creatures stalking their prey, teeth bared for the kill. The frisson that ran over her at the idea was pleasing, her readers would surely agree.

Prue jolted as a sharp rapping upon her bedroom door forced the wicked duke from her mind and dragged her back to reality.

"Prue! Mama wants to know if you're getting ready." Her cousin Minerva's sharp tone concealed none of her irritation at being sent to fetch Prue. No doubt she'd been preparing for this evening since the moment she got out of bed this morning.

Damnation.

"Er... yes," Prue replied, lying through her teeth. She glanced up, realising with a sinking heart that the skies had darkened into evening and she'd not even noticed.

"Well, you'd better be. We leave in fifteen minutes."

Prue cursed a bit more and hurried to put her writing away. A loose floorboard in her room had proven a useful hidey-hole for things she needed to keep private and away from Minerva's prying eyes. The young woman did not enjoy Prunella's company and found a good deal of enjoyment in causing her aggravation. Prue endured Minerva's presence with the fortitude of one who had no option, but did not hold her tongue as often as she ought. In her less prudent moments, the two of them fought like cat and dog.

With a great deal of haste and very little skill, Prue dragged a comb through her hair and pinned it up in a style more haphazard than fashionable, before attempting to wrestle herself into her dress. She looked around as their maid of all works hurried through the door and rolled her eyes.

"I knew it," the woman muttered, tsking and setting herself to fastening the back of the dress.

Prue sighed and gave the woman a fond smile over her shoulder. "Thank you, Sally. I don't know what I'd do without you."

"You'd cop a deal more nagging from Mrs Butler than you already do, as if you ain't got enough to be going on with," Sally replied tartly as she shook her head over the state of Prue's coiffure. "She'll not like that, I can tell you."

"Oh, what does it matter?" Prue replied with a shrug. "The worse I look, the more her lovely Minerva can shine."

Sally pulled a face. Prue snorted before leaning in to give the older lady a fond kiss on the cheek. She was a ruddy faced woman, of generous proportions and an equally warm heart, and she had quickly become Prue's saviour. Sally was an ally in the battle for her sanity.

Prue looked around the room for her gloves and cursed under her breath. She seemed to have a problem with gloves; they were never where she thought she'd left them. The maid sighed.

"I found them on the path by the front gate; lucky for you I washed them. They're downstairs in the hallway."

Prue bit her lip and tried to look contrite for her sins. She knew she failed. "You're an angel. You know that, don't you?"

With a roll of her eyes, Sally ushered her out the door.

"Have a nice quiet evening without us, Sally," Prue said as she headed for the stairs, adding in an undertone: "You have no idea how much I envy you."

"Oh, aye? You can polish the silver then, miss. I'll leave it out for you."

Prue gave a snort of laughter, knowing Sally wouldn't believe her if she protested it was better than the evening ahead of her, even if Prue really thought it was.

At least the rout party was being held by Charles Adolphus, Baron Fitzwalter, who lived at the 'big house' and held a position of authority and respect. The old man was a good sort and not like the stuffy busybodies that seemed to populate the rest of their tiny village. So, it was possible there would be some interesting conversation, if she could wrest him away from the other guests. For reasons best known to himself, the baron seemed fond of her despite her awkwardness in social situations and her utter disinterest in improving said awkwardness, as her aunt constantly pleaded for her to do.

The sooner Aunt Phyllis gave up on the idea she would marry and stop being a burden to them all, the better. Not that Prue *was* a burden. Her contribution to their household made a significant difference to her widowed aunt and Phyllis' only daughter Minerva, who both lived perilously close to the edge of shabby genteel respectability. Aunt Phyllis was not in fact her aunt at all, but her deceased mother's cousin, though *Aunt* Phyllis always seemed easier than explaining the ins and outs of their relationship to others.

Prue had every intention of getting out from under Aunt Phyllis' roof as soon as she could, but marrying to do it was not a feature in her plans. Far from it. Prue intended to be an independent female, and she was well on her way to being just that. If her aunt had the slightest suspicion of her scandalous plans, and—even worse—how she intended to do it, she'd likely suffer an apoplexy.

"Oh, there you are," the woman herself said, emerging from the parlour amidst an aggressive cloud of violet perfume. "Honestly, Prunella. Is it too much to ask that you are ready to leave at the appointed hour? I chaperone you to these events out of the goodness of my heart, when I have my own daughter's future to think of. A more ungrateful creature would be hard to find."

As that was entirely true, Prue opened her mouth to say something to soothe her relation's ruffled feathers and instead gave a violent sneeze.

Phyllis' mouth compressed into a thin line and her faded blue eyes widened in despair as Prue's hand rose to cover her mouth and nose.

"Look at the state of your hands!" she exclaimed. "What have you been doing, and where are your gloves?"

Prue blanched and hurried to cover up her inky fingers.

"I'm not even going to comment on the state of your hair," Aunt Phyllis said with a disapproving sniff, though she then contradicted this statement by doing just that for the next several minutes, and in detail, as they walked to the grandest house in the village.

It was a handsome red brick building, as solid and impressive as the baron himself, who was also a touch on the florid side. He was still a large man, despite his advancing years, and he greeted her aunt and Minerva with gracious attentiveness, though Prue was aware he couldn't stand them. Her aunt's ingratiating ways irked him, and he believed Minerva was no better than she ought to be.

It was one reason they got on so well.

"Ah, and Miss Chuffington-Smythe," the baron said, turning to Prue with a wide grin. "How are you? Recovered from your recent bout of ill-health, I hope?"

The old man's eyes twinkled with conspiratorial glee, as if he'd guessed that she had been telling fibs. She sent him a look, half glare, half amusement that he'd figured her out. It was true: Prue had sworn off a recent dinner party, claiming to be laid low with a dreadful megrim. Prue had never suffered a megrim in all her life, but they were a handy excuse when the next social event on the calendar struck her as being unendurable, or the next chapter in her novel could not wait.

"Quite recovered, thank you," she said, giving him a sweet smile.

"And how is your nephew, *the duke*, my lord?" her aunt demanded, with such a proprietary air that any casual observer might suppose she was well acquainted with the man himself. The baron, perfectly used to such tactics, replied with little more than a twitch of his lips, unnoticed by any but Prue.

"His grace is in fine fettle, last I heard, Madam. I thank you for the gracious enquiry." He turned back to Prue, holding out his arm. "Miss Chuffington-Smythe, I wonder if I might borrow you? I have recently acquired a wonderful copy of Claudius Aelianus' *Variae Historiae*. It's an intriguing collection of excerpts and anecdotes of a moralising nature, and I should like your opinion. I know what a love of books you have and feel certain you will appreciate the quality of the binding."

Prue stared at him, attempting to keep a straight face.

"Indeed, my lord," she said, her tone even lest her amusement become apparent. "I should be pleased to see it."

"I'm not sure it's at all the thing for a young lady to take an interest in dusty old books, my lord," Aunt Phyllis said, before the baron could usher Prue away to the library which had been set up as a card room for the evening's entertainments. "I mean, my Minerva has never read a book in her life and look at her."

Prue choked as Baron Fitzwalter eyed the pretty blonde at her aunt's side. Minerva looked up at him with what Prue guessed was supposed to be a sweetly shy expression from under her lashes. To Prue's eye she looked like her shoes were pinching her, but then she knew Minerva too well to be fooled.

"Er, yes... indeed," said the baron, a noncommittal answer that Aunt Phyllis seemed to take as one of approval.

"There, you see, Prunella? Even his lordship does not approve."

Prue fashioned her expression somewhere between a smile and a grimace and decided it best to keep her mouth shut. Occasionally she thought before she spoke. Rarely enough, but still.

"If you would excuse us, Mrs Butler, Miss Butler."

She gave a sigh of relief as the baron bore her away.

"Claudius Aelianus?" she queried, looking up at her companion.

He gave an unrepentant shrug. "It was all I could think of. My dear, how do you stand it? It's beyond anything. You know we really must get you suitably married."

Prue gave an impatient tut and shook her head. "Please, my lord, do not begin on this hopeless path once again. My aunt is really very kind, and her vulgarity stems only from a desire to see myself and Minerva well established. As for marriage, you know very well I have neither fortune nor beauty, nor any talent for housekeeping, added to which I have no interest whatsoever in becoming any man's chattel." She laughed at the heavy sigh the baron gave at that comment and turned to him with an impatient tone, as they'd discussed this many times before. "Being added to a list of belongings, my person subsumed by the rights of my husband? No, I thank you. I shall guard the keys to my destiny like Cerberus guards the gates of hell."

The baron looked down at her with an indulgent eye. "A rather violent metaphor, don't you think?"

For a moment Prue allowed her thoughts to drift back to her childhood, and the spectre of a man who ought to have been her and her mother's protector. "Yes, it is. I think it rather apt."

She felt the old man's gaze upon her and avoided it.

"Now then, what's the gossip?" Prue asked, turning the subject and forcing away the ghosts of the past, preparing instead to enjoy a comfortable chat with her most favourite source of news and intrigue.

Once they had turned over every aspect of life in the village and beyond to their satisfaction, the baron wandered off to mingle with his guests. Prue found a book she had not read—the baron had given her free run of his library some time ago—and settled down in a quiet corner. She had barely read the first line when a voice hailed her.

"Prunella?"

Prue looked up, startled to have been called with such obvious enthusiasm.

"Oh, it *is* you!"

A young woman hurried towards her. A slender and delicate redhead, she was as fragile and petite as a porcelain shepherdess.

"Alice!" Prue exclaimed, and jumped to her feet in such a hurry her book almost tumbled to the floor. She caught it before it hit the rug at her feet and then straightened to find Alice laughing at her.

"I might have known I'd find you skulking in the corner with a book in hand," she said, grinning with such affection it was clear there was no criticism in her words.

"I was *not* skulking," Prue retorted with a sniff. "I was just...."

She trailed off as Alice arched one elegant red-gold eyebrow. "Oh, well, yes. I was skulking, but honestly Alice, what else is there to do?"

"Avoid my mother?" the young woman suggested with a twinkle in her eyes.

Prue snorted and took her friend's arm. "Oh, that goes without saying, but tell me, why are you here? I didn't know you were coming."

"Nor did I," Alice replied as Prue put the book down and they set off on a walk about the grand house. "My uncle lives at Dunton Green and his wife has taken ill. Mama brought me to help her with the children for a few days until she's feeling better. It was all very last minute, so I didn't have time to write and tell you."

"But, if that's the case, why are you here tonight?"

Alice rolled her eyes, giving a despairing shake of her head. "My mother has made such a song and dance to my uncle about the difficulty of getting me suitably married that he took pity on her. I'm here with friends of the family. They have a son...." She grimaced.

"Oh, lord," Prue said, with heartfelt sympathy. "Is he ghastly?"

"Buck teeth, bad breath, *and* a stutter," Alice said on a sigh. "I mean, really, I do try not to be too fussy but—"

"But?"

"But there's something about him, Prue," Alice said, lowering her voice. "He ... he's very attentive but he makes me feel—" Alice shuddered, and Prue grasped her hand.

"What?"

"He frightens me a little."

"Good heavens, Alice," Prue exclaimed, turning to stare at her in horror. "There's fussy and there's ..." It was her turn to run out of words, at a loss for what could possibly induce her friend to even consider the idea for a moment. The idea of lovely Alice married to a man who might be even a little like Prue's father. She closed her eyes. "You can't be considering such a match, Alice, truly. You cannot marry a man who frightens you. It's not as if you're penniless or at risk of destitution. Surely, you're not so desperate to get out from under your mother's clutches?"

"Not *so* desperate," Alice agreed, sounding thoroughly desperate.

Prue sighed. "Oh, well. The season is almost upon us, and you can husband hunt to your heart's content."

Alice cut her a look. "Oh, yes, because I was so successful last season."

"It was your first year," Prue said with a huff. "You've got some town bronze now; you know what's in store, so it won't come as such a shock."

Their eyes met and both gave a heavy sigh. Yes. They did indeed know what was in store, and Prue well knew that Alice dreaded it every bit as much as she did.

Chapter 2

Dear Prunella,

Oh heavens. Not only buck teeth, bad breath and a stutter. He thinks women ought not to read lest it give them opinions. I had the most appalling row with mama about it, who quite agrees with him. Sadly, he is quite obscenely wealthy and is the youngest son of an earl, which is naturally the only thing she cares about. I won't do it though, Prue. I won't. There is a season to come yet. I shan't give in. Not yet.

—Excerpt of a letter from Miss Alice Dowding to Miss Prunella Chuffington-Smythe.

***

5th April. Otford. Kent. 1814

Prue reached for another sausage and ignored Minerva's grimace of disgust. Her cousin had spent the last ten minutes nibbling at a piece of toast like a dainty mouse. Well, if she wanted to starve herself to look fragile and waif like, it was entirely her own affair. Prue couldn't think on an empty stomach and, as she often forgot to eat lunch when the words were flowing well, a hearty breakfast was a necessity.

"Oh, do look at this one," her aunt exclaimed, turning the latest copy of *The Lady's Weekly Review* to show Minerva one of the fashion prints. "Isn't it lovely?"

Minerva dropped her toast with a little squeal of excitement and Prue rolled her eyes.

"There's a small fortune in the lace alone," Prue observed, aware of her aunt's slender finances and her penchant for frittering it away on frivolous items they could ill afford.

"I wasn't asking you," her aunt snapped, glaring from under an extravagant lace cap that she'd bought the day before, and which rather proved Prue's point.

Still, her aunt was quite correct. It was not her affair. Once she had enough money put aside, and hopefully a commission to write another novel, she would be free to leave. If she was careful, she had calculated she would be safe to do so by the end of this year. Fond imaginings of a dear little cottage filled her mind's eye, somewhere close to friends, where she could see them often. Why, they might even come and stay with her.

That idea was more than a little problematic, as a woman living alone would be a scandalous creature. Prue had hoped to convince one or more of her friends to join her, for their mutual benefit and to ease the costs, but she knew it was a lot to ask. There were few women who would countenance such a situation. She, however, was one. Anything for her freedom, her independence. The idea made her smile, though she suppressed it at once as Minerva caught sight of her.

"What are you looking so pleased with yourself for?" her cousin snapped. "I know you think I'm stupid, but I need new dresses for the season, you know I do. I shan't let you stop us buying them. Not this time."

Prue pursed her lips and bit back the retort that was brewing there. It would only cause a row which would make her late getting upstairs and back to the Duke of Bedsin. If Phyllis was such a pea-brain as to get them both into debt, why should she care? Yet despite her impatience with the two frivolous creatures, her aunt had taken her in when no one else had. Prue owed her a good deal for that. She was grateful and tried to help where she could.

"I don't do it to spoil your fun, Minerva," she said, wishing she was better at sounding reasonable instead of merely irritated. "Only to ensure you have enough to pay your rent and put food on the table. We all have limited funds and you must see that a gown like that would use every penny your mother has saved, and more besides. It isn't feasible."

Minerva's temper erupted with a flash of fury and she stood, her chair toppling over backwards with a crash. "You're just jealous, that's all! I might not be as clever as you, but I will catch a duke, you miserly old Prune," she said, using the childish nickname she'd saddled Prue with years ago. "So, it doesn't matter how much we spend. When I've hooked him, he'll pay for everything. He'll beg to do it."

Prue stared at her and then turned to her aunt, waiting for her to suppress her daughter's idiotic flights of fancy, but Phyllis only gave a nervous little laugh.

"Oh, Min, dear. We said we'd not talk of this to anyone, did we not?"

Minerva gave a snort of disgust. "It's only Prune, it's not like *she's* anyone. Not anyone that counts. Besides, she'll see soon enough."

Prue blinked, wondering what manner of madness had possessed them. She'd always known Phyllis had hopes of her lovely daughter catching a title, and she *was* lovely—and penniless and without connections—but a *duke*?

An unpleasant shiver of foreboding crawled down her spine and she turned back to face Minerva.

"Which duke?" she demanded.

Minerva righted her chair and made a show of smoothing out her skirts and sitting down again, a prim little smile settling over her bow shaped mouth.

"The Duke of Bedwin."

Prue gasped and looked to Phyllis, who had the grace to colour a little and would not meet Prue's eye.

"If you hadn't spent all night sitting in a corner with your nose in a book, you'd have heard the news," Minerva continued, turning Prue's attention back, her voice sweet but laced with arsenic. "His grace is on the lookout for a new duchess."

The idea was horrifying enough to make Prue gape in astonishment. Her gaze flew once more to her aunt.

"You can't be serious! You would want Minerva married to… to such a man?"

Aunt Phyllis put her chin up. "He's a duke."

As if that was all the answer required.

"Aunt Phyllis," Prue continued, her heart thudding in her chest. "You know the rumours as well as I do. He's a libertine, depraved! My God, they say he murdered his first wife!"

Phyllis made a waving motion with her hand, brushing the argument aside. "For heaven's sake, Prunella, even you said you set no store by such scurrilous stories. You did say that," she added, wagging a finger.

Prue nodded, unable to deny it. For all the stories that had circulated about his grace, she had not believed the one about his wife's untimely demise. That he was a rake and blackguard however, the *ton* had circulated those stories widely enough and they were such common knowledge there had to be some truth in them. Indeed, anyone getting a glimpse of the man would be hard pressed not to conclude it without even ever having heard the stories.

Prue swallowed down a sigh as she remembered the last time she'd caught a glimpse of him. He'd looked like sin on a moonless night, dark and forbidding and full of unseen pleasures.

"Nonetheless, Aunt, he could ruin Minerva and even if he does seek a wife, surely he'd choose—"

"I told you she was jealous," Minerva said to her mother, before Prue could finish the sentence. "You're jealous, Prue, because you're plain and dull and boring, and no man will ever want you."

Prue's breath caught at the spite of her words, which was foolish. She ought to be used to such outbursts from her cousin by now, and besides, she knew it was true enough. Plain might have been a little harsh, but she really could not deny it, and whilst she didn't believe herself dull or boring, she could not pretend to find enjoyment in the things most young ladies seemed to go into transports over, either.

"Now, now, Minerva, that will do," Phyllis said, frowning a little. "That was rather uncalled for."

"No," Prue said. Her smile felt a little too tight, but there was no point in pretending otherwise about things that were true. "Minerva is correct, which is why I have no intention of marrying."

Both women gaped at her.

"Well, you need not think you'll be living off my charity till the end of your days," Phyllis snapped, looking affronted.

"I don't live off it now," Prue pointed out dryly. "I pay you for my room and board, and have never asked you for a penny towards my upkeep."

Aunt Phyllis' face darkened, and Prue sighed. "I have no say in how you spend your money, or what plans you make for the future. It is entirely your affair and none of mine. If Bedwin is what you want, then I wish you every success with him."

Minerva returned a dazzling and somewhat unnerving smile. "Oh, don't fret, Prune. I'll be a duchess before the year is out, and I'll make sure his grace finds you a little cottage somewhere. You could keep cats," she added, and though she kept the smirk from her mouth, Prue could hear it loud and clear.

"Yes, that sounds ideal," Prue replied, amused that Minerva thought it such an appalling fate. The young woman's expression faltered, a look of curiosity in her eyes as Prue got to her feet. "If you'll excuse me."

***

"Hell and damnation!"

Robert Adolphus, the Duke of Bedwin, flung aside the latest copy of *The Lady's Weekly Review* in fury. His sister, Helena just smiled and gave a little shrug as she piled marmalade onto her toast.

"I know it's awful," she said, her voice full of sympathy. "But it is awfully good, too."

Robert turned to glare at her and she blushed, giving him a rueful grin. "Well, it is, you know. I mean, if one must be thought a villain, then best to be the kind that makes women swoon and long to be debauched—"

"Helena!"

How his eighteen-year-old sister even knew such a word… good god, he'd been a terrible brother. The dreadful creature gave an unrepentant gurgle of laughter. "Well, really, Robert. You've done very little to disabuse people of the notion. Quite the contrary. I can't help but think you rather enjoy your dreadful reputation."

Robert sent her a dark look that suggested she close her mouth. As terrifying as his reputation might be among the *ton*, however, his baby sister was not in the least bit impressed.

279

"Oh, pooh. Glare all you like, it's at least partly your own fault and well you know it."

He folded his arms, seething even though he knew there was truth in her words. She reached out and patted his arm to soothe his prickly temper.

"I know Lavinia made a horrible mess for you, dearest, and I know it haunts you, but sooner or later you must start over. It's time, don't you think? The rumours already fly you're in search of a wife. Why not make them true?"

Robert said nothing. His sister was far too mature for her years, mostly because of his idiotic actions as a young man. He knew she had suffered from his behaviour, not that she'd ever complained. That she was the one giving him good advice now though, was bad enough. He ought to have protected her, and yet all he'd done was make everything as black as bloody pitch.

Damn it.

The day had got off to a bad start. He was in a wretched temper and unwilling to be reasonable about anything now. If he didn't loathe wasting a day, he'd go back to bed and be done with it. Yet that would be unproductive and it was, at least, a glorious spring morning. He'd just have to find something to take his mind off things.

"I'll write to them," he said, perking up at the notion. "Tell them I'll sue if they don't withdraw the story."

Helena gave an impatient huff. "Honestly, Robert, you may as well admit that the Duke of Bedsin is you and hold your hands up for murder. It's what they'll all think."

"So, I'm supposed to let this anonymous lunatic author destroy my character and write such... such ludicrous nonsense?"

His sister shrugged and took another bite of toast, chewing with the air of someone with something to say. "If you don't want things to get worse, yes," she said once she could, and reached for her tea. "It will only last so long, and then there will be someone else in the spotlight and you'll be forgotten. Unless you make a huge scandal of it, then it will take years to die down and everyone will believe you've really something to hide."

"Everyone thinks that now!" he raged, frustrated by his inability to act.

Helena smiled, her green eyes—the same shade as his own, the same as their mother's had been—warm with affection. "No, they don't. Not everyone. Not the people that matter. If anything good came of the whole disastrous affair, at least we discovered who our friends were."

Robert snorted. "Oh, yes, that was marvellous," he said, dry as dust. He snatched up the paper again, waving it in his sister's face. "I wouldn't mind so much if it wasn't so preposterous. Listen to this…."

He cleared his throat and turned to the offending page.

"Lydia trembled in the darkness as she realised, she'd been tricked. She ought never to have come, ought never to have slipped away from the ball and the lights, and sought the shadows. She ought never have been tempted by the velvet night, soft and warm with promise, but now there was no going back. He was there before her, full of wickedness and dark pleasure. Her breath caught." Robert gave his sister an *I ask you* look but found nothing but rapt concentration in her eyes. "Oh, for God's sake. What utter rubbish!"

Helena gave a heavy sigh, smiling a little.

"I think it's romantic."

"Romantic?" Robert spluttered, staring at her in horror. "The bloody man is set on ruining an innocent girl, and no doubt murdering her too if they follow the story to its logical conclusion. In what perverse world could you believe that romantic? And," he added, thoroughly unsettled, "you're never being let out of this house again! Heaven alone knows what I'll find you about. Romantic, indeed."

Helena returned a scathing look. "I'd like to see you enforce that."

"And," Robert continued, too irritated to stop now, "that's supposed to be about me. I'm your brother, for God's sake!"

"More's the pity," Helena muttered before giving a huff of annoyance as he glared at her. "Oh, for heaven's sake, Robert. The *ton* might think it's you, but I know it isn't. I can assure you my villain doesn't look a bit like you," she added with a dreamy smile.

"How terribly reassuring."

She grinned at him and Robert sighed, reaching for her hand.

"Sorry," he muttered, feeling like an arse. Helena was his staunchest ally and she'd not had an easy time. His first wife, Lavinia, had tainted her reputation just as she had his own, and Helena was entirely innocent in a way he was not. To cap it all her come out had been delayed by their mother's death, whose kind and loving presence they both missed sorely.

At least she had put off those dreadful blacks now for half-mourning, and the pale lavender she wore today looked charming.

"Idiot," she said, giving him a sweet smile even as her eyes twinkled with mirth. She enjoyed insulting him. He snorted and went to withdraw his hand but, to his surprise, she kept hold. "Seriously, though, Robert. It's time we put the past to rest. Start over. You need to go back into society, let them see you're not the monster they have painted you."

Robert hesitated. "And what if I am?"

Helena squeezed his hand tighter. "That, I will never believe. You... You allowed the darkness of life to swallow you up for a while, that's all, but you've promised me that part of your life is over, and I believe you."

He frowned, staring down at the table, unwilling to meet her eyes. God, he was a bastard for having put her through this.

"You must go back out there, Robert, and you must meet people and make friends and... fall in love."

Robert jolted and snatched his hand away. "This is what comes of reading such twaddle," he said, revolted by the notion. "As if I would, after the mess I made the first time around?"

Order your copy here: To Dare a Duke

Want more Emma?

If you enjoyed this book, please support this indie author and take a moment to leave a few words in a review. *Thank you!*

To be kept informed of special offers and free deals (which I do regularly) follow me on *https://www.bookbub.com/authors/emma-v-leech*

To find out more and to get news and sneak peeks of the first chapter of upcoming works, go to my website and sign up for the newsletter.

http://www.emmavleech.com/

Come and join the fans in my Facebook group for news, info and exciting discussion...

Emmas Book Club

Or Follow me here......

http://viewauthor.at/EmmaVLeechAmazon

Facebook

Instagram

Emma's Twitter page

TikTok

About Me!

I started this incredible journey way back in 2010 with The Key to Erebus but didn't summon the courage to hit publish until October 2012. For anyone who's done it, you'll know publishing your first title is a terribly scary thing! I still get butterflies on the morning a new title releases but the terror has subsided at least. Now I just live in dread of the day my daughters are old enough to read them.

The horror! (On both sides I suspect.)

2017 marked the year that I made my first foray into Historical Romance and the world of the Regency Romance, and my word what a year! I was delighted by the response to this series and can't wait to add more titles. Paranormal Romance readers need not despair however as there is much more to come there too. Writing has become an addiction and as soon as one book is over I'm hugely excited to start the next so you can expect plenty more in the future.

As many of my works reflect I am greatly influenced by the beautiful French countryside in which I live. I've been here in the South West for the past twenty years though I was born and raised in England. My three gorgeous girls are all bilingual and the youngest who is only six, is showing signs of following in my footsteps after producing *The Lonely Princess* all by herself.

I'm told book two is coming soon ...

She's keeping me on my toes, so I'd better get cracking!

KEEP READING TO DISCOVER MY OTHER BOOKS!

Other Works by Emma V. Leech

(For those of you who have read The French Fae Legend series, please remember that chronologically The Heart of Arima precedes The Dark Prince)

Rogues & Gentlemen

Rogues & Gentlemen Series

Daring Daughters

Daring Daughters Series

Girls Who Dare

<u>Girls Who Dare Series</u>

The Regency Romance Mysteries

<u>The Regency Romance Mysteries Series</u>

The French Vampire Legend

Audio Books!

Don't have time to read but still need your romance fix? The wait is over…

By popular demand, get your favourite Emma V Leech Regency Romance books on audio at Audible as performed by the incomparable Philip Battley and Gerard Marzilli. Several titles available and more added each month!

Click the links to choose your favourite and start listening now.

Rogues & Gentlemen

The Rogue ***

The Earl's Tempation

Scandal's Daughter

The Devil May Care

Nearly Ruining Mr Russell

One Wicked Winter ***

To Tame a Savage Heart *****

Persuading Patience

The Last Man in London

Flaming June ***

The Winter Bride, a novella ***

Girls Who Dare

To Dare a Duke

To Steal A Kiss ***

To Break the Rules ***

To Follow her Heart

The Regency Romance Mysteries

Dying for a Duke ***

A Dog in a Doublet **

The Rum and the Fox **

The French Vampire Legend

The Key to Erebus (coming soon)

** Available on Chirp

*** Available on Chirp and Audible/Amazon

From the author of the bestselling Girls Who Dare Series – An exciting new series featuring the children of the Girls Who Dare...

The stories of the **Peculiar Ladies Book Club** and their hatful of dares has become legend among their children. When the hat is rediscovered, dusty and forlorn, the remaining dares spark a series of events that will echo through all the families... and their

Daring Daughters

Dare to be Wicked

Daring Daughters Book One

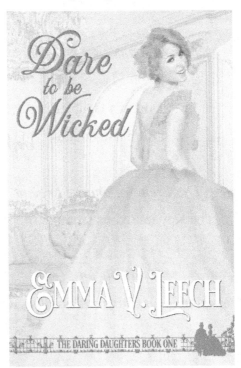

Two daring daughters ...

Lady Elizabeth and Lady Charlotte are the daughters of the Duke and Duchess of Bedwin. Raised by an unconventional mother and an indulgent, if overprotective father, they both strain against the rigid morality of the era.

The fashionable image of a meek, weak young lady, prone to swooning at the least provocation, is one that makes them seethe with frustration.

Their handsome childhood friend ...

Cassius Cadogen, Viscount Oakley, is the only child of the Earl and Countess St Clair. Beloved and indulged, he is popular, gloriously handsome, and a talented artist.

Returning from two years of study in France, his friendship with both sisters becomes strained as jealousy raises its head. A situation not helped by the two mysterious Frenchmen who have accompanied him home.

And simmering sibling rivalry ...

Passion, art, and secrets prove to be a combustible combination, and someone will undoubtedly get burned.

Pre Order your copy here: *Dare to be Wicked*

Interested in a Regency Romance with a twist?

Dying for a Duke

The Regency Romance Mysteries Book 1

Straight-laced, imperious and morally rigid, Benedict Rutland - the darkly handsome Earl of Rothay - gained his title too young. Responsible for a large family of younger siblings that his frivolous parents have brought to bankruptcy, his youth was spent clawing back the family fortunes.

Now a man in his prime and financially secure he is betrothed to a strict, sensible and cool-headed woman who will never upset the balance of his life or disturb his emotions ...

But then Miss Skeffington-Fox arrives.

Brought up solely by her rake of a step-father, Benedict is scandalised by everything about the dashing Miss.

But as family members in line for the dukedom begin to die at an alarming rate, all fingers point at Benedict, and Miss Skeffington-Fox may be the only one who can save him.

FREE to read on Amazon Kindle Unlimited.. Dying for a Duke

Lose yourself in Emma's paranormal world with The French Vampire Legend series.

The Key to Erebus

The French Vampire Legend Book 1

The truth can kill you.

Taken away as a small child, from a life where vampires, the Fae, and other mythical creatures are real and treacherous, the beautiful young witch, Jéhenne Corbeaux is totally unprepared when she returns to rural France to live with her eccentric Grandmother.

Thrown headlong into a world she knows nothing about she seeks to learn the truth about herself, uncovering secrets more shocking than anything she could ever have imagined and finding that she is by no means powerless to protect the ones she loves.

Despite her Gran's dire warnings, she is inexorably drawn to the dark and terrifying figure of Corvus, an ancient vampire and master of the vast Albinus family.

Jéhenne is about to find her answers and discover that, not only is Corvus far more dangerous than she could ever imagine, but that he holds much more than the key to her heart …

Available at your favourite retailer:

The Key to Erebus

Check out Emma's exciting fantasy series with hailed by Kirkus Reviews as "An enchanting fantasy with a likable heroine, romantic intrigue, and clever narrative flourishes."

The Dark Prince

The French Fae Legend Book 1

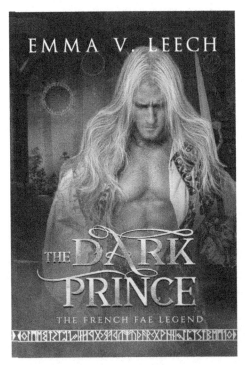

Two Fae Princes
One Human Woman
And a world ready to tear them all apart

Laen Braed is Prince of the Dark fae, with a temper and reputation to match his black eyes, and a heart that despises the human race. When he is sent back through the forbidden gates between realms to retrieve an ancient fae artifact, he returns home with far more than he bargained for.

Corin Albrecht, the most powerful Elven Prince ever born. His golden eyes are rumoured to be a gift from the gods, and destiny is calling him. With a love for the human world that runs deep, his friendship with Laen is being torn apart by his prejudices.

Océane DeBeauvoir is an artist and bookbinder who has always relied on her lively imagination to get her through an unhappy and uneventful life. A jewelled dagger put on display at a nearby museum hits the headlines with speculation of another race, the Fae. But the discovery also inspires Océane to create an extraordinary piece of art that cannot be confined to the pages of a book.

With two powerful men vying for her attention and their friendship stretched to the breaking point, the only question that remains...who is truly The Dark Prince.

The man of your dreams is coming...or is it your nightmares he visits? Find out in Book One of The French Fae Legend.

Available at your favourite retailer:

The Dark Prince

Acknowledgements

Thanks, of course, to my wonderful editor Kezia Cole.

To Victoria Cooper for all your hard work, amazing artwork and above all your unending patience!!! Thank you so much. You are amazing!

To my BFF, PA, personal cheerleader and bringer of chocolate, Varsi Appel, for moral support, confidence boosting and for reading my work more times than I have. I love you loads!

A huge thank you to all of Emma's Book Club members! You guys are the best!

I'm always so happy to hear from you so do email or message me :)

emmavleech@orange.fr

To my husband Pat and my family ... For always being proud of me.

Can't get your fill of Historical Romance? Do you crave stories with passion and red hot chemistry?

If the answer is yes, have I got the group for you!

Come join myself and other awesome authors in our Facebook group

Historical Harlots

Be the first to know about exclusive giveaways, chat with amazing HistRom authors, lots of raunchy shenanigans and more!

Historical Harlots Facebook Group

Made in the USA
Monee, IL
18 April 2024

57119986R00177